What the critics are saying...

"Fans of contemporary romances will adore Elizabeth Jennings' latest release from Cerridwen Press, Homecoming. Written with verve and charm, this is a delightful story which is impossible to put down! Warm, witty and heartwarming, Homecoming is an excellent contemporary romance. Elizabeth Jennings is a fantastic spinner of tales who enchants her readers from the very first page. Homecoming is a delightful tale which will make you laugh and cry. It is peopled with a heroine you can't help but love, a hero who will make you pulse race and a supporting cast of characters and a town which you will take straight to your heart." ~ *ECataRomance Reviews*

"The story of Federica and Jack is a beautifully written love story…I look forward to reading other books by Ms. Jennings. I recommend it to everyone." ~ *The Romance Studio*

"I truly enjoyed Ms. Jennings' skillful use of e-mails and faxes to tell part of the story and I fell in love with Jack and the crazy people of Carson's Bluff." ~ *Lighthouse Literary Reviews*

"Homecoming is a romance that takes the reader away to a town where time seems to stand still. The author, Elizabeth Jennings has a way of creating a tapestry of beauty with words when describing the small town where everyone matters. Homecoming is a very charming story that will steal your heart away." ~ *Fallen Angel Reviews*

Also by Elizabeth Jennings

∞

Dying for Siena

About the Author

∞

Elizabeth Jennings has always loved words—big ones, little ones, fat ones, skinny ones… She's been a wordsmith all her life, as a simultaneous interpreter, translator and now as a writer. She lives in southern Italy, which she loves, together with her wonderful, high-maintenance husband and son. Who could ask for anything more?

Elizabeth welcomes comments from readers. You can find her website and email address on her author bio page at www.cerridwenpress.com.

Elizabeth Jennings

Homecoming

Cerridwen Press

A Cerridwen Press Publication

www.cerridwenpress.com

Homecoming

ISBN #1419954121
Edited by Kelli Kwiatkowski
Cover art by Syneca

Electronic book Publication September 2005

Trade Paperback Publication September 2006

Cerridwen Press is an imprint of Ellora's Cave Publishing, Inc.®

HOMECOMING

Chapter One

May 15th, from Inter Airways flight 4410 en route to Hong Kong

FAX MESSAGE TO: Sheriff J. A. Sutter, Sheriff's Office, Carson's Bluff, California

FAX MESSAGE FROM: F. H. Mansion

Sheriff Sutter,

I'm sending this fax to you because I seem to be unable to contact Mayor Sutter—who I assume is a relation of yours—to discuss the possible sale and restoration of a property inside the city limits of Carson's Bluff.

The property is known locally as "Harry's Folly" and my lawyers have been unable to discover if it is known by any other name. Nonetheless, as you probably know, since I have been trying to get in touch with either you or the mayor for over three weeks now, Mansion Enterprises, which I represent, is interested in contacting the city authorities. Apparently, it is the city which holds a lien on the property. Mansion Enterprises is thinking of either acquiring a majority interest or purchasing the property outright.

I have been totally unsuccessful so far in establishing contact with any member of the Carson's Bluff City Council. I am operating on a tight schedule, but could make a brief visit in the second half of May, preferably sometime after the 25th, after my return from Singapore.

In my previous messages, you will find the number of my cell phone and my email address. My itinerary is as follows: May 16th, Hong Kong, May 22nd, Singapore, May 25th San Francisco. You can reach me at the Mansion Hotels in each of these cities or leave messages with the San Francisco or New York administrative offices, which will forward any messages.

Best, F. H. Mansion

~~~~~

Carson's Bluff

Note taped to Jack Sutter's refrigerator door

Hey Jack, the Cossacks have faxed again. I guess this F. H. guy's just not giving up. You're going to have to answer, otherwise this workaholic yuppie will just turn up on our doorstep some fine day and drink us out of all our white wine. You know how much Dad would appreciate that.

Cavendish broke through the fence again. He chewed the top half of your favorite boots. Maybe Norman can repair them. Sorry about that.

Lilly

~~~~~

FAX TO: Ellen Larsen c/o Inter Airways, Logan Airport

FAX FROM: Federica Mansion, en route to Hong Kong

Hi El,

You won't be surprised to hear that I'm going to have to cry off our date in Paris. My beloved uncle has tacked on a quick tour around the Pacific Rim hotels before the Paris trip—it seems quarterly profits are up only seventy-five percent instead of ninety percent and he wants to know why—so that's been postponed by a week. You'll be in London by then. This is the second time I've cancelled in a row. Forgive, forgive.

How did the date with the Great Dane go? Lucky you, you get to date. I don't remember the last time I had dinner with a man who didn't consider me a proxy for Uncle Frederick.

Love, Federica

~~~~~

May 16th, Paris

FAX TO: Federica Mansion, c/o Hong Kong Mansion Inn

FAX FROM: Ellen Larsen, Roissy-Charles De Gaulle Airport, Paris

Hi honey,

That's okay. We'll meet up eventually. The date wasn't with the Dane, it was the Swedish Captain for SAS. I don't know why I bother. The date came to an early end. He started mistaking my breast for a joystick before we even got out of the taxi. It must be part of the job description for pilots—they have to have high testosterone levels and be oversexed. I'm still working to get the taste of his beery tongue out of my mouth. Am just about willing to throw in the towel and join you in celibacy. What's it like?

Are you going to Podunk in Northern California at the end of May? We could meet up in the beginning of June. If you let me know, I'll put in a bid for the California route.

Don't work too hard making another zillion for your uncle. He doesn't need it. What he really needs is a brain transplant and a heart.

Love, El

~~~~~

Hong Kong

FAX TO: Mayor Sutter, Carson's Bluff
FAX FROM: F. H. Mansion

Mayor Sutter,

I wonder if the entire Town Council of Carson's Bluff has disappeared? I didn't know the area was part of the Bermuda Triangle. My faxes to you and to Sheriff Sutter have gone unanswered. I am sending a copy of this to the City Treasurer, c/o your town hall. Someone, somewhere, must be alive out there.

As you must know by now, Mansion Enterprises is interested in purchasing Lot 448 of the local land register—otherwise known as "Harry's Folly"—either partially or in its entirety. My lawyers have checked the public records. The property has a debt burden of over $100,000 in back taxes and is a drain on the community. It seems impossible to me that the Town Council would not leap at the opportunity to make a profit and see a thriving business grow in their community. However, the original offer has been cut by $10,000 dollars and shall fall by that amount every day my messages go unanswered.

F. H. Mansion

~~~~~

Carson's Bluff
Sticker on fax message from F. H. Mansion

Jack—this is the latest fax that shark sent. Now I know what those weird lawyer types were doing poking around our records last week. Do you think City Hall should have a fire, tragically burning all our registers? What are we going to do? Can't you try a little unfriendly persuasion?

Wyatt

~~~~~

FAX TO: F. H. Mansion, c/o Administrative Headquarters, Mansion Enterprises, San Francisco, CA

FAX FROM: Sheriff J. A. Sutter, Sheriff's office, Carson's Bluff, CA

Sorry I haven't answered your faxes. Me and some men from Carson's Bluff have been out to Harry's Folly clearing brush. This is brushfire season and the brush hides all the rattlers. They get pretty big this time of year. Some have been known to carry off babies. Any time you want to come out, that's fine by us. "Us" meaning the Town Council, which is mostly me (I'm the mayor, too) and my brother, Wyatt, who's City Treasurer. Since you're interested in Harry's Folly, we'll fix up a room for you there if you want. It's a little isolated, up in the mountains, but we'll try and make it cozy for you, put some sheeting on the roof, clear out the black widows.

By the way, what does the F. H. stand for?

```
    P.S. Don't worry. We'll leave a snakebite
kit next to the bed.
    Sheriff J. A. Sutter
```

<p align="center">~~~~~</p>

May 17th

EMAIL FROM: F.H.Mansion@mansent.com

TO: f_mansion@mansent.com

Federica,

Why haven't you made that appointment with the City Council of Carson's Bluff yet? Our lawyers have already been in to check out the legal situation, and the engineering offices have come up with a timetable for the restoration. It's in a perfect location for business seminars and there is plenty of room for a helipad. We want to get on this right away.

Have you found out anything about our Pacific Rim properties? You might want to fire someone out there. Just pick someone out and fire him. That'll make them sit up and take notice.

Uncle Frederick

<p align="center">~~~~~</p>

May 18th

EMAIL FROM: f_mansion@mansent.com

TO: F.H.Mansion@mansent.com

Dear Uncle Frederick,

It is now 11:00 p.m. my time—their time, Hong Kong time, whatever. I only landed two hours ago. The meeting with the Hong Kong manager is scheduled for 7:00 a.m. Will know more tomorrow. Strongly advise against firing anyone. Received message from mayor of Carson's Bluff upon arrival. Will schedule meeting soonest.

Federica

~~~~~

May 18th/19th, Hong Kong

FAX TO: Ellen Larsen, c/o Inter Airways, Roissy-Charles De Gaulle Airport, Paris

FAX FROM: Federica Mansion

Hey El,

I'm not too sure what day it is anymore. I'm in Jet Lag from Hell phase and have only just started this swing through the Rim. Sorry the Swedish captain didn't pan out. At least you're seeing some action. What does celibacy feel like? Dunno. I don't feel much of anything below the neck these days.

Uncle Frederick wants me to fire someone out here. I don't think it makes much difference who, he just wants to make a point.

I have actually established contact with Carson's Bluff City Council, in the person of its sheriff (who is also the mayor!), and I might be edging closer to an appointment. For some reason, they seem to want to scare me off.

That nutcase wrote that the rattlers on the property are big enough to carry off babies. Anyway, if I do manage to actually make an appointment with these people, we could meet in San Francisco end of May/early June.

What do you say? We could take in a show or two. You could stay with me, sleep in my spare room. I do have a spare room, don't I? I can't

seem to remember. I don't even remember the
last time I was there.

   Love, Federica

~~~~~

May 19th

Note stuck under Lilly Sutter Wright's windshield wiper

Hi Lil,

Stopped by your studio but you weren't there. Cavendish did me a favor, those boots chafed at the top. Tell your good-for-nothing husband that he can cook me a meal instead of repairing my boots. I haven't had a home-cooked meal since the last time the two of you had me over.

I think I might have stopped the Mansion Enterprises juggernaut. Told him Harry's Folly was overrun with giant rattlers and black widows, but don't know how long I can hold out. Maybe we should have a town caucus.

   Love, Jack

~~~~~

EMAIL: e.larsen@aol.com
TO: f_mansion@mansent.com

Federica,

Let's meet in California, that would be great. Confirm soon, because I have to bid the flight in a few days. I imagine that the Town Council is spinning tales because they don't want to be taken over by Mansion Enterprises.

Your Uncle Frederick belongs under a rock. Our boss at Inter Airways is like that. He would fire his grandmother. Eat this email.

Don't you ever dream of the perfect man? Six-foot-two, bright blue eyes, sexy as hell? If you're dead below the neck, what do you dream of?

You have a spare room, trust me on this. Let me know soonest if we can meet because the bidding wars have begun.

Love, El

~~~~~

May 20th

FAX FROM: F. H. Mansion c/o Hong Kong Mansion Inn

FAX TO: Sheriff J. A. Sutter, Sheriff's Office, Carson's Bluff, CA

Sheriff Sutter,

I will be arriving in Carson's Bluff on either May 31st or June 1st. Shall advise exact date in a few days. I would appreciate if you could convene a meeting of the City Council by the 1st or 2nd of June.

Don't worry about the rattlers. My bite is deadlier. Will bring my own snake kit. If it's brush fire season, should I pack my asbestos pajamas?

Isn't it illegal to be both sheriff and mayor?

I was named for my uncle—Frederick Henry Mansion.

Best, F. H. Mansion

~~~~~

EMAIL FROM: f_mansion@mansent.com

TO: F.H.Mansion@mansent.com

Dear Uncle Frederick,

I met with Mr. Chen, our Hong Kong manager, and he assured me that the slight downturn in profits was due to cancellations after the Air Swift disaster. It makes sense. He showed me preliminary figures for the next quarter and it looks as if profits will be back up to par soon. If you give him a little slack, he'll produce more.

Have made provisional appointment with Carson's Bluff City Council for June 2nd.

Love, Federica

~~~~~

EMAIL FROM: F.H.Mansion@mansent.com

TO: f_mansion@mansent.com

Federica, don't let yourself be blinded by figures. Did you check what Chen showed you? The Air Swift disaster should have been followed by an aggressive ad campaign. Tell Chen he is borderline.

Firm up CB Town Council meeting. We will expect report by June 5. If sale is made by June 15, schedule will be met. Don't fail me.

Uncle Frederick

~~~~~

May 21st

Notice tacked on oak tree in front of City Hall, Carson's Bluff

Citizenry,

I think we're in deepest shit. Outside forces are moving in. We're calling a town meeting for the day after tomorrow in the courthouse at 7:00 p.m. We want everyone to be there. AND THAT MEANS YOU!!

Jack Sutter

~~~~~

FAX FROM: Mayor J. A. Sutter, Mayor's Office, Carson's Bluff, CA

FAX TO: F. H. Mansion c/o Administrative Headquarters, Mansion Enterprises, San Francisco, CA

Dear F. H. Mansion,

We are happy to hear that you can come to Carson's Bluff in early June. Early June tends to be landslide season… Still, if the roads give out, the City Council can always send a rescue squad. Use a four-wheel drive. The bigger the better.

You'll probably be tired when you return. We can always reschedule. Carson's Bluff operates on slow time. There's no hurry.

I'm sheriff and mayor because no one else wants to be. Ditto for my brother Wyatt, who is City Treasurer, and my sister, who is Town Clerk. Carson's Bluff people aren't real big on civic-mindedness.

I was named John Augustus, but no relation. My Mom was a Western history buff. She called my sister Lilly after Lilly Langtry and my brother Wyatt after Wyatt Earp. Friends call me Jack. Do your friends call you Freddie?

J. A. Sutter

~~~~~

FAX FROM: F. H. Mansion, c/o Hong Kong Mansion Inn

FAX TO: Ellen Larsen, c/o Inter Airways, Heathrow Airport, London

Hi El,

Hope I remembered your schedule and that you're in London and not Bombay or Caracas. Thanks for reminding me about the spare room. It's all I can do to remember what country I'm in.

My dreams right now are very prosaic. I dream of one good night's sleep. In my own bed. Isn't that sad?

For the record, all the six-foot-two blue-eyed hunks I've met lately are out for Uncle Frederick's money. I get all my romance vicariously through books. Did you finish *Love's Eternal Torment*? Wasn't it great when she told him she was fine but she really had tuberculosis? I cried buckets. Is that sick or what? Springsteen is playing on the 3rd in SF. Should I have the company accountant buy tickets? Am leaving for Singapore this evening.

Love, Federica

~~~~~

May 22nd

Singapore

EMAIL FROM: f_mansion@mansent.com
TO: F.H.Mansion@mansent.com

Dear Uncle Frederick,

I was able to meet with the hotel manager, Mr. Jackson, only this afternoon, as I was slightly ill in the morning. He is very anxious to show me the projected figures for the second semester later this evening. There are four international congresses scheduled for the fall, which should make up for the slight drop in profits this spring.

Will collect the documents and study them in my hotel room. I'm not feeling very well. I can always go over them on the flight back to San Francisco and can email him regarding our assessment.

The Carson's Bluff appointment is firming up.

Love, Federica

~~~~~

EMAIL FROM: F.H.Mansion@mansent.com

TO: f_mansion@mansent.com

Federica,

Too bad you weren't able to fully carry out the mission. Am very disappointed. Would remind you that the Singapore Mansion Inn is lagging far behind in our Pacific Rim line-up. Jackson had better have a good excuse. I imagine he took advantage of the fact that you didn't conduct a thorough survey. I'll have our people look over the figures when you get back. Can you make a stopover in New York to talk to Leslie Brooks? Would appreciate it.

Uncle Frederick

~~~~~

Fiumicino Airport, Rome

FAX FROM: Ellen Larsen, Inter Airways

FAX TO: Federica Mansion c/o Mansion Inn, Singapore

Hey honey,

My schedule was changed at the last minute, so now I'm in the Eternal City, but haven't seen anything but the airport. Unfortunately, the Big Boss has decided that henceforth, we lazy bums can work double shifts, i.e. we can't rest between flights. God I hate that man. Eat this fax.

I hope I can make it to SF by the 2nd or 3rd. Am crazily shifting schedules. Did you read *Terrible Temptation,* where he throws himself in front of the wagon train to save her? I smuggled it onto the flight and couldn't put it down. I think some passengers complained when they didn't get their coffee. I think I'm ready to quit. If your Uncle Frederick were

human, I'd ask him for a job. Let me know if the Springsteen tickets are for real. You can reach me tomorrow at Tegel.

Love, El

~~~~~

Singapore

FAX FROM: F. H. Mansion, Singapore Mansion Inn

FAX TO: Sheriff J. A. Sutter

Sheriff,

I can't set a date now, but our San Francisco office will be in touch soonest. I'm thinking of between the 31st of May and 2nd of June, depending. Thank you for your warm welcome. Mansion Enterprises has four-wheel drives, off-road vehicles and helicopters at its disposal, so whether Carson's Bluff has a landslide in that time span or not doesn't really make much of a difference.

John Augustus Sutter? Who was he? Lilly Langtry? Wyatt Earp I've heard of. Wasn't there a TV show a long time back?

No, my friends definitely do not call me Freddie.

Best, F. H. Mansion

~~~~~

May 23rd

FAX FROM: F. H. Mansion, c/o Singapore Mansion Inn

FAX TO: Ellen Larsen, c/o Inter Airways, Tegel Airport, Berlin

Dearest El,

I hope this gets to you. I wanted to fax sooner, but I just flaked out. Seems I've got a bit of a temperature. One-hundred-three degrees, actually. Mr. Jackson, the hotel manager here, is so obsequious that he had the hotel doctor up in three seconds. The doctor said I needed rest. Ha. He's never met my Uncle Frederick.

Anyway, I hope to wrap things up here in a day or two, then fly back. Have to make a stopover in New York, so won't be back in SF until the 27th. God knows where I'll find the strength to get to that hellhole in Northern California. The mayor kindly informed me it's landslide season.

What will he think of next? Black holes? Still, who can blame him? They're afraid of being taken over by Mansion Enterprises. I'd be afraid of being taken over by Mansion Enterprises, too.

Can you make it? I'm so looking forward to seeing you. Did you read *Endless Night*? Wasn't the hero divine? All that luscious *sex*.

For the record, Marcus Jackson is five-foot-two, bald and married. The hotel doctor had mossy teeth and hadn't changed his shirt in a week, I swear. I think I'll stick to books.

Don't pig out on the sauerkraut.

Love, Federica

~~~~~

Minutes of town caucus, Carson's Bluff, May 23rd

Meeting began at 7:00 p.m. The meeting was called to order by Mayor J. A. Sutter. 1,378 people were present, holding 2,390 proxies, for a total of 3,768. The population of greater Carson's Bluff being 2,682, the validity of proxies will be checked at a later date, when people (that means you, Lester) sober up.

Mayor Sutter informed the citizenry that Mansion Enterprises, a San Francisco-based hotel chain, has expressed interest in Harry's Folly. The property has back taxes of more than $100,000 and is therefore, according to California state law, up for public auction.

It being the informed opinion of Mayor J. A. Sutter, Sheriff J. A. Sutter, Treasurer W. E. Sutter and various citizens whose opinions the mayor was able to sound out, that the purchase of Harry's Folly by a big hotel chain would irrevocably change the pace of life in Carson's Bluff, the mayor put it to the citizenry how best to stave off the takeover.

After various illegal and immoral suggestions had been rejected, it was decided by the town caucus that the best thing to do is to convince Mansion Enterprises that Harry's Folly would be a foolish investment and that they'd be really sorry afterwards.

The motion was put to a vote to make Mansion Enterprises sorry. Ayes: 1,552. Nays: zero. The town caucus retired to Stella's Bar & Grill at 7:32 p.m.

Signed, this day of the 23rd of May, 2005

Town Clerk

Lilly Langtry Sutter Wright

~~~~~

May 24th

FAX FROM: Ellen Larsen, Zaventem Airport, Brussels

FAX TO: Federica Mansion, c/o Singapore Mansion Inn

Sweetie,

How's the temperature? One-hundred-three is no joke. The last time you were sick, as far as I know, was when we were in college together and you challenged that creepy jock to a beer-drinking contest. Whatever happened to him?

What do you mean, you'd hate to be taken over by Mansion Enterprises? You *have* been taken over by Mansion Enterprises. What do you think you've been doing for the past eight years? Having fun?

Against my better judgment, I accepted a dinner invitation from a passenger. I know better. Tell me I know better. I don't know what was worse—his conversation or his breath. Why don't I just throw in the towel? Good sex just isn't going to happen any time soon.

Do I at least have Springsteen to look forward to or is Uncle Frederick going to stand in the way of that, too?

Kisses, El

~~~~~

May 25th

EMAIL FROM: f_mansion@mansent.com
TO: F.H.Mansion@mansent.com

Dear Uncle Frederick,

I'm sorry but you'll have to cancel the New York meeting. I worked with Mr. Jackson until midnight, and we managed to settle a lot of things. I think some of the problems might lie in a lack of communications with the head office.

I seem to have this stubborn temperature of one-hundred-three and the hotel doctor won't let me travel. Sorry. Tell Leslie Brooks that he can email me the documentation in PDF format and I'll get out there as soon as possible. Am going to bed now.

Love, Federica

~~~~~

May 26th

EMAIL FROM: F.H.Mansion@manent.com
TO: f_mansion@mansent.com

Federica,

Very sorry you let Leslie Brooks down. He wanted to go over the quarterly reports with you. Hope you won't renege on the Carson's Bluff meeting.

Uncle Frederick

~~~~~

May 27th

24

FAX FROM: J. A. Sutter, Sheriff's Office, Carson's Bluff, CA

FAX TO: F. H. Mansion, c/o Administrative Headquarters, Mansion Enterprises, San Francisco, CA

The town caucus met and decided to review your offer. Let us know when you will be arriving and we will arrange transport. Landslides permitting.

There is an old legend that says that Harry's Folly is haunted, but of course you won't believe that nonsense. Still, if you want, Stella's Bar & Grill has upstairs rooms to let out. I think Stella provides sheets, too.

How come you don't know who John Augustus Sutter was? I thought you were from California?

J. A. Sutter

~~~~~

May 28th

From Changi International Airport, Singapore

FAX TO: Mayor J. A. Sutter
FAX FROM: F. H. Mansion

Sheriff,

I will be arriving in Carson's Bluff by chauffeur around 11:00 p.m. on the 29th. I will be most happy to stay in Harry's Folly. I will provide my own bedding, thank you.

I'm sorry I'm not up on local folklore. I *am* from California, sort of. I mean, I was born there, but—never mind. Could you arrange for a

Town Council meeting on the morning of the 30th?

    Best, F. H. Mansion

<div align="center">~~~~~</div>

May 30th

Early morning

"Jack?"

"Christ, who is this?"

"It's Lilly, Jack. Your sister. Tell me you're not drunk."

"Of course I'm not drunk. I'm asleep. What the hell are you calling me for at this hour—what time is it?"

"It's one o'clock."

"What's wrong? Did Norman feed Cavendish the leftovers?"

"Very funny. Listen, Jack, about this Mansion person—"

"Yeah? Well, I imagine he's pretty much settled up in Harry's Folly by now. He's going to be in for a few surprises. I can't wait."

"Jack—"

"Yeah?"

"Jack, F. H. Mansion is a girl."

"He's a *what!*"

"A girl, Jack. She's a girl. A human of the female persuasion."

"Well, fuck. How can you tell?"

"The car stopped at Stella's for directions."

"Well, maybe Stella was wrong. You know how she gets after a few beers."

"I was there, Jack. F. H. Mansion is a girl. Believe me. A pretty one, too."

"Well, hell, maybe he's a transvestite."

"Nope. Trust me on this one. She's small and blond with big blue eyes, and she looked very sick."

"Oh, shit."

"Yeah."

"Tell Norman to get rid of the booby traps."

"I already did."

Chapter Two

May 30th

Federica opened her eyes slightly, saw daylight, then closed them again. Where was she? She had no recollection whatsoever of the night before. Or the night before that, for that matter.

The bed was unfamiliar, but that was no surprise. Most beds were. Most nights she spent in an unfamiliar hotel room in an unfamiliar city.

She rolled over, every muscle aching, and wondered where the wall was. Where the bathroom was.

She felt awful. She wanted to call down to the front desk, but realized with a hazy terror that she hadn't the faintest idea what language she should speak.

It didn't make much difference. Nearly everyone in the Mansion Inn chain spoke excellent English. Still, she couldn't quite see a Mansion calling down to reception and saying, with a note of wild panic, "Excuse me. I seem to have lost my bearings. What day is today? What country am I in?"

Wherever she was, the sun was rising. A faint, pearly gray sky was visible through the window.

She didn't want to face the new day. Couldn't.

Whimpering, she turned her face into the pillow and fell into a restless sleep again.

"She alive?"

"I guess so. She's breathing. If she's breathing, there's a pretty good chance she's still alive."

"I knew all those years of veterinarian correspondence courses weren't wasted on you."

"Thanks, Jack. What are we going to do about her?"

"Mmmm?"

"Jack?"

"Yeah?"

"Quit mooning and start thinking. So okay, she's pretty. But don't forget she's the enemy."

"She's not the enemy now, Lil. Now she's just a very sick and very tired young woman."

"Tired I can believe. Did you see that airline ticket she had on the dresser? It looked like an accordion, it was so big. Did you know that she's been traveling nonstop for over three months?"

"Since when did you turn into a snoop, Lil?"

"I was curious to know what we were up against."

"Well, what we're up against now looks like a temperature, exhaustion and maybe the flu. And coming in from Singapore, flu is no joke. Is Doc Alonzo around?"

"I saw him playing poker at Stella's a couple of hours ago."

"Well, let's go get him. While we're at it, we'll have Stella prepare her some hot soup, and I want to talk to that chauffeur of hers."

"Okay. Jack?"

"Yeah?"

"She looks awfully...I don't know...small and lonely curled up in that bed. Not like an enemy at all."

"Yeah, I know, Lil. I know. Let's go get her some help."

Jack Sutter stepped into the cool darkness of Stella's Bar & Grill and waited until his eyes made the adjustment from the bright sunshine outside. He removed his Stetson and slapped it against his denim-covered thigh to remove some of the dust from the van ride down from the Folly.

He saw Doc Alonzo in the far corner seconds before the man gave a loud whoop of joy and reached out his arms to pull the pile of beans in the center of the poker table over to him. He took a hefty slug from a glass of Diet Coke.

Ten years ago, the pile of beans would have been several thousand dollars' worth of chips, Carson's Bluff would have been Reno, and the Diet Coke would have been good whiskey. Ten years ago, Dr. Alonzo Garcia y Fernandez had had a fancy practice in San Diego, with a fancy house and a fancy wife, until a taste for poker, blackjack and alcohol had robbed him of all three.

Now, he mended broken bones and cured colds in Carson's Bluff, drank soda and played a mean hand of poker with beans as the stake, which was all anyone would play him for. And—to his astonishment—it kept him satisfied.

Jack grinned. Like many in Carson's Bluff, Doc Alonzo had been given a second chance here. A second chance in life was what Carson's Bluff was all about.

Jack ambled over to the stained wooden counter, lifting a booted foot to the brass railing running along the bottom and settled his dusty hat on a nearby barstool. The bar was over one-hundred-forty years old. He should know. He'd helped the other men in town sand it down when Stella had inherited it from a great-aunt. He'd found a little brass plaque under the counter. *Schmidt & Sons. Fine Woodworkers. St. Louis. 1864.*

A tall, shapely brunette put down the tea towel she'd been using to wipe glasses and walked over to where he was standing.

"Hey, Jack."

"Stella."

"How's the lady doin'?"

"Not too well, Stella. That's why I'm here, to get Doc Alonzo and to talk to that chauffeur of hers. And while I'm doing that, why don't you throw some grub together, and put some hot soup in a thermos?"

"Sure thing. I'll tell you, I was all set to hate that guy and do everything to drive him away. And then when it turns out he's a *she* and she looked so—so helpless, you know?"

"I know, Stella. Throw some food together for me, will you? And see if you can find that chauffeur."

"Sure thing." Stella walked around the counter and approached a husky man with shiny, mahogany-colored skin. She spoke quietly and pointed at Jack. The husky man rose, unsmiling, and walked slowly over to Jack.

"You Ms. Mansion's driver?"

The man nodded.

Jack stuck out his hand and tried not to wince at the ferociously strong grip. "Name's John Sutter. Most people call me Jack. I'm the sheriff and the mayor around here."

He scowled. "Erle Newton. Just call me Newton."

Jack got his hand back and tried to shake it surreptitiously under the counter to get the circulation going again.

"Pleased to meet you, Newton. I take it you drove Miss— ah, Ms. Mansion up here?"

"Yes, sheriff, I did." The man's voice was deep and soft.

"Well, we have a problem."

The man's big body tensed. "A problem?"

"Yes. We can't seem to get her to wake up. I've been going up with my sister every couple of hours or so to see if she's gotten up, but she's still in bed. I sent my sister in to shake her, but she just smiled, closed her eyes again and rolled over. I'm going up again with my sister now to bring Ms. Mansion some food and I'll take our local doc with us. But I need to know if there's some problem there—"

"If you're thinking what I think you're thinking—" the big man started angrily.

Jack held up a hand. "Whoa. I was thinking medical problem, like diabetes, something the doctor should know about."

"Ain't nothing wrong with Miss Federica a kinder family and a little rest won't cure."

"Kinder family?"

The man drew himself up to his full height, a few inches taller than Jack's six-one, and gave Jack an intimidating stare. "You didn't hear that."

Jack didn't intimidate easily and he recognized protectiveness when he saw it. He grinned and slapped the side of his head with an open palm.

"Damn, but my hearing goes now and again. So what were you saying? That there are no medical problems I should know about?"

"No medical problems at all. Miss Federica is as healthy as a horse. Has to be, the way they—the way she works. Just let her be. She's exhausted. I picked her up directly from the airport and drove her here. Orders."

"A seven-hour drive after she'd flown halfway around the world?"

"Yessir. And she's been doin' that for nigh on eight years now. I think she deserves a little sleep, don't you?" The big black man's eyes met his. "I'd like to see that she gets it."

"No problem by me," Jack said cheerfully. "She can sleep for the next ten years, far as I'm concerned. Harry's Folly is there—clean and empty."

"They'll be looking for her soon," Newton said slowly.

"'They' being a boyfriend?" Jack's voice was studiously casual.

"No. Uncle. Frederick Mansion." Newton's face went blank. "He'll call and call and then his secretary will start sending faxes."

"Well." Jack scratched his whiskered chin and reminded himself to have a quick shave before heading back to the Folly. Who knew if the gorgeous Miss Mansion was awake? "Mr. Frederick Mansion is not going to have too much luck in calling, Newton, because I'm not in my office and my secretary just had a baby. And damned if our fax didn't just break down a few minutes ago and the answering service will be on the blink. So maybe Miss Federica can get her sleep after all."

A white grin split the darkness of the man's face. "Owe you one. Sir."

Jack felt a grin creep over his face. So pretty Miss Federica Mansion had a wicked uncle and no boyfriend, did she? "Think nothing of it, my good man." He playfully jabbed a right to Newton's shoulder and met solid muscle. "Think nothing of it."

"Come on, honey, sit up."

Federica mumbled, "Go away," and tried to turn over, but gentle hands turned her back. She swatted at them, but they were firm.

A cool hand felt her brow and stuck a thermometer in her mouth and she drifted back to sleep, then someone was shaking her gently awake again.

Without wanting to, she found herself sitting up, pushing hair out of her eyes, leaning against a hard shoulder.

"Drink up, honey. You need to get something in you." A woman with an interesting face, high broad cheekbones easing down into a determined chin, was bending down to her, holding a steaming oversized cup. Her intense blue eyes were kind, and she had a soft Western accent.

Suddenly, Federica realized she was starving. She accepted the cup and began trembling. To her horror, she found that her shaking hands couldn't support the big cup, and she was about to spill what smelled like soup all over herself when a large, brown hand cupped hers. She sipped cautiously, then eagerly. It was delicious.

She followed that brown hand up a checked plaid arm until she met another pair of intense blue eyes disturbingly near hers. She blinked.

"Better?" a deep voice asked.

He looked like the woman, only with tanned leathery skin and curly black hair instead of the woman's soft brown. He smiled encouragingly and Federica found herself smiling back.

"Yes," Federica replied cautiously. "I think so. It's just that I—I'm so sleepy."

"Doc, what do you think?"

"Nothing some more bed rest and a few more of Stella's meals won't cure." The third person in the room, a portly Hispanic man, smiled at her from the shadows.

"Who—" Federica began, but the word turned into a yawn. "Who are you?"

"Jack Sutter," the man beside her said. He was so close she could feel the vibrations of his deep voice in his chest. "That's my sister Lilly, and that fat man over there is Doc Alonzo. Don't look like much, I know, but he's a pretty good quack. Hasn't buried too many of his patients, and he says you're okay."

Someone had attached lead weights to Federica's eyes. The hot soup nestled warmly in her stomach. "Jack Sutter," she murmured. "Lilly." Her eyes closed and she slid back down into the bed. "Pleased to meet you, Mr. Mayor," she said, and fell asleep.

The three let themselves quietly out of her room, and walked down the huge banistered staircase of Harry's Folly and into the bright morning. Carson's Bluff could be clearly seen a few miles down the valley, looking closer than it was because of the pristine clarity of the mountain air.

"Well, Jack," Lilly said, amusement lacing her voice. "I'll bet that was a real first for you."

"What's that, Lil?"

"Most girls fall at your feet. First time I've seen one fall fast asleep on you."

~~~~~

May 31ˢᵗ

FAX FROM: Ellen Larsen, c/o Inter Airways, JFK Airport, New York

FAX TO: F. H. Mansion c/o Mayor's Office, Carson's Bluff, CA

Hi Federica, I thought you'd have called me by now, but I imagine you were tired when you got in. Trust Uncle F. to send you straight off without a chance to recover from jet lag. Just like our boss, El Shithead. Eat this fax.

I bid the California route, just in case you finish your business early, and asked for the 2nd and 3rd off. Even if we can't see each other, we can at least chat on the phone without making the phone company rich.

I wonder if the sheriff has come up with any other little problems Carson's Bluff might have, like giant man-eating spiders or space pods. Isn't Northern California *Invasion of the Body Snatchers* country or am I thinking of the wrong movie?

Let me know if we're going to be seeing the Boss.

Love, El

MESSAGE NOT RECEIVED/NO SIGNAL

~~~~~

May 31st, 3:00 p.m.

INTERNAL MEMO, Mansion Enterprises
From: Frederick Mansion
To: Russell White

R.W. — I've been waiting for two days now for that building and restoration schedule for the Carson's Bluff property. Federica hasn't contacted me, but I imagine she's working on the sale. McClellan over at Sandford & Co. has assured me they would be booking a week a month in the second quarter of next year, and Neal Haar has been making interested noises. The retreat could be a big money spinner, but we have to stay on target. Carson's Bluff is our last scheduled construction project until next year, and if it's not online by Christmas, I might have to shut down your department.

F. M.

~~~~~

3:30 p.m.

INTERNAL MEMO, Mansion Enterprises
From: Russell White
To: Frederick Mansion

F.M. — It's hard for my department to come up with accurate planning since we don't have all the data on Carson's Bluff yet. For all we know, there might be municipal zoning problems. I don't think shutting down my department would be cost-effective, as you'd just have to start from scratch again in setting up the engineering team next year, and good engineers are hard to find. Let's sit on it a minute.

R. W.

~~~~~

4:15 p.m.

INTERNAL MEMO, Mansion Enterprises

From: Frederick Mansion

To: Russell White

Good engineers are a dime a dozen in India, and our accounting department has already given me the figures for closing down your department and outsourcing if we don't get the Carson's Bluff property. The figures look pretty damned convincing. Get moving.

B. M.

~~~~~

    FAX FROM: Frederick Mansion, Mansion Enterprises

    FAX TO: Federica Mansion, c/o Mayor's Office, Carson's Bluff

    Federica—your silence is highly irresponsible. As you know, we're operating on a tight schedule. Please give immediate report on the status of negotiations. Did you warn the City Council that the offer falls by $10,000 a day?

    Uncle Frederick

    MESSAGE NOT RECEIVED/NO SIGNAL

~~~~~

June 1st

Birdsong filtered into the darkened room. Federica opened her eyes and lay staring at the ceiling shrouded in shadows.

This time she knew where she was. She was in Carson's Bluff. There was something she had to do here, something urgent, but nothing seemed to penetrate her befogged brain.

She had a vague memory of people coming into her room and forcing her to eat. An old rocking chair sat in the corner with an afghan haphazardly laid across it, and she seemed to recall someone spending the nights there, though night and day tended to blur in her memory.

No matter. She didn't want to think of the past. She didn't want to think of the future. She didn't want to think of anything.

Throwing off the covers, she walked slowly to the shuttered windows and flung them open, closing her eyes against the bright sunlight.

A tall stand of oak shed filtered dappled sunlight across a wide, untended lawn. Wild roses grew in profusion and Federica could hear the soft buzz of bees. The sun was halfway up a brilliant blue sky. She smiled, yawned and turned back to the room.

A door in the far wall was ajar. She remembered that it was the bathroom, and she could vaguely remember someone helping her to it more than once. She frowned, but the memory wouldn't jell further.

It was an old-fashioned bathroom, with a claw-footed tub and a big, no-nonsense showerhead. For the first time in years, it wasn't necessary to figure out the super-modern workings. All she did was turn the hot water faucet clockwise, fiddle with the cold water faucet until it was exactly to her liking and stand under the refreshing jet. Still dripping, she padded into the bedroom.

Her suitcase lay on the floor, open, the elastic straps still in place. Usually, the first thing she did when arriving somewhere was unpack and try to make the temporary hotel room as homey as possible.

Her traveling wardrobe was either business suits or casual wear for the hotel room. She rummaged, and brought out black leggings and a turquoise silk top.

She felt as if she were moving under water. Black wings of anxiety—*there was something she had to do*—brushed fleetingly across her mind, but she couldn't hold onto any thoughts as she descended slowly, carefully, down a big wooden staircase to the ground floor.

She was in a beautiful building. That much penetrated her benumbed senses, but it had no meaning, as impersonal as the sun shining through the big transom window over the front door, as right and timeless as the oaks and the roses and the buzzing bees.

She stepped out onto a wide veranda and breathed deeply. The air smelled as sparkling as champagne.

The sound of an engine changing gears as it climbed the mountain road filtered through the morning's silence.

Federica sat down on the top step and waited for what the morning would bring, bare feet curling into the rough wooden planking. She felt as if she were living each moment, each second, anew, as if she had never done anything but sit in the morning sunshine on a wooden veranda, and would stay there forever.

A dusty van rounded a corner and the driver killed the engine. Slowly, the sounds of the forest began again—a gentle soughing of wind, the soft hum of bees.

A tall man unfolded himself from the van and walked with an easy, lanky grace up the driveway, carrying a large paper bag. The Mayor. The Sheriff.

Dispassionately, Federica saw that he was handsome, in a rough, very masculine way, totally unlike Russell—but that thought escaped her as quickly as it formed. He had intense blue eyes, set in a strong, bluntly carved face tanned a deep brown. He had the kind of tan that came from working in the sun, not lying in it.

She watched him walk up and shaded her eyes against the bright sunlight.

"Sheriff."

He stopped a few feet away, tipping back his Stetson with a thumb. He held up the bag. "Brought breakfast."

She smiled. "Right neighborly of you, Sheriff."

He climbed the steps to the veranda and sat down beside her. He opened the bag and peered inside. "Let's see what Stella packed this time. A thermos of," he unscrewed the cap and smelled reverently, "coffee. Stella's coffee is famous in three counties. A couple of Danish and four apples."

There were some paper cups in the bag. Jack poured them two cups and handed her one.

They sat in a comfortable silence, sipping coffee. The morning fog was clearing quickly, revealing a handful of wooden buildings down in the valley, beautiful even from up at the Folly.

"What's that?" Federica pointed with her cup. "Brigadoon?"

"Not quite." The sheriff smiled. "But close."

"It's pretty." She sighed. "Peaceful."

"That it is." He slanted her a close look. "Folks around here would like to keep it that way."

"That I can imagine." She tilted her face into the sun and closed her eyes.

"So," he said quietly as he put the cup of coffee down, "how're you feeling?"

"I'm not sure." She still had her face to the sun, like a soft sunflower. Slowly, she lowered her head until it rested on her knees and turned her face to him. "I think—I think I'm having a nervous breakdown."

His expression didn't change. "That so?"

"I'm not so sure, because I've never had one before, you see, but it certainly feels like one."

"Well," he grinned suddenly, "you've come to the right place. We've all had one—it's practically a precondition for citizenship of Carson's Bluff." A shadow passed briefly across his face, so quickly it was gone almost before she could notice it. "I've had mine. Lilly's had hers. Hell, Doc Alonzo's had a couple."

She smiled and rested her forehead on her knees. "I guess I'm in good company then."

He crushed the paper cups and leaned back on his elbows. They sat for a long while, watching the sun rise above the oaks. A rabbit crossed the lawn, not warily but bold as brass, stopping halfway and staring at them, nose twitching, as if they were intruders on his turf.

Jack stared out across the lawn. "Phone lines seem to be down," he said.

She looked at him and didn't speak.

"Fax isn't working either," he continued pensively. "I guess anyone looking for you is going to come up empty-handed."

"Guess so," she said softly, and the corners of her mouth lifted in the ghost of a smile. "I appreciate it, Sheriff."

"Jack."

"Federica, then."

The comfortable silence returned. Federica watched a hummingbird flit among the morning glory, which climbed the walls of Harry's Folly.

"I think," she said to Jack, "I'll go back up to bed for a nap. It's been a strenuous morning."

~~~~~

FAX FROM: Frederick Mansion, San Francisco Administrative Headquarters, Mansion Enterprises

FAX TO: Federica Mansion, c/o Mayor's Office, Carson's Bluff

Federica,

I have sent you five email messages. I can only hope that this long silence means that you are locked in twenty-four-hour negotiations with the Town Council of Carson's Bluff. Still, you could have had one of the secretaries send me a fax in code. Why is your cell phone switched off?

You have our negotiating parameters, and I expect you to stick to them. This silence is extremely annoying and I trust you will contact me soon.

Uncle Frederick

MESSAGE NOT RECEIVED/ NO SIGNAL

~~~~~

FAX FROM: Ellen Larsen, Inter Airways, SFO Airport

FAX TO: Federica Mansion, c/o Mayor's Office, Carson's Bluff

Federica—you there? Knock twice if you're among the living. I've been trying and trying to call you, but to no avail. Have left any number of messages on your answering service. You're not answering your emails.

I can only imagine that you're tied up in business, but do get in touch the minute you're free. I'm off tomorrow and the next day, so we could get together here if Uncle Frederick slips the leash a bit. You'll find me at the usual Inter Airways hellhole. This time he's found a place to put us all up at for $34. He's overpaying. Eat this fax.

MESSAGE NOT RECEIVED/ NO SIGNAL

~~~~~

Federica awoke from her morning nap and contemplated starting her afternoon nap early when she heard a deep male voice calling her name from downstairs.

Jack.

She smiled and swung her legs over the bed, searching with her toes for her flip-flops and finding them. Going barefoot twice was perhaps a bit much.

Something, somewhere in the back of her mind told her that when she had been someone else, in another incarnation, she had been relentlessly formal. She had never encountered anyone unless she had been dressed, coiffed and made-up properly for the occasion.

Federica shook her head.

So much wasted energy.

She combed her fingers through her hair, gave a quick, disinterested glance at herself in the mirror on the dresser, and went out to the Folly's spectacular staircase and leant on the balustrade, looking down into the immense foyer.

Jack Sutter stood in the center of the mosaic-tiled floor. He smiled up at her and held up a big paper bag.

"Lunch," he announced.

Federica felt a sharp tug, somewhere in the vicinity of her heart.

"Why sheriff," she said. "Déjà vu all over again."

Chapter Three

They had lunch on the Folly's immense lawn, soaking up the sunshine.

When the sun was directly overhead, they moved beneath the shade of a century-old oak, watching the leaves shimmer in the light breeze.

"This picnic," Jack announced, "is a compendium of the talents of Carson's Bluff. Stella cooked, my second cousin Rose Franklin wove the tablecloth, Lilly made the plates and my brother Wyatt made the beer."

He spread an exquisite linen tablecloth on the crabgrass, laid out gray and blue earthenware plates and matching earthenware glasses, and opened two bottles of beer. He handed one to Federica and she looked at the label.

The hand-printed label was a copy of a sepia print of an old saloon, above it the legend, Prime Pigswill.

"Wyatt's finest," Jack said, and chugged a slug from the bottle.

Federica poured half the bottle in her glass, admiring the glaze of the earthenware glass and the solid heft of it. She took a sip and her eyes widened.

Jack noticed and smiled. "Good, eh?"

"It's great," Federica said sincerely. "As good as Korean beer."

"Better," Jack said absently, as he opened Stella's picnic basket. He pulled out a roast chicken.

Federica was suddenly curious. "How do you know? Have you been to Korea?"

"Couple of times," he said curtly, and pulled the tinfoil off a bowl of potato salad.

Something about his tone and the suddenly shuttered expression on his face told her he didn't want to talk about it.

That was fine with Federica. She didn't want to pry. She didn't want to pressure him. She didn't want to do anything but sit in the shade of an old oak tree, sip beer and eat Stella's delicious food.

She crossed her legs at the ankles and took another sip.

"Tell me about the beer. When did your brother start making it?"

Jack leaned against the tree trunk. "When Wyatt was eighteen," he began, in a storyteller's singsong cadence, "and even more hormonal than he is now, he saw a rerun on TV of an old chestnut called *The Vikings*. Kirk Douglas as a Viking chieftain and Tony Curtis as his slave, believe it or not. You ever see it?"

Federica shook her head and drank deeply from her glass.

"Well, what really attracted Wyatt about the movie were these scenes where a lot of blonde bimbos walked around half-dressed, skimming beer off a big vat and pouring it into horns for the heroes to drink. I guess it really struck a chord with him. Anyway, Wyatt got a book on brewing from the library, went to the butcher and had him prepare a bull horn, poured his first effort for our dad and asked him what he thought of it."

"And?"

"And Dad said it was prime pigswill. Wyatt improved on that first batch and he's never looked back since."

"Does he market it?"

"Yeah, he sells to a few bars around here, but he keeps the quantities down. He says if he made larger quantities, it would be too much like working."

Federica smiled, and bit down on a drumstick. It tasted of free-range chicken, rosemary and garlic.

They munched happily in silence, moving the tablecloth when the sun rose higher in the sky. Federica tackled the potato salad and sighed with pleasure. She rolled her shoulders experimentally and felt something odd. She waggled her head.

"Anything wrong?" Jack asked lazily.

"I don't know," she said, lifting a shoulder cautiously. "I feel...funny."

"No tension," Jack said, and helped himself to more potato salad. "Takes a while to get used to it."

Stella had packed half an apple pie. By the time she had finished her share of it and had started on her third bottle of Prime Pigswill, Federica was feeling replete and had a pleasant buzz. She stuck her legs out in the sun and leaned back in the shade.

She had the feeling she was in the eye of the hurricane. Dark forces were gathering on the horizon and soon the storm would strike, lashing everything in its path. But right now, the day was sunny, the bees were humming and she felt an unaccustomed bone-deep contentment.

"Why don't you let me clear these things up and you can go have your afternoon nap," Jack said. "You've had a really tiring day."

~~~~~

FAX FROM: Ellen Larsen, c/o Inter Airways, SFO Airport

FAX TO: Frederick Mansion, San Francisco Administrative Headquarters, Mansion Enterprises

Hello, Mr. Mansion, do you remember me? I'm Federica's best friend. We met on Christmas Eve last year, when I was visiting Federica. I wouldn't ordinarily bother you, but I can't seem to contact her. We had a tentative date here in San Francisco tomorrow. I know that she's in Northern California on business and I wonder if you could relay a message to her and tell her I'm here. She knows where to contact me. Thank you.

Best regards, Ellen Larsen

~~~~~

FAX TO: Ellen Larsen, c/o Inter Airways, SFO Airport

FAX FROM: Office of Frederick Mansion, Mansion Enterprises

Dear Miss Larsen,

Mr. Mansion regrets to inform you that he is unable to contact Miss Mansion, who is away on company business.

Best, R. P. for F. M.

~~~~~

INTERNAL MEMO: Mansion Enterprises

From: Frederick Mansion

To: Russell White

R. W.,

Unfortunately, I have to leave for Prague immediately. The Czech government is apparently changing its laws on foreign ownership, and the Foreign Trade Council has appointed me its representative. We must be there to protect our interests. In the interim, I am putting you in charge of the Carson's Bluff project. Don't forget your department is on the line. Keep in touch by email.

F. M.

~~~~~

FAX FROM: Frederick Mansion, San Francisco
FAX TO: Federica Mansion, c/o Mayor's Office, Carson's Bluff

Federica, your silence is most irresponsible, indeed. I trust you are in the midst of negotiations, but switching your cellular phone off, not answering emails and not checking to see whether that hamlet's faxes are working is unconscionable. I am leaving for Prague this afternoon—you remember we were warned that the Czech government might reverse its policies. Your liaison will be Russell White while I'm away.

Uncle Frederick

MESSAGE NOT RECEIVED/NO SIGNAL

~~~~~

Note taped to door of Jack Sutter's office.

Jack—I realize you're having a lot of fun up at the Folly, and I'd love to let you while your time away in Neverland forever, but...if we don't reconnect the fax soon I'm going to have to take a trip down to Shelby *myself. By car.*

You know how much I hate putting myself out like that. Come on. We're going to have to get in contact with the outside world at some point. See you at Lilly's tonight.

Wyatt

~~~~~

FAX FROM: Ellen Larsen, c/o Inter Airways, SFO airport

FAX TO: Federica Mansion, c/o Mayor's Office, Carson's Bluff

Honey, I'm starting to get worried. This isn't like you at all. Are you okay? I'm here in SF waiting for you to get in touch at the Inter Airways Roach Motel. Eat this fax.

Love, El

MESSAGE NOT RECEIVED/NO SIGNAL

~~~~~

Note taped to Jack Sutter's fridge.

Jack, why don't you bring down the hermit from the Folly this evening? I'm cooking. I promise her okay food and superb earthenware. How can she resist? See you around seven. Bring something for Cavendish.

Love, Lilly

~~~~~

Federica woke up around five, stretched, yawned and lay back in the big four-poster with her hands behind her head. She contemplated the ceiling and her situation.

She was here to do a job. No matter that the very idea of engaging the Carson's Bluff City Council—in the person of the very handsome and laid-back sheriff, his likeable sister of the beautiful pottery and his brother of the delicious beer—in a *mano a mano* over Harry's Folly made her nauseous. No matter that the idea of hauling out her laptop with its spreadsheet full of schedules and appraisals made her ill.

The very idea of bestirring herself to do the job she had come here for made her feel as if she were wading through molasses.

I don't want to do this, she told the ceiling.

The ceiling didn't answer back.

After a while, she got up. She thought she would go back down to the veranda and watch the grass grow.

Walking down the staircase, she fully realized, for the first time, the extraordinary beauty of Harry's Folly. Originally, it must have been a saloon, probably like thousands of other Western saloons in the nineteenth century, though Federica had never seen one close-up herself except in movies. Though the layout was probably perfectly standard, the workmanship was anything but.

Master carpenters had lovingly worked over every fine detail, from the graceful wooden balustrade to the oak bird and flower frieze carved along the top of the wainscoting. Some unsung genius had painted a fresco of a heavenly chorus on the vaulted ceiling, the fresco perfect down to the cherubs' tiny, superbly proportioned toenails.

It was clear that Harry's Folly had been in a state of decay and that someone had been restoring it. Wooden scaffolding covered the far wall of the downstairs area, a dark, sooty area visible beneath the netting.

Federica had once gone into the wrong bedroom upstairs, and had discovered that all the upstairs rooms were moldy, with cracked plaster walls and broken hardwood flooring, except her own bedroom — a miracle of light and grace.

When Harry's Folly was completely restored, it was going to be spectacular, she thought uneasily. Worth every penny Uncle Frederick was bidding, and more. Probably the grounds alone were worth what he was offering.

Dark snatches of thoughts of duty buzzed around her head like gnats as she walked out onto the veranda.

She sat down in her now familiar position on the top step and watched the sun start to settle behind the tops of the oaks.

It was so easy to lose herself here, to imagine that life was sleeping in that gorgeous four-poster bed with its cotton and linen flowered bedspread which she imagined Jack's cousin had woven, and eating Stella's delicious food out of Lilly's imaginative plates.

It was easy to imagine that she could stay here forever, watching the sun go up and down in the sky and thinking of nothing but how good she felt.

But she couldn't, of course. A prickle of unease ran up her back. The storm hadn't broken, but the clouds were gathering.

Federica smiled when she heard a familiar powerful engine change gears on the way up.

She watched Jack drive up and wondered what he would be bringing her for dinner, vaguely surprised when he stepped out of the van without his usual paper bag.

"Hi." He smiled up at her.

"Hi." She scooted over and made room for him on the top step. "I'm watching the sun set. Join me?"

"Don't overdo all this frenetic activity," Jack said, as he folded his long legs to sit next to her.

They sat in silence.

"I guess I'm not eating tonight," she said, looking at his empty hands.

"You're eating all right. My sister Lil has invited you for dinner. It's a real privilege. She hates to cook. Her husband Norman usually does the cooking, but he's busy on some project."

"Someone from Carson's Bluff working? I thought 'take it easy' was the town motto."

"It is. Today is an exception. So—you want to run up and grab a sweater or something?"

"I don't know." Federica's voice was light. "I'm not really up to much traveling these days." She folded her hands carefully to disguise the trembling, but his eyes were sharp. He saw.

He was quiet for several minutes. "About how much of a range do you have?" he asked, finally.

Federica hadn't been home in six weeks. She thought of her extended business trip and remembered Paris, Rome, Berlin, Prague, Frankfurt, Madrid, New York, Honolulu, Singapore and Hong Kong as one long, exhausting blur. Just the thought of it, of another foreign city and another plane—or even moving from exactly where she was—had a band tightening across her chest and her breath catching in her throat.

"I don't have much of a range at all. Couple of miles maybe. If I push it," she replied. She caught her hands under her knees, because the trembling was getting worse.

"Well, you're in luck, because Lil and Norman live about a mile and a half away," he said. "You could sort of close your eyes in the van and pretend you're not going anywhere."

Federica looked at him in silence. *He understands*, she thought in wonder. And then, confused, *understands what? What on Earth is happening to me?*

She opened her mouth to refuse and surprised herself by saying, "I think I could swing that."

~~~~~

FAX FROM: Ellen Larsen, c/o Inter Airways, SFO Airport

FAX TO: Federica Mansion, c/o Mayor's Office, Carson's Bluff

Federica,

Hon, you've really got me worried. I faxed your uncle, but he was no help. Had his secretary answer. I suppose you're wrapped up in company business, but I'd really like to know what you're doing. I've got tomorrow and the next day off and had to push my supervisor to get it. For a dime, I'd quit. Springsteen's probably off, but maybe we could still have a day together. You okay?

Love, El

MESSAGE NOT RECEIVED/NO SIGNAL

~~~~~

FAX FROM: Russell White, c/o SF Administrative Headquarters, Mansion Enterprises

FAX TO: Federica Mansion, c/o Mayor's Office, Carson's Bluff

Federica,

Hello, long time no see. Your uncle has put me in charge of the Carson's Bluff project until his return from Prague. Imagine you're working very hard on this project, though you really should get in touch soon with the SF office. We're a little behind in planning and we need more input. We'll be working together on this until your uncle's return. I trust our shared personal history will not intrude on business.

Russell

MESSAGE NOT RECEIVED/NO SIGNAL

~~~~~

Lilly and Norman lived in a charming cottage at the foot of the road leading to Harry's Folly. Brambler roses in full bloom climbed the freshly painted wood walls. The doors and windows were painted a bright green and the picket fence surrounding the garden was blue.

As Jack pulled the van up, Federica could see a goat tethered on the lawn munching on the grass. A kennel abutted the cottage and wild barking erupted as soon as the van pulled up.

"Pipe down you guys!" Jack shouted, as he walked around the van and opened the passenger door, helping her out of the vehicle. He opened the gate latch, then walked over to the kennel door. He had barely unlocked it when two German shepherds nosed the door open and jumped him, wriggling with delight and vying to lick his face.

Jack laughed. He knelt and hugged the squirming dogs, trying to avoid two wet tongues. He looked up at her, his arms full of dog. "Sorry about that. Lil's raised them, and she's not too good about discipline."

Federica watched him wrestle with the dogs, then was distracted by a litter of kittens emerging from under the door stoop. They were red tabbies and she smiled as they tumbled over each other, scuffling and trying to bite each other with tiny white milk teeth.

Jack finally got the two German shepherds back in the kennel and took her elbow. As they walked toward the house, the mother tabby yawned and watched them out of slitted, contented eyes.

Jack pointed to the goat. "That's Norman's. He says it beats mowing the lawn."

"I can see that people in Carson's Bluff believe in conservation of energy," Federica replied.

"Jack!" a voice shouted from behind the house. "We're in the backyard."

As they walked around the little cottage, Federica saw a potter's kiln. Set in ledges built into the wall of the kiln were vases, plates and pitchers. Gorgeous shapes, gorgeous colors. The smell of honeysuckle and jasmine almost overwhelmed her.

"Hey," Lilly said, coming toward them. She hugged Federica. "Glad you could make it."

"I'm glad, too," Federica said sincerely. The backyard was bigger than the front garden. It sloped down to a river, and was flanked by flowerbeds and two weeping willows. A big brick barbecue held glowing embers.

A tall blond man stood up, as did another man…

"Newton!" Federica cried, and rushed into the big man's arms. Federica hugged him tightly, then pulled away. "Oh, Newton." How could she have forgotten about him? She had been so wrapped in herself up at the Folly… She swiped at a tear. "I'm sorry. God, I forgot all about you—"

"No problem, Miss Federica." Newton smiled down at her and rubbed a hand over his big belly. "Stella's been taking care of me."

"Oh, Newton. I just didn't think, I've been sleeping and sleeping—have you been staying at Stella's? But I didn't bring sheets for you."

"Sheets?" Newton sounded confused. "Stella has everything. What do you mean, sheets?"

Federica turned toward Jack, looking at him through narrowed eyes, but he was petting the big tabby, which had followed them into the backyard. Feeling Federica's gaze, he raised innocent eyes.

"Never mind, Newton," Federica said. "I'm so glad you're still here."

"I'm here as long as you are, Miss Federica," Newton said gently.

Federica hugged him tightly again, then let go. Somehow Newton was always there. He had always been there. He had been there when Federica had come back from Europe, a frightened eighteen-year-old. He had been there when she had graduated from business school, the only one to celebrate her graduation, bearing a congratulatory telegram from Uncle Frederick. He had been there when Russell—

"Federica, meet my brother Wyatt," Lilly said, tugging on the arm of a tall, handsome blond man.

"He of the marvelous beer," Federica grinned.

"Me of the marvelous beer," Wyatt agreed, sticking out a hand.

Federica took it. Wyatt Sutter was incredibly good-looking. He resembled Lilly and Jack both, but where Lilly's looks were soft and feminine, and Jack looked hard and masculine, Wyatt just looked good. And kind. He shared that with his sister and brother. All three looked kind-hearted.

"Wyatt. Nice to meet you."

"Same here," he replied. "We've all been curious about the recluse up at Harry's Folly. I just knew you'd come down some day."

Federica knew why she was there, and so did everyone else. It should have made for an embarrassing situation, but somehow it didn't. Everyone was genuinely welcoming. Federica could tell, because she had never felt that warmth before.

Usually, a visit from a Mansion heralded trouble, and she was used to a wary, defensive posture from the people she encountered.

"Even recluses come down from the mountain," she replied. "Recluses have surprises."

"Hey, surprises I like."

They both laughed.

Lilly threw some steaks on the embers and the smell rose sharp and pungent on the evening air. Through an open window, Federica could hear the familiar sound of someone pounding on a computer keyboard.

Jack put a glass in her hand and opened a bottle. "Let's celebrate your emergence from hermithood."

The glass was a stoneware sculpture of a hand holding a glass. Her own flesh-and-blood hand fit perfectly around the ceramic one. She laughed aloud in delight. "Lilly, you're a genius."

Jack poured some Pigswill into her glass, so quickly it foamed over. Federica licked some off the rim. "Do you sell your stuff?" Federica asked Lilly.

"Yes. There's a gallery in Sacramento that sells my sculptures. And an upscale boutique in Fresco that sells my house wares. The funny thing is, I've discovered that the less I produce, the more I can ask for my work."

"Supply and demand," Federica intoned solemnly, raising her glass. "I propose a toast to the market economy."

"Hear, hear," Jack said, and drained his glass.

The sound of tapping continued to drift out the window.

"Uh, oh," Lilly said, consulting her wristwatch. "It's time."

"Time?" Federica asked. "Time for what?"

"For Norman to quit working," Jack explained. "He's been at it a couple of hours now. Lilly rations his computer time. Otherwise, he'd never stop."

"Norman!" Lilly shouted. "Quitting time."

The tapping increased in tempo. Lilly sighed.

"Sorry, Lil," Wyatt said gently. "You know what he's like. You're going to have to go in and drag him out."

Lilly rolled her eyes and got up. Something about the way she moved attracted Federica's attention. She tugged on Jack's sleeve as she watched Lilly go in the kitchen door.

"Jack, is Lilly, uh, is she—"

"Yes, she's expecting," he said, as his eyes rested fondly on his sister disappearing through the door. "About time another Sutter came into the world. There are only five of us."

"Five?" Federica asked. "You, Wyatt, Lilly and—"

"And my folks."

"Your parents are alive?" Federica asked softly. Her breath caught in her throat.

"Well, yes, though I'm not too sure about Dad—"

"Our parents are alive," Wyatt interrupted, shooting an exasperated glance at Jack. "It's just that our father is a very relaxed man. It confuses people. Even Jack."

"Well, when we go fishing, he doesn't really respond when the fish bite," Jack pointed out reasonably, then looked at her through narrowed eyes. "Where are your folks?" he asked.

"Dead," Federica replied. "A long time ago."

"Brothers and sisters?"

"None," she replied.

"Don't you have any family at all?"

"Well," Federica said slowly, "there's Uncle Frederick."

Newton choked on his beer. He wheezed and brought a hand to his throat. Jack slapped him on the back.

"Uncle Frederick was very good to me," she said reprovingly to Newton. "After all, he paid for my education."

Newton was silent a moment, considering, then took a long drink. "What the hell," he said into his glass. "Might as well have my say. He might have paid for your education, honey," he said gently, raising his eyes to Federica, "but he's never let you forget it for one single second. And you've been working like a dog for him for the past eight years."

The back door opened, and Lilly led a bewildered-looking man out by the hand. He was of middling height, balding and with a fuzzy blond beard.

"Come on, Norman," Lilly coaxed. "It's all right."

"But Lil," he protested. "I haven't finished yet. I've got one more spreadsheet. Just one, Lil, I promise, and then I'll stop. Just let me—"

"No," she replied firmly. "Your time is up and you know it."

She sat him on the bench and looked at him sternly. "That's it. You're done for the day now, aren't you?"

"Yes, Lil," the man replied obediently, "of course." But his eyes strayed with longing toward the door.

"Norman's a recovering workaholic," Lilly explained to Federica, as she grabbed the big barbecue fork. "We've come a long way. We're taking it one day at a time."

Norman's eyes were still glazed.

"Here," Wyatt said kindly, and pushed a bottle toward Norman. "Have a beer. Maybe it'll help."

Norman took the bottle blindly and took a long pull. But when he put the bottle down, his eyes were still glued on the back door.

Lilly laughed and took his hand. She placed it on her belly and Norman lost that glazed look. He fondled her stomach and they exchanged a loving glance.

Lucky Lilly, Federica found herself thinking in spite of herself. *Lucky, lucky Lilly. A husband, two brothers who adore her. Parents. A child. A rose-filled cottage. A job she does well and loves.*

Stop it, she told herself sternly. *Envy is nasty. It doesn't become you. You have so much more than she does.*

Federica thought of her life. Lilly's cottage was charming, but small. Federica had an enormous condo on Nob Hill, owned by Mansion Enterprises and leased to her on privileged terms. She didn't even know what to do with all the space she had. She traveled the world. She was an executive, with great authority and responsibility in one of the world's most important hotel chains. The hotel chain bore her name.

And…and she hadn't seen her apartment in six weeks. She hadn't seen a friendly, familiar face in the same time. She had no friends at all, come to think of it, except for Ellen, who led the same life she did. She had no family of her own. And the way she was going, she never would.

That's enough. It was pointless getting maudlin. She was here for a purpose. The fact that the purpose was to earn her uncle even more money than he already had didn't make her feel any better. She wasn't here to mull over her empty life, she was here to —

A bell rang distantly.

"Federica?" Lilly was wrestling with a recalcitrant steak. "Would you do me a favor?"

"Sure, Lilly," Federica smiled.

"That was the oven. The potato casserole is cooked. Would you bring it out here? The pot holders are hanging inside the door next to the oven."

Federica walked to the kitchen door.

Jack's eyes followed her every step of the way.

"Hey, bro," Wyatt grinned, and gave a whoop once Federica had disappeared. "She's pretty rich for your blood, isn't she?"

"I don't know what you're talking about," Jack began huffily.

Then they heard the scream.

Chapter Four

Federica's scream was still echoing in her ears when Jack burst into the kitchen, eyes narrowed.

"Something slithered by me!" Federica took a shaky breath and pointed vaguely in the direction of the little living room visible through an archway. "Something big and...and furry. Like a *rat*, only bigger!"

Wyatt and Norman stood framed in the kitchen door. Lilly's head peeped over their shoulders. A worried-looking Newton appeared, and Lilly put a reassuring hand on his massive arm.

"Poor little thing," Jack crooned softly. He started forward and Federica half-turned to him in gratitude, only to watch him move past her.

"He's scared, poor sweetheart." Wyatt's voice, too, was low and soft.

"No—no, really. It's okay." Federica lifted a hand to her still thundering heart. "It's just that—" She stopped.

He? He's scared?

Jack went into a half-crouch, hand extended, making cooing noises, closely followed by Wyatt and Norman. Lilly leaned against a counter, arms crossed over the slight swell of her stomach, and watched her men with a half-smile on her face.

Curious, Federica peered into the living room. For a moment she was distracted by the riot of colors. Each wall was painted a slightly different shade of turquoise, the cornice and ceiling a pale shell-pink. Two 'fifties couches, reupholstered in a cheery daisy yellow, were strewn with throw pillows in every color of the rainbow. A royal blue bookcase filled with paperbacks covered one wall.

A sage green dresser held a cornucopia of pottery in bright, swirling colors — pitchers in the shape of lemons, a dark-green platter shaped like a fig leaf, a duck teapot with a bill for a spout... Federica was entranced.

She thought of her own living room, a vast expanse big enough to grow corn in. It was larger than Lilly's entire house and decorated expensively and anonymously in every hue of beige by the same woman who designed the hotel rooms for the Mansion Enterprises West Coast hotels. The only thing her living room had in common with Lilly's was four walls and a ceiling.

There it was again! Out of the corner of one eye, Federica caught a dark brown blur and watched, astonished, as Jack slowly straightened with a fur collar around his neck. The collar twitched and two black button eyes glared at Federica. Jack and Wyatt were petting it and Norman fed it pieces of meat he had snagged off the kitchen counter.

Norman looked over his shoulder at Federica. "You scared him." His voice was reproachful. "He's trembling."

"*I* scared *him*?" Federica sucked in an indignant breath. "I thought I'd have a heart attack. What is he — it?"

"He's a mongoose, honey." Lilly sounded annoyed. "And a lazy, shiftless, voracious one at that. Which is why the menfolk love him so much. They identify with him. Norman, why is Cavendish out of his cage?"

"Come on, Lil. Have a heart. Cavendish looked so lonely in there. Even mongooses have a right to company." Norman held out his hand and Cavendish flowed smoothly from Jack's neck to Norman's shoulder. Three men and a mongoose looked at Lilly and Federica with three innocent expressions and a crafty one.

"Men." Lilly turned in disgust and took Federica by the arm. "Come on, Federica, Newton. Anyone for another beer?"

They trooped back through the kitchen and out into the garden. On his way out, Jack bent to peer with interest into the oven door.

"Hey Lil," he called out casually. "Are the potatoes *supposed* to be black?"

With a cry, Lilly rushed back into the kitchen, grabbed the oven mitts and pulled out a smoking pan. "My casserole," she moaned.

"That's okay, Lil. I brought along an extra case of Pigswill and these." Wyatt pulled out one of two bottles nestled in a plastic bucket of ice resting against one of the table legs. "This will wash out even the taste of *your* cooking. Dad's best vintage."

Curious, Federica checked the handmade label and laughed. The label showed the stylized profile of a man with a stem glass held to his lips. Above, in impressive Gothic script— *Plonk du Patron. Grand Cru 2004.*

Lilly was fussing with the table settings. "Norman, you sit here, Newton here. Wyatt, you'll be pouring, so you sit here. Jack," she said, her voice casual, "you sit next to Federica. And as for *you*—" she plucked Cavendish off Norman's shoulders, and carried him to a cage set against the pink-washed stucco wall. "You eat in the guest room."

"Aw, Lil." Three male voices rose in protest.

Lilly latched the cage and walked over to the barbecue. "Not another word out of you three or you'll be eating in the guest room, too." She forked the steaks onto a massive marbleized platter. Norman jumped up and took the platter out of his wife's hands.

The food was indifferent. The steaks were tough and overcooked, the potato casserole over-salted and burnt, and the salad was watery. Federica didn't care. It was so pleasant out in the garden, with the smell of charcoal and jasmine floating on the gentle summer breeze, and the glistening river just visible through the willows providing a soft background murmur.

"Sorry about the food. Particularly since you've been eating Stella's fare." Lilly smiled at Federica and Newton. "Norman's the real cook around here, but he's in the middle of a job and as you saw, he's out of it when he's working. It's a good thing I ration him to one account a month, otherwise we'd starve to death."

"What do you do, Norman?" Federica asked.

Norman winced when he put a bite of steak in his mouth. He hesitated a moment, then chewed, swallowed and gratefully put down his fork. "Well, now I keep the books of a few local businesses. I draw up the odd business plan or two, as well. That's what I'm doing now. A local software company has asked me for advice. Three very smart kids. Silicon Valley refugees after the dot-com crash. We get a lot of those around here."

"Are they planning on expanding?" Federica was having trouble keeping her mind on the conversation. The bench was small, and Jack was so close she could feel his body heat. He had on a short-sleeved polo shirt and Federica tried to keep her eyes off the fascinating play of muscles in his forearm, but it was hard. Jack's hands were large and strong and Federica gave herself a shake when she found herself following his hands as he heaped his plate and hers.

Stop that right now, she told herself sternly. Was this part of a nervous breakdown? It must be, because she couldn't remember the last time she'd been mesmerized by a man's hands. Large, gorgeous, thoroughly masculine hands, but just *hands,* for heaven's sake!

She was here for business. Just business. She had to remember that.

Actually, she should be steering the conversation around to the sale of Harry's Folly. She should be angling for an appointment with the Town Council. It wouldn't be hard. The Carson's Bluff Town Council was right here with her, sitting around a picnic table, guzzling beer.

She tried to concentrate on the sale, then Jack's thigh brushed hers, and her thoughts melted and slid warmly down her spine to pool in her middle.

"No, they aren't planning on expanding," Norman, and for a moment Federica wondered what he was talking about. Then she remembered she'd asked a question. "Just the opposite, in fact." He carefully cut around the charred part of the potato casserole. "That's the problem. They've had an exceptional year, too much work to handle comfortably with current staff levels, and they want a plan to scale down without losing market share." He paused with his fork halfway to his mouth and his eyes lost their focus. "Non-growth is a tricky problem, because there are a lot of things you have to factor in, like client weight, pluri-annual contracts as opposed to jobbing…"

"Norman," Lilly said gently.

"And of course, advertising has to be scaled accordingly and very carefully placed—"

"Norman—"

"—and you have to watch your quarterly estimates and calculate FICA—"

"*Norman*!"

"*What?*" He sounded aggrieved.

"Work time is *over*, Norman."

He sighed and pushed his plate away.

"Have you always been a freelancer?" Federica asked.

Norman grimaced. "No. I used to be a vice president at Longthorn, Pace and Feldstein." He took a long swallow of Pigswill. "In a previous life."

"They keep our accounts," Federica said, startled. Longthorn, Pace and Feldstein was one of the largest accountancy firms in the state and far and away the best. It was also known for its shark-like accounting practices and for walking the finest line possible between clever bookkeeping and tax evasion. Which was why, Federica thought uncomfortably, it kept Mansion Enterprises' books.

The firm was also famous for treating its employees like the pharoahs treated the workers on the pyramids. "I know Longthorn, Pace and Feldstein very well. If you were a vice president, you must have worked sixty-hour weeks." It was hard to square that with Norman's present lifestyle.

"Seventy-hour weeks, actually. I had one heart attack and was barreling straight into my second when I met Lilly." He reached for his wife's hand and smiled into her eyes. "Best thing that ever happened to me. Saved my life in more ways than one." Norman looked around the table. "Of course, the downside to that is that my wife comes with a couple of flatliners for brothers, but what the hell. Her folks are nice and it's not that big a price to pay."

"I'll drink to that." Wyatt was grinning as he walked out of the kitchen with a tray of wine glasses. He set the tray down and uncorked the bottle of wine, deftly filling the glasses. "Here's to Dad. Long may he vint, if that's the word I want."

Jack handed Federica a glass and watched with a smile as she sniffed, then took a sip.

Federica rolled the wine around her tongue and swallowed. She took another sip and closed her eyes in delight. It was like tasting sunlight. The wine was a full-bodied red, with a very faint fruity aftertaste, and it went down like a dream. Federica opened her eyes to find everyone watching her.

"So what do you think?" Jack's eyes bored into hers. Against his deep suntan, the electric blue of his eyes was startling. An incredible blue. The bluest blue this side of—

"Heaven," she said without thinking. And blushed.

"Dad laid this down the year Norman and Lilly got married." Wyatt pushed back a shock of blond hair and Federica was struck again by how good-looking he was. He was better looking than Jack, his features more even and less craggy. But it was to Jack's face that her eyes kept wandering. "He said 'one down, two to go'."

"He also said that you two would never get married." Lilly was nestling comfortably in Norman's embrace. "He said you were too flighty and Jack was too serious."

Federica was mulling this over when an extraordinary apparition rounded the corner of the cottage.

"Lilly, blast it all, where are you, woman? My mug's broken and I need a new one. How can I drink my whisky out of a broken mug?"

An ancient man, bent almost double over a cane, hobbled into view. The hand clutching the cane was twisted with arthritis. Nonetheless, he covered ground surprisingly quickly. He stood for a moment while Jack got him a chair, then sat down, pulling off a battered black felt beret and revealing a bald, brown liver-spotted pate.

"Goddammit. I shouted myself hoarse out front." His black eyes, as crafty as Cavendish's, surveyed the picnic table, and the empty bottles of Pigswill scattered over the tabletop like so many fallen soldiers. "Of course, if I'd known you people were out here getting pie-eyed, I would have saved my breath and joined you earlier."

"Here, Horace." Wyatt uncorked another bottle and poured the old man a full glass of wine. "Dad wants to know what you think of it."

"Don't mind if I do, boy. Don't mind if I do." The wine disappeared down the old man's throat in two long swallows. "Ah…" He smacked his lips and held out the glass. "Okay, now I've primed the pump."

Wyatt had been holding the bottle ready and topped the glass up again. The next sip was worthy of a sommelier. The old man chewed the wine for a moment, then wiped his mouth with the back of his hand.

"Chateau Sutter." He nodded slowly. "Tell old Charlie it's better than the St. Emilion I used to drink in Paris."

Federica gasped and took a closer look at the man. Most of the light had drained from the evening sky and a few stars had come out, but it was still possible to see. The skin was more flaccid and the monk's rim of hair had gone, as had a few teeth, but the face was the same as the one on the back cover of one of her favorite books.

Horace.

Wyatt had called him Horace. Of course.

Horace Milton, author of America's most famous dirty books. He had written movingly, lyrically, lewdly, hilariously about his life and loves as a struggling artist in Paris during the Depression years. Federica had learned a lot about life—and love—by reading his forbidden books. Horace Milton. But how could Horace Milton be here? *Now?* He had been in his twenties at the start of the Depression, which made him...

"I thought you were dead," Federica blurted.

The old man turned his head slowly. He stared at her out of coal-black eyes which, for all their age, had lost nothing of their sharpness. For a moment, Federica felt stripped to the bone as he seemed to stare straight into her soul.

"Dead?" The old man's lips widened in a smile to reveal a mouthful of blackened stumps. "No, sweetheart. Not as long as there's a Republican majority I'm not. Though there are a lot of husbands who would have been happy to dance on my grave." Federica stared for a moment into his lively, ferociously intelligent black eyes. "*Ha!*" he suddenly cackled, and Federica jumped. "Outlived them all!"

"I used to read you in school," she breathed.

It was hard to believe he was here, at a picnic table with her in a small town in Northern California. He was forever fixed in her mind in the corner of a smoky bistro in Montmartre with a girl in one hand and a filter-less cigarette in another.

Again, she had the impression that he could see straight into her as he stared at her. "Good God, girl. Don't tell me I'm being taught in school now. I'd hate to be required reading in some asinine syllabus."

"Actually," Federica smiled, "I read you under the covers at night with a flashlight."

Horace Milton cackled. "That's more like it. Who are you, girl?" He looked around. "Come on, who is she? She's pretty. I want her."

"Horace Milton, meet Federica Mansion." Lilly's voice was quiet in the deepening darkness.

"*Mansion!*" The bantering tone was gone. Horace Milton took another long look at Federica, all the flirtatiousness and good humor vanished in an instant. Milton stared at Jack accusingly. "You didn't tell us at the meeting that this Mansion monster was a woman."

"We didn't know he was a she, either." Jack answered evenly.

Milton scooted his chair closer.

"You listen to me girl, and listen good." He pressed a nicotine-stained finger into her chest. "I know the Mansion Hotels. Godless, soulless places, all of them. Well, we don't want that here. We don't want any truck with your kind of commercialism. This is one of the last unsullied spots left on Earth and we all want to keep it that way. And as long as I'm alive, I'll fight you to my last breath. I don't care if I die in the process. You get me?" He jabbed hard at her chest and Newton half-rose in his seat. *"Do you understand me, girl?"*

Federica shook her head at Newton, then turned to meet Milton's hostile, black-eyed gaze. "Yes," she said quietly, "I understand."

Horace Milton turned in his chair and surveyed the Sutters and Norman, glaring at each in turn.

"And *you*—you should be ashamed of yourselves. Aiding and abetting the enemy. You know what this place will turn into if the Mansions ever get hold of Harry's Folly. The whole town will change. We'll be overrun by business types and they'll start laying down rules and regulations to protect their investment and we'll be prettified and regulated out of existence. They'll take the town over. Don't you remember what we said at the caucus?" Milton stared at his half-empty wine glass and pushed it away in disgust. "Lost my taste for it. Can't drink when I'm upset. Spoils the spirit of wine. I'll be back when we're in better company." After a sharp hostile glance at Federica, Horace rose slowly and hobbled away, leaving a long, uncomfortable silence.

Federica stared down at her uneaten steak. The air had grown suddenly chilly and she shivered.

"I'm sorry, Federica," Lilly said gently into the silence. "But no one can stop Milton when he wants to have his say. No one has ever been able to shut him up, and that includes the government. We wouldn't want to shut him up even if we could." She drew in a long breath. "That's part of why he likes it here in Carson's Bluff. Everyone is free to do and say exactly what they please here."

Everyone's free to do and say exactly what they please here. The words burned like acid in Federica's mind. She hadn't drawn a free breath in eight years.

"That's okay, Lilly." Federica smiled wanly. It was as if some giant black hole had opened up over Northern California and had sucked out all the pleasure and ease of the night. "Well." She placed her hands on the table and stood up. "It was a lovely dinner, Lilly, thank you. Wyatt, please congratulate your father on his wine for me." *Congratulations from a Mansion,* she thought. *That ought to go over big.* "Newton, I wonder if you could —"

"I'll drive you back, Federica." Jack already had her sweater on her shoulders and a hand at her elbow.

"If Miss Federica wants me to take her up, then that's what I'm doing." Newton towered over Jack, and his deep voice sounded threatening.

"That's all right, Newton." Federica laid a hand on his arm. Sweet, loyal Newton. His evening had been spoiled, too. Well, tense evenings in a hostile atmosphere were what being a Mansion was all about. Newton should know that by now. "I'll go up with the sheriff. Thank you all very much for a lovely evening. Good night."

She turned away, leaving the rest unspoken. But it hung in the air.

And good-by.

~~~~~

FAX FROM: Ellen Larsen, c/o Clairmont Hotel, San Francisco

FAX TO: Federica Mansion, c/o Sheriff's Office, Carson's Bluff

Hi, honey. It's 10:30 at night and I'm turning in. My supervisor offered me the Black Death Paris run tomorrow (turnaround time only two hours!) in exchange for another three-day free period starting the 5th. Since I haven't heard from you, I accepted. Nobody knows what's going on with you. Getting information out of the SF office of Mansion Enterprises is like asking the CIA for its list of agents. Their reaction ranges from silence to stony silence. Like trying to get information out of Inter Airways when a flight is late. I didn't say that.

Anyway, no one's talking, least of all that louse Russell White. I'm starting to get worried. Did you come down with the Ebola virus? Legionnaire's disease? Have you been kidnapped? Knock twice if you're there. See you on the 5th (I hope).

Love, El

MESSAGE NOT RECEIVED/NO SIGNAL

~~~~~

FAX FROM: Russell White, c/o Mansion Enterprises, San Francisco

FAX TO: Federica Mansion, c/o Sheriff's Office, Carson's Bluff

Federica,

Your emails are bouncing, so I'm sending another fax.

I'm trying to get on top of the Carson's Bluff project, which I'm temporarily heading pending F. M.'s return from Prague. I told you that in a previous fax, but the machine on your end was switched off. I'm prioritizing this so we can stay on schedule. We're looking at a June 10 deadline, but there's a lot of work to be done before we can seal the deal. We need more input this end. You're not checking your email, so will try the fax again. Contact head office soonest.

Russell

MESSAGE NOT RECEIVED/NO SIGNAL

~~~~~

EMAIL FROM: pcobb@mansent.com
TO: F.H.Mansion@mansent.com

Frederick,

I'm encrypting this, decrypt your end. Message below:

It's 11:30 p.m. over here, 7:30 a.m. your end, so you should be reading this soon. I understand that this business with the Czechs is serious and I was told that the Czech President himself is keeping a close eye on the course of negotiations (he knows he needs the backing of the business community if he wants to be re-elected), so you just take your time over there and make sure our investments are protected.

Next year, Carlson will be retiring as head of the FTC and there is a good chance that you'll be appointed, which will put Mansion Enterprises' foreign holdings on a very good footing, indeed. So I would advise you to stay long enough to do the job right.

Everything is under control here, except for our Muau Loi property. Apparently some mistake was made in the original surveying and our property was built under a still active volcano, which has started erupting. Lava is flowing very slowly down the hill and will take more than a week to reach the Muau Loi Mansion Inn, by which time our geologists assure us that the eruptions should cease and the lava will cool.

Ordinarily, we'd just fly in a Vegas performer, Wayne Newton or someone like that, or an extra chef to keep the guests distracted, but we had a real stroke of bad luck. One of the anchors for the local TV station fancies herself Pulitzer Prize material. She raised a fuss about the risks to the hotel's guests. The editorialist for the local paper called up Henly, the Muau Loi manager, for confirmation, and caught him by surprise. The man made a few unfortunate remarks and four-fifths of our guests checked out the next morning. We almost had a riot on our hands.

Of course, measures have been taken. Henly has been fired and Mansion Enterprises has withdrawn its advertising from the TV station and from the newspaper. I've been assured that there is very little likelihood of the lava flow reaching the hotel— nonetheless the damage has been done and we should be seen doing *something*.

It would be nice if Russell White could come out and oversee the construction of a lava break, but of course he's busy with the Carson's Bluff deal. So I guess that means we'll have to go through the added expense of hiring an outside engineer. Pity.

On a happier note, I was golfing the other day with Walker from AmeriBancorp, and he said that if we add golf links to the Carson's Bluff executive retreat, he'll have the bank sign up for six weeks a year at the premium rate. It's beginning to look like the Carson's Bluff property will pay for itself in the first year and be turning a healthy profit in the second. Of course, everything depends on the final sale price and on the cost of restructuring, which is Russell White's lookout.

By the way, Walker also gave me (in confidence) an interesting tidbit about White. It seems he asked AmeriBancorp for a second mortgage, which was rejected after the bank checked his credit rating.

Looks like White has been making a series of very bad investments playing the arbs, hoovering up bad stocks. He's in debt up to his armpits. I passed on word to our Personal Finances Office to turn down any requests for a loan from White. Are we doing the right thing in entrusting the Carson's Bluff project to him?

Federica hasn't checked her email box for four days and she's done something to make her emails bounce, so all messages are undelivered. What's going on?

Paul

~~~~~

INTERNAL MEMO: Mansion Enterprises
From: Paul Cobb, Executive Vice President
To: Russell White

Russell,

Finances really needs those estimates on the Carson's Bluff property. Factor in a fourteen-hole golf course and make sure it's far enough away from the helipad.

Paul

~~~~~

Jack watched Federica out of the corner of his eye as he negotiated the dark switchback road up to the Folly.

She looked somehow smaller, curled up close to the door.

Goddammit, Horace was right. Of course he was right. If a big international conglomerate bought up the Folly, it would change the pace of life in Carson's Bluff forever. Mansion Enterprises was pure unadulterated poison. For him, his family, his friends.

But that didn't make him feel any better about having Federica Mansion curled up like a lost waif in the corner of his van. She was shivering. He switched on the heat.

The ride up was endless and yet too short. He pulled up in the Folly's driveway and killed the engine. Federica already had the door open.

Her words came out in a rush. "Thanks for the ride, Jack. Don't worry about me tomorrow. I'll have Newton drive up and —"

"Whoa, there." Jack clamped a hand on her wrist. It was small, delicate and soft. "Not so fast."

"Let me go, Jack." Federica twisted her hand, but his grip was too tight. He could almost feel the tears vibrating in her throat. "*Let me go*!"

She was hurting herself.

Jack released her wrist and she shot out of the van and into the night.

Federica rushed up the drive. She pounded up the steps then stopped when she reached the veranda. Though the night had turned cool, she hated the thought of cooping herself up in the Folly.

She sat down on the top step, looping her arms around her knees and letting the tears fall. She rested her head against her knees until the tears slowly receded, then lifted it again. Soon, the bright, starry night sky stopped being a blurred, watery mass overhead.

She looked up at the heartless sky. The swollen pale moon was waning. It had been a full moon back in Singapore. She'd watched it traversing the sky for hours, huddled in the requisite pale beige armchair, staring out the picture window of the thirtieth-floor penthouse suite.

I wish I had another job, she thought dully. *Another life.* But she didn't. This was the only job she had. And the only life, for that matter.

Federica tried to concentrate on what needed to be done. She should get onto negotiations right away. She'd wasted enough of her time. Her uncle's time. Mansion Enterprises' time.

But it wouldn't come together. Every time she tried to establish a strategy, the thoughts would burst and fragment into a thousand pieces. It was like trying to push against a black rubber wall. The harder she pushed, the more it resisted.

It was useless. In her head was a jumble of words—Harry's Folly, sale, lien—all meaningless, except for the heaviness they created in her mind and heart.

It was a clear night and the Milky Way was a creamy ribbon spiraling across the sky. The last time Federica had seen so many stars so clearly had been at the Tahiti Mansion Inn last year, though of course the constellations had been in the southern hemisphere, and therefore different and unfamiliar.

It was easier thinking about the stars than about her life. Safer.

She tried to recall a sky chart she'd once had as a child. She'd been fascinated by the constellations, the mythology, and had spent many long hours looking out her bedroom window, matching the charts to the stars.

Just as Federica realized that she hadn't heard the van's engine start up, there was the sound of boots on gravel, and the broad-shouldered black outline of a man blotted out Ursa Minor.

Jack climbed the steps and sat down next to her. They sat that way, in silence, for a long time.

Jack tilted his head and studied the night sky. "The ancients used to think that the Milky Way was a staircase to heaven. Some think humans became explorers because they wanted to follow the Milky Way to the end."

Federica didn't answer. The tall oaks blotted out great clumps of bright starry sky. In the distance, down in the valley, lights went out, one by one, until only one building was visible.

"Looks like Stella's is still open," she said finally.

"Looks like it," he agreed.

Another long silence followed, broken only by the sudden eruption of a cricket's seesawing cry and the soft hooting of a night owl. If not for the lights still burning at Stella's down in the valley, they could have been the only humans on Earth.

Federica rested her forehead on her knees. "How much time do I have?"

He was smart. He'd know what she meant. How long could they hold off the start of negotiations? How much time could he give her? She didn't even want to think of the real question.

How much time do we have?

Jack turned his head to her, considering. "I'd say…four days. Five if I push it. Then I'll have to plug us back in and put Carson's Bluff back on the map." He paused for a long moment. "Will that be enough?"

"I don't know," Federica whispered. Four days. Maybe five. It was as if a dense fog had come down and cut her life off four, maybe five, days down the road. She couldn't see anything beyond the four or five days Jack had just given her. She couldn't think about what was waiting for her in the fog. "I guess it'll have to be."

"I guess it will." His deep voice was soft. Federica wondered what he was thinking.

She wondered what *she* was thinking. Her mind had switched off.

But her body hadn't.

She could feel Jack's body heat, though she could barely see him, a large black mass in the surrounding blackness of the night. She needed to turn to him as a sunflower needed the sun.

Without thinking, she reached out with her hand and found it captured in his large, hard one. He pulled slowly, gently, until she rested her head against his heart, listening to the solid, heavy beat. Her own heart had gone into overdrive. Without any conscious thought of what she was doing, she lifted her head just as his descended. His hand moved through the mass of short curls and held her head still, mouth hovering just above hers.

Then Jack's mouth covered hers, moving gently until she opened her lips, and he began a slow, heady invasion.

Excitement. Comfort. Promise. Danger. They were all present in his long, slow kiss. Federica heard small, breathy moans and thought, *that can't be me.*

But it was.

She was dizzy with desire when he finally lifted his head. One hand rested on his chest, just over his heart, which had begun thudding almost as heavily as hers.

His face was stark in the moonlight. He wasn't smiling as he lifted his head.

"I was afraid of that," he said, the muscles in his jaw jumping. He released her, stood up and walked back down to the van.

Chapter Five

June 2nd

EMAIL FROM: F.H.Mansion@mansent.com
TO: pcobb@mansent.com

Paul,

I'm sending this encrypted. Message below.

Thanks for the update on our Muau Loi property. There is no reason whatsoever to hire an outside engineer, certainly not when we're keeping Russell White on staff. If it means an extra workload for him, tough.

If he's in debt, he needs the job.

But I do want you to find out exactly how much he's in debt. A worried employee is a careless employee and I don't want him making mistakes on our dime. Talk to Walker at AmeriBancorp and have him give you particulars of White's current account.

If Walker won't cooperate, hint that Mansion Enterprises could take its business elsewhere. If Walker still won't play along, play hardball. In double encryption, you'll find the name and address of a hacker who will get past AmeriBancorp's firewalls and access data on White's credit profile.

The hacker charges $300. Don't pay a penny more.

Frederick

~~~~~

EMAIL FROM: F.H.Mansion@mansent.com

TO: ruswhite@mansent.com

Russell,

This Prague business is going to take more time than I thought. We were supposed to meet today with the Deputy Prime Minister, but he's out of the country. It might very well be a stalling tactic, but the Foreign Trade Commission intends to wait it out. Which means that I'm here for the duration. In my absence, report to Paul Cobb.

We need you to go out to Hawaii to oversee the construction of a lava break. I want you to leave immediately, on the first flight out. You'll find a round-trip ticket at the airport.

Of course, I expect you to continue to stay on top of the Carson's Bluff project, but we can let the deadline slide by five days, bringing it up to the 15th of June. Keep in touch by email. I know it's an extra workload, but we have to justify keeping your office open and keeping a staff engineer.

I had our Finances office look into the estimates for hiring out whenever we needed engineering work done, instead of having you and your crew on staff, and the figures looked good. Get going.

F. M.

~~~~~

FAX FROM: Russell White, Mansion Enterprises, SF

FAX TO: Federica Mansion, c/o Sheriff's Office, Carson's Bluff

Federica,

I have to leave for Hawaii today, but I shouldn't be gone for more than three or four days. In my absence, please fax or email the following information regarding the Carson's Bluff property to the SF office.

1. The original surveyor's certificate. Some of these small towns have the original documents dating back to the nineteenth century.

2. The last official survey of the property and any geological reports available.

3. Find out if the local agency of the USDA has carried out any soil composition testing, and if so, what the soil composition is over the entire property, and not just at the building site.

4. Any records regarding the structure of the property, also known as the "Folly". Was there an architect on record, and if so, who was he? Are the original blueprints available? Has the building undergone any structural changes or have there been any additions to the original plans?

That will do for starters, though of course more information will be necessary during the course of negotiations.

The $10,000 a day clause will lapse for the period during which I'll be in Hawaii, since you won't have a Mansion Enterprises representative this end.

I trust that you will emerge from the first round of negotiations today. We haven't been able to get in touch with you up to now and it is, quite frankly, rather bothersome. Why aren't you checking your email?

Russell

MESSAGE NOT RECEIVED/NO SIGNAL

~~~~~

EMAIL FROM: wgreenlee@mansent.com
TO: ruswhite@mansent.com

Hey Russ,

I called to confirm our squash date tonight and your office said that you're off to Hawaii. You lucky stiff. The farthest I've traveled for Mansion Enterprises is Sacramento to lobby for tax breaks.

Should I reschedule the squash court for next Tuesday?

By the way, sorry to have to turn your loan application down.

Will

~~~~~

Federica woke up very late, very suddenly. She had slept through the usual early morning cacophony around the Folly. Sunrise at the Folly was to the accompaniment of blue jays and robins chattering at each other and a brisk breeze soughing through the oak stand. By late morning, though, the noise died down and a peaceful hush enveloped the Folly.

The light was slanting in at a high angle through the half-open window and there was a deep hush, so she knew it was late.

As always at the Folly, she had slept well and dreamlessly. If only she could bottle the peace of Harry's Folly and take it with her, she thought wistfully.

For months now, her sleeping had been fitful. She would wake up in some strange hotel room with a dry mouth, unrested, her head full of half-remembered images. Not like now, waking up totally refreshed, thinking of Jack's mouth on hers…

Federica bolted up in the bed. *Had she really kissed Jack Sutter last night?*

It was unthinkable. She barely knew the man. Not to mention the fact that he was slated to be on the opposite side of the bargaining table. Once she could force herself to sit down at it—whenever that would be.

If there was one thing she should have learned from her brief and disastrous affair with Russell White, it was that work and romance do not mix.

Ever.

Though that heavenly blend of excitement and ease she felt when in Jack's presence was not what she had felt with Russell.

She was here for a purpose and that purpose was to leave Jack Sutter, Mayor, Jack Sutter, Sheriff, Wyatt Sutter, Treasurer, Lilly Sutter Wright, Clerk, and God knows how many other cousins and friends facedown in the dust and to tip Carson's Bluff into the maw of Mansion Enterprises.

Horace Milton was right, she thought glumly. Within a year of the purchase of the Folly, the Town Council would be stacked with Mansion Enterprises lackeys, most of the shops would be mere service providers to the executive center up at the Folly, and nothing that could be even remotely considered detrimental to Uncle Frederick's interests would ever happen in the town.

Of course, she hadn't seen Carson's Bluff in the flesh, as it were. Maybe Carson's Bluff was a charmless dump, a pimple on the face of beautiful Northern California, and no great loss. Somehow she didn't think so.

And she, Federica Mansion would be the one to change its nature. For she would win.

She always won, both because she was good at what she did and because she had the vast financial and logistical resources of Mansion Enterprises behind her. Carson's Bluff would fight and Carson's Bluff would lose. There was no doubt about that. Just as there was no doubt about the fact that the Sutters and the rest of the Town Council would prove to be honest but ineffectual adversaries.

They would be eaten alive.

Kissing the man she was destined to engage in a dogfight with — and the man she was going to send spiraling down in flames — was not a good move.

Suddenly Federica had a thought that made her cheeks burn. Surely Jack didn't think that she was trying to *seduce* him into surrender?

What had he said? *"I was afraid of that."*

As if he had suspected that a potent kiss, a kiss she hadn't even known she had in her, was a wily trick she could pull out of her ostrich-skin briefcase. Why, that would make her no better than…no better than…

Federica's stomach rumbled and she remembered that between the quality of Lilly's cooking and Horace Milton's harangue, she hadn't eaten more than a few bites last night.

Jack's little care packages from Stella were obviously no more, so she'd have to see about feeding herself, presumably for the next few days.

Moving out from the seductive peace of Harry's Folly was painful to think about, and it was highly unlikely that the magic of the Folly ran to a Breakfast Fairy who would show up every morning with a couple of Danish and heavenly coffee. It was time to start taking care of herself.

Feeding herself. Dressing herself. Even hauling out clothes from her still unpacked bags. It all felt like too much, when what she really wanted to do was snuggle up in the Folly's big four-poster forever.

Her stomach rumbled again as she heard the familiar sound of Jack's van rolling up in the Folly's driveway. She was astonished at the unstoppable rush of pleasure welling up inside her. The rush was followed immediately by a desperate desire to hide away. Maybe if she didn't show, Jack would leave a paper sack on the veranda and steal away.

Federica waited in her bedroom for Jack to drive off, but there was only silence.

It was clear she was going to have to face him.

Federica took a leisurely shower, then wrapped a big bath towel around herself. She rummaged in her suitcase for something to put on, fingering the various suits she'd worn on her travels, discarding each one. Just the thought of her work clothes was enough to give her hives.

She had power suits and power pumps and power blouses. And for off-work time, two silk shells to go with the black leggings. By now, both shells were grungy. With a sigh, she opted for the turquoise one, which she'd worn the day before and the day before that, and descended the staircase.

Federica opened the front door and there was Jack, in his usual position on the top step of the veranda.

"Good thing I brought lunch, too." He didn't turn around. He was sitting on the top step, big hands dangling over his knees. "You're late."

Hungrily, Federica took in Jack's broad shoulders, the lean muscles visible through the white polo shirt, his strong, tanned neck, the indented ridges of his spine. He was so good to look at it was sinful. She shouldn't be looking at him the way she was. She certainly shouldn't be thinking what she was thinking.

Federica sat down next to him, mimicking his posture, wrists poised on her knees, hands dangling. "I didn't think I'd see you today."

"You thought I'd just let you starve?" His hard profile didn't change, but his voice sounded amused. "You don't strike me as the kind of woman who can trap and skin her own food."

"No, I—I guess I thought Newton would come up."

"You thought I'd avoid you?" They both looked out over the Folly's lawn. A small falcon suddenly swooped down like a brown, feathered bullet, but it missed its prey and flew up again, talons empty. "To tell you the truth, I won't say that it was easy convincing Newton that I should come up. We, um, discussed it at length. He seemed to think that he had to defend you against me."

"I guess after last night…"

Jack looked up at the cloudless sky. "Before or after I took you home?"

Before or after I kissed you?

He might as well have said the words aloud.

"Before."

"Ah." His face was still in profile, and as enigmatic as an Easter Island head. "Well, when Newton puts his mind to something, he's pretty convincing." Jack finally turned to smile at Federica and she gasped. His left eye was bloodshot and he had the beginnings of a world-class shiner.

"Oh no, Jack." Federica reached out to gently touch the bruised skin of his cheekbone and drew her hand back when Jack winced. "Who on Earth…" Federica's heart lurched. "Not— not Newton? *Please* tell me you didn't fight with Newton."

"Okay," he said agreeably. "You didn't fight with Newton."

"I can't believe this." Her voice was flat, exhausted.

This was worse than she could possibly have imagined. In a few days, she'd managed to convince the Carson's Bluff Town Council that she was a basket case. She had kissed and practically fallen into a warm puddle at the feet of her main adversary. And now her chauffeur would probably be hauled into court for assault and battery of the town's mayor. It couldn't possibly get any worse, unless…

"And Newton?" Federica tried to keep the panic out of her voice. "How is he? Is he—"

"He's fine." Jack smiled faintly. "Last time I saw him, he was putting away his third bottle at Stella's. Which I paid for, by the way."

"He isn't hurt?"

"Nope," Jack replied. "I didn't even get close." Considering that Newton had started his days as a heavyweight contender, Federica wasn't surprised. Jack fingered his chin, where a dark bruise had started. "That man sure packs a mean punch."

"Mansion Enterprises will reimburse you for any damage," Federica said stiffly. "I hope you won't press charges."

"Press charges? Weren't you listening, woman? I bought him a drink. Several drinks. Any man who can get the drop on me like that is a friend I want in my corner."

Federica looked at him, forgetting to blink. She was still very, very tired, which was probably why her mind wasn't functioning as well as it should. Either that or he wasn't making any sense.

"A friend?" she asked carefully.

"Yup. A friend."

"You, you…" Federica tried to think of a polite way to phrase it. "The two of you engaged in fisticuffs, you've got a black eye and God knows what else and the two of you have become *friends?*"

"It's a guy thing," he said kindly. "You wouldn't understand. We ready for breakfast yet?"

~~~~~

EMAIL FROM: F.H.Mansion@mansent.com

TO: f_mansion@mansent.com

Federica,

Head office tells me you haven't been picking up any of your email messages and apparently you aren't answering faxes either. I find this kind of behavior intolerable. The only thing I can imagine is that you are disturbed by the idea of working with Russell White.

Russell is in charge of negotiations in SF until I return from Prague, which might be several weeks, so you had better get used to the idea. This silence is costing us money, Federica.

Due to a minor emergency, our Carson's Bluff deadline has been shifted to the 15th of June. You will finish on the morning of the 15th and I expect you to be in San Francisco by late afternoon, where you will be debriefed.

On the 16th of June, I want you to fly out to New York on the 5:30 a.m. flight.

Your schedule for the rest of the month is New York, June 16–20, where you'll be meeting with Leslie Brooks, which you should have done after Singapore. London, 20–25th. Hamburg, 26th. Copenhagen, 27–30th. From Copenhagen, you will proceed directly to Kiev, where Mansion Enterprises is scouting for property.

Plan on staying at least a month.

Uncle Frederick

~~~~~

FAX FROM: ELLEN LARSEN, c/o Inter Airways, JFK

FAX TO: FEDERICA MANSION, c/o Sheriff's Office, Carson's Bluff

Dear Federica,

I'm stuck in JFK. We had what Inter Airways charmingly calls an "incident" about an hour out from New York. The right engine suddenly stopped functioning for about three minutes. The longest three minutes of my life. We lost a thousand feet in those three minutes. Then, luckily, the engine kicked back in.

I was really impressed with the pilot and the rest of the flight crew. They were very calm and laconic, very macho. But the pucker factor must have been extremely high because the cabin crew had to spray air freshener in the cockpit afterwards.

There was a dentist in first class who'd been giving me a hard time, a real jump seat sniffer. When he thought he was going to die, he shouted something about going out in style, grabbed me and started checking my fillings with his tongue. I had to bang him over the head with the in-flight magazine to get him to let me go.

The plane is undergoing a revision and I think we'll be departing soon on another plane. Or at least, I *hope* on another plane.

You must still be in Carson's Bluff, because your answering service message in SF is still the same. Your emails are bouncing back. Honey, I sure hope you're okay. Was the sheriff really kidding about the man-eating rattlers and black widows? Will try to get in touch from Paris.

Love, El

MESSAGE NOT RECEIVED/NO SIGNAL

~~~~~

It had turned into a hot day, so they stayed in the cool shade of the veranda. Breakfast somehow segued slowly into lunch. Stella had outdone herself. Thick slices of honey-cured ham between equally thick slices of home-baked bran bread, a tomato and potato salad, chunky wedges of a sharp country cheese, half an apple pie and lots of Pigswill. After half a sandwich and a slice of cheese, however, Federica was full. She sat with her back against the railing post, nursing a bottle of beer, and watched Jack demolish the lot.

"You're not leaving much for my dinner," she observed.

"No." Jack carefully folded the wax paper Stella packed the cheese in, took a fork and started on the apple pie. "I'll be feeding you tonight." He slanted her a glance. "You up to going out?"

"Not very far," she warned. "And not with other people." Last night had taught her a lesson.

Jack uncapped a thermos of coffee. "Well, that's fine, because I was planning on cooking for you myself. And don't worry, I'm a better cook than Lilly."

"I like Lilly." Not only did Federica like Lilly, but she was grateful to her for organizing the first relaxed evening she'd had in a long time. Or, at least it *had* been relaxing until Horace Milton had hobbled along.

"Well, I like Lilly, too, but she's no cook." Jack passed Federica a steaming cup. "Here. Don't let it interfere with your sleep."

Federica cut off a yawn. "Sorry," she said, embarrassed.

"Don't worry about it." Jack watched her down her coffee in slow sips. "Come here," he said softly.

Federica blinked. Jack was sitting about a foot away. "Where?"

"Right here," he said, and held out his right arm. There was a Federica-shaped space between his shoulder and elbow. "Let me tell you the story of Harry's Folly."

"Well, with that for an inducement, how can I resist?" Federica scooted over until her left arm touched his side. He looped his arm around her shoulder in such a way that Federica just had to rest her head on his shoulder if she wanted to be comfortable. She had kept her voice light, but the truth was that the idea of snuggling up to Jack Sutter was tempting beyond words.

His hold was perfect. Just strong enough to make her feel protected, just loose enough for her to be able to free herself anytime she wanted to. Though right now, the thought of being anywhere but leaning up against the solid shoulder of Jack Sutter was too insane to even contemplate.

For the first time in forever, Federica felt perfectly in tune with her life. She was replete with excellent food and better beer, the air was hot, but not too hot, the shade of the veranda was cool, but not too cool, and she was in the arms of a man who made her hormones hum.

She shifted until she found the perfect fit. Jack's right hand cupped her elbow and she felt his chin rest on the top of her head. She shifted again until her back was to Jack's chest and his other arm came around to clasp her around the waist. She was surrounded by warm, strong male.

"Once upon a time," Jack said, his deep voice low, "there was a man and an idea. The man's name was Harry Carson. No one knew where he came from or even if his real name was Harry Carson."

There was a faint spicy scent in the air, either the pine trees in the distance, or Jack's aftershave, or simply the smell of happiness. Federica closed her eyes and savored the smell, the feel of Jack's strong body against hers, the thrum of his steady heartbeat against her back. Her breathing slowed as her eyelids drooped.

Jack paused a moment, casting about for the right words, trying not to be distracted by the soft feel of Federica Mansion in his arms. He had an ulterior motive in coaxing her into his arms.

He wanted to tell her the story of Carson's Bluff, how the town had evolved, how Harry had won the money for his Folly and what he did with it and why. He wanted her to understand just how unique Carson's Bluff was, what a magic refuge it was. How precious it was to him and its inhabitants.

It was hard to find the words and there were undercurrents everywhere. Something was happening with him and Federica. He hadn't felt this way about a woman in a long time. Maybe never. Not even his ex-wife had stirred this deep curiosity mixed with admiration he felt whenever he looked at her.

But of course, he couldn't forget that they were adversaries. On opposite sides of a life-or-death question. The citizens of Carson's Bluff had elected him their representative in the upcoming battle. Carson's Bluff versus Mansion Enterprises. He represented Carson's Bluff and Federica represented Mansion Enterprises.

She represented more than just Mansion Enterprises. She was a stand-in for everything he and his family and friends hated and had resisted so far. Big Business. Money over quality of life. Power over people. Stress and battle and competition. He had to make her understand why they were fighting so hard to keep Mansion Enterprises away.

Right smack in the middle of this mess was the wild attraction between them. Federica needed to know the score.

He took a deep breath and continued.

"So one day Harry Carson came to a place called Libertyville. It wasn't much more than an encampment. Just a few lean-tos and maybe thirty tents. A place where drifters didn't want to stay for very long because they were all going to get rich quick. And go somewhere else."

Jack opened his mouth to continue the story of Carson's Bluff, but something about Federica's breathing and the slight snuffling sounds from her chest stopped him.

He looked down at her and shook his head, smiling.

She had fallen fast asleep.

Chapter Six

June 2nd

Note taped to Jack Sutter's front door.

Jack, please tell Federica I'm sorry the evening had to end like that. Norman was so upset that he had a relapse. At three o'clock in the morning, I found him at the computer, going over the files of old clients.

Horace was brutally truthful, as usual, but you know Horace. The United States Government couldn't get him to shut up, and of course neither can we. Horace isn't afraid of the truth and I suppose we shouldn't be, either. I think we need to talk about this. Do you want to come over for a bite tonight? I promise that I'll make Norman cook.

Love, Lilly

P.S. We're all really worried, Jack. About you, too.

~~~~~

Message left on Jack Sutter's answering machine.

"Jack, hi this is Wyatt. I had a vision last night, or rather, a voice spoke to me in the darkness. The voice sounded a lot like Obi Wan Kenobe. He said, and I quote, *'Why doesn't Jack seduce Federica into surrender and recruit her for Carson's Bluff?'* Sound good? I mean, with those eyes and that figure, we're not exactly talking hardship duty, bro. I still need to get down to Shelby. May the Force be with you."

~~~~~

EMAIL FROM: pcobb@mansent.com
TO: F.H.Mansion@mansent.com

Dear Frederick,

I'm double-encrypting this whole message. I'm tempted to send this snail-mail, or at least send it by courier because your Mister...your hacker has made me utterly paranoid about our computer security. He gave me everything but Russell White's neck size in two hours and I'm sure he'd have given me that if I'd asked.

It was actually rather frightening what I was able to learn about White, including medical records. In case you're interested, Russell White is healthy, except for his blood pressure, which is one-eighty over ninety. He was almost thrown out of Stanford for suspected cheating, he came up negative with the National Crime Information Commission, he is HIV-negative, he has a penchant for Mercedes-Benzes and Armani suits and he is $250,000 in debt.

Your man was even able to give me the exact record of White's indebtedness. White has consistently spent thirty percent more than his salary over the past four years and has tried to make up for it day-trading on the stock market, though with no success since he aims at short-term profits and isn't good enough at high-risk stocks. He took a real drubbing in derivatives a month ago. From what I've been able to see, White is fundamentally a loose cannon on deck. Should we throw him overboard?

Paul

~~~~~

Note taped to Lilly Langtry Sutter Wright's refrigerator.

Hi Lil,

Thanks for the invitation, but I've invited Federica over tonight. She'll be getting some real food. Sorry Norman fell off the wagon. Tell him to just say no, then put his laptop under lock and key with a timer. Don't worry about me, Lil, everything's under control. I think. You'll find some leftover hamburger for Cavendish on a red plastic plate I put in your fridge. See you tomorrow.

Jack

P.S. I don't want you coming through the gate tonight asking to borrow some sugar, understood?

~~~~~

Federica woke up in the late afternoon. At first she was disoriented. The last thing she remembered was leaning up against Jack's broad chest, listening to his low deep voice talking about… She frowned. Talking about something. Something to do with Carson's Bluff.

She sat up, swinging her legs over the side of the bed. She took a deep breath of Carson's Bluff air. It was sweet and cool.

Cool. She and Ellen used to fight over whether cool could still be used as an adjective.

Ellen.

Federica closed her eyes.

Oh God, Ellen. Her best friend in the whole world. The one constant in her shifting life. The friend she'd had a date with.

Springsteen, yet.

How could she have forgotten Ellen? If anything could make Federica frightened that she was losing—no, had *lost* her grip, it was that. Forgetting a date with Ellen.

How could she?

Federica mulled over how to get in touch with Ellen without getting in touch with anyone. Contact with the outside world was still too much to contemplate.

Feeling logy, Federica stepped under the big showerhead and turned on the cold water full blast, and stood there for fifteen minutes, hoping for her old self back. Her old self was always invigorated by a cold shower. But there she was, twisting this way and that under the cold spray, with no ambition greater than to spend some time with Jack, puttering around his house, putting together a meal...kissing him...feeling his lips, his tongue against hers...

Federica turned the water spout off with a jerk of her wrist when she realized that it felt like steam on her overheated skin.

She had no business thinking about Jack's kisses. No business wanting a repeat of last night. As soon as she was herself again, whenever that would be, she would, she would...

But the thoughts just wouldn't form. Every time she tried to think about the future or her duty, she pulled a blank.

"Federica!" Jack's voice sounded from below. She was so out of it, she hadn't even heard the engine.

"Coming!" she shouted back contentedly, and went down.

Jack was standing in the foyer, face tilted up. Federica started down the beautiful old staircase, then suddenly stopped, hand on the banister, one foot up and one foot down, looking at Jack and feeling her heart go into double overdrive. She just looked and looked, and at that moment, Jack was the most beautiful man in the world and everything she had ever wanted, had ever dreamed of having, was right here, in a gorgeous old mansion in the mountains. She started trembling as a stab of desire so strong it nearly brought her to her knees pierced through her.

"Federica?" Jack peered uncertainly up at her. "You all right?"

No, she wanted to answer, *I'm under attack. Alien hormones have taken over my body.*

"Federica?"

Federica opened her mouth to answer, but as she breathed in air it was like fire in her lungs. Her whole body was aflame and she was sure her face was burning.

"Federica?" Jack sounded worried now and he started up the stairs.

"*No!*" If he came too close right now, she'd blow up in a conflagration. "No," she said, more calmly, walking down on wobbly knees. "I just had a-a dizzy spell, that's all. I'll be okay."

"Must be the altitude."

"The altitude," she said. "Right."

~~~~~

FAX FROM: Ellen Larsen, Inter Airways Terminal, JFK

FAX TO: Federica Mansion, c/o Clerk's Office, Carson's Bluff

Honey,

This is my last attempt at communication stateside. The Inter Airways terminal here at JFK is in a state of utter chaos because my flight almost crashed. We're on go/no-go status. Flights are being delayed by four-five hours and there are so many irate passengers storming the citadel that the local manager just locked his office and has taken off for parts unknown.

I'm being besieged by desperate requests for information which I don't have, an overly amorous dentist I whacked over the head is threatening to sue me and it's too much for me to take, so I've slipped into our office here for some respite and a final stab at communicating with you.

I called the local telephone company to find out why the sheriff's fax isn't answering and they said it was switched off. I asked for the number of the mayor's fax and they said it was the same number. So then I asked for the number of the clerk's fax and I can only hope that this one is switched on.

I'm really, really worried. It's not like you to forget a date or to be out of touch like this. Something very strange is going on. The SF Mansion Enterprises office isn't giving out any information and it seems like there's no way to communicate with Carson's Bluff.

Are you in any danger? Maybe it was the close brush with the Grim Reaper on the flight, but really weird thoughts are going through my head—like you've been kidnapped and are being held for ransom. Tell me it isn't so and that it's the usual—Uncle Frederick asking you to work three hundred hours a day. Just like Inter Airways.

Maybe we should both quit. I'll move out West. Surely there are some jobs for smart, overweight brunettes in California? Maybe in Silicon Valley—one look at my hips and thighs and they'll realize I'm a software expert.

I'm flying straight back to California from Paris. Can you leave a message at the usual hotel in SF?

Love, El

MESSAGE NOT RECEIVED/ NO SIGNAL

~~~~~

Jack's house was charming, Federica wasn't surprised to see. It was next door to Lilly's, but the wisteria growing in fat clumps over a high wooden fence effectively shut out Lilly's house and enclosed Jack's house in a private, purple embrace.

"It must be nice living so close to your sister," Federica said wistfully. Most of the luxury flats in her high-rise were owned by corporations for the convenience of out-of town executives, and she didn't know any of her neighbors. It didn't really matter, since she spent so little time there.

"Yeah." Jack hauled out two deck chairs and started wrestling obstinately with one. "Sometimes she has a little difficulty in distinguishing between mine and thine, though. Ah." The chair opened miraculously and he waved at it with a flourish, inviting Federica to have a seat. He looked at the other one with narrowed eyes. "But don't worry. She's got strict instructions to stay on her side of the fence tonight."

"I'm not worried." Federica eyed the deck chair and realized that if she sat down, she would sink into it and fall asleep again.

It was late afternoon and the sun was so low it peeped through the willows and oaks and dazzled and lulled her. She bit back a yawn. How could she be sleepy and aroused at the same time? Embarrassed, she cast about for something to say. "Your picnic table looks like Lilly's."

"It should. Wyatt made both of them."

"Wyatt is a professional woodcarver?" Federica asked, startled.

"Nah." Jack shot her an amused glance. "He just dabbles in woodworking. But he's good at picnic tables and shelves." He looked at her closely. "Listen, why don't you go down and look at the river while I cook? It's real pretty and relaxing. It's also a part of the history of Carson's Bluff. It's where gold was found in 1878 and every hungry drifter west of the Rockies came rushing over. I seem to remember telling you the whole story," he smiled slyly, "but you slept right through it."

"I'd had—" Federica began defensively.

"A hard day. I know." Jack went into the house and came out with a wet cloth and some plates. Gorgeous plates, Federica couldn't help noticing, in Lilly's distinct vivid colors. He wiped the picnic table. "Look, you go on down and commune with the river while I fix dinner. Just don't fall asleep."

"I'll try not to." Federica shot him a wry look. Probably everyone in Carson's Bluff thought she suffered from narcolepsy.

"You want leather or feather?"

The steak the night before had been tough and undigestible. What could go wrong with chicken? "Feather."

"Right." Jack shooed her away. "Go and relax. You've had—"

"—a hard day," Federica finished for him. She wondered if he knew she ordinarily put in twelve-hour days.

Maybe he did.

She smiled and tipped back an imaginary ten-gallon hat with her thumb. "Thanks. Well, pardner," she said in a very bad imitation of John Wayne, "think I'll just mosey on down to the river and rest mah weary bones."

"Don't work too hard while you're at it."

"Nope," she assured him. "Shore won't."

She wandered down a charmingly unkempt lawn with more clover and alfalfa than grass, until she came to the steep riverbank she'd had just a glimpse of at Lilly's. Federica sat down on the rim of the bank and watched the river flow gently past.

It was hypnotic. The river shone silver in the late evening sun and she could count two trout at least, maybe more, making bubbles and shimmers in the water.

The water was so clear she could see the gray stones and beige sand of the bottom. The water burbled by, flowing neatly over a large granite boulder, making a rippling noise Federica found incredibly soothing. Two giant willows on either side of the bank dangled drooping green tendrils in the water. She was hypnotized by the peace and beauty of the river. She let herself sink into a place where there was no yesterday, no tomorrow, only an endless, peaceful now.

This is meditation, she thought.

How many times she'd tried to meditate in an anonymous hotel room, hoping to quiet jangled nerves and prepare herself for a nerve-wracking meeting. She even had her own mantra, but it never worked.

This was the first time she truly understood all those New Age truisms. *Go with the flow. You are a part of the Universe. You are part of the tapestry of life.*

They'd all seemed such hackneyed phrases, until she found herself melting into the flowing river, dissolving into the willows, part of the peace of the sunlit evening. Federica didn't even notice the passage of time until she felt Jack's hand on her shoulder. It felt as right, as elemental, as the river and the trees and the trout.

"Feels good out here, doesn't it?" he asked quietly.

He knew. Somehow he knew.

"Mm-hmm."

"When you're ready, I'll feed you."

The food was delicious. Somehow, Federica was surprised.

"More?" he asked.

A massive appetite had roared out of nowhere. She'd had two chicken breasts with mushrooms, heaps of steamed broccoli with sesame seeds and several slices of wholemeal bread.

"I shouldn't…" she hesitated.

"Of course you should." Jack ladled more broccoli onto her plate. "You need to keep your strength up."

"Actually, all I seem to be doing is sleeping lately."

His eyes met hers. "If you need it, do it."

If you need it, do it. The words hung there in the air, heavy with meaning. What she wanted to do, *needed* to do, was exactly what she shouldn't do.

"Is that a Carson's Bluff motto?"

"No, it's mine."

"Oh."

She sucked in a breath and made a conscious effort to shift the conversation into a more…comfortable mode. Not that she wasn't comfortable. Actually, she was spectacularly comfortable. And spectacularly aroused. It was the weirdest feeling in the world to have all her muscles lax with contentment while anticipation and excitement tingled through her nervous system.

Jack stretched out his legs under the table, coming into contact with Federica's legs. She glanced up, startled, then blushed at the expression in his eyes.

"Jack," she whispered.

Jack's whole body tightened. He wanted to trap Federica's legs between his and drag her under the table with him. He was barely able to restrain himself. From the red blush tingeing her cheeks, she was as affected by the contact as he was.

Casual affairs weren't his style. They never had been. That was Wyatt's scene, stuck in perpetual adolescence.

What could there possibly be between him and Federica but a casual affair, an affair that would haunt them and taunt them later?

He'd bought her—and them—a few days by pulling the plug on Carson's Bluff. That wasn't hard. Carson's Bluff citizens didn't like the outside world that much, anyway. But if not today, then tomorrow or the next day, sooner rather than later, the proverbial fecal matter would hit the proverbial fan.

Federica was a wealthy woman, an executive for one of the most powerful hotel chains in the world. A hotel chain that bore her name.

It was clear that she'd arrived in a state of exhaustion, on the edge of collapse, like a soldier who'd been in the line of fire for too long. And it was also clear that these few days were merely a little R&R for a busy executive. When she recovered, who knew what she'd morph into?

Well, he knew. Ms. Yup, that's who. Ms. International Yup, with one of those fancy watches with two dial faces so you could always know the time in Singapore, and wallets with separate zippers for different currencies.

Jack had had enough of grasping women. Women who calculated the odds before making any kind of a move. Right now, though, Federica didn't look calculating at all. She looked soft and unbearably inviting. He had to clamp down on the hard edge of desire that had him looking at her hungrily. Wanting her with a fierceness that surprised him.

He sighed. This was going to end badly, he could feel it. Getting involved with Federica Mansion was a big, big mistake. He knew that.

He was going to make that mistake anyway.

He got up from the picnic table and crossed around to her side.

"Come with me," he said, holding out his hand.

Federica looked up at Jack, at his outstretched hand. She placed her hand in his and he tugged her to her feet. He led her to the deck chairs, which he'd placed side by side, facing the river and the setting sun. "Come sit down and watch the sunset with me."

"Okay." Federica would have cheerfully followed him if he'd said, "Come with me and watch the hogs being slaughtered."

She walked on weakened knees and sank heavily into the canvas deck chair. Jack only touched her lightly, guiding her by the elbow, and she felt as if she were on fire.

"You want a chaser for that meal?"

"What?" His voice came to her dimly, as if he were talking through several layers of glass.

"A chaser. I've got some good bourbon."

"Bourbon." She shook her head, trying to get rid of the fog. "Sure. Who made it? A cousin?"

"Nope." Jack came back from the house with a bottle and two glasses. He poured one for her then peered at the label. "Rickety Bridge. Old Virginia brand. They only make two hundred bottles a year."

Federica sipped her bourbon, though she didn't need anything to make her feel light-headed. Jack sank into the deck chair beside her with a sigh.

He was inches away from her and her hands literally itched to touch him. Thank goodness one hand was occupied with a glass. Something was going to have to give, and soon. She felt like reaching over and touching him, grabbing him, anywhere. She, of all people, who had cultivated her touch-me-not persona for so long it was nearly perfect. So many businessmen on the road assumed that because she was on the road too, and away from home, she was an easy mark.

So she had a lot of experience with icy refusals but not much with jumping bones. To keep her hands busy, she sipped her drink and wished that Ellen were here. Ellen would know exactly what to do. Too bad she couldn't have Ellen at the other end of a hidden mike, like a Secret Service agent. That way Ellen could give her instructions. She could almost hear Ellen's voice, coaching her.

Women don't jump men's bones, Federica. That's crass. Women eat men's bones. Delicately. And spit them out afterwards.

Now slowly, very slowly, sidle your hand close to his, as if you weren't aware of what your hand was doing, and make a conversational gambit.

Federica plopped her hand on the arm of Jack's deck chair, then stared at it.

That wasn't very subtle. Now, think of something to say.

Jack looked down at her hand, then at her, and Federica started drowning in those deep blue eyes.

Talk, Federica! Say something!

"Er—that was a wonderful meal," she said finally. Her voice sounded choked and distant. "How come you cook so well?"

"What?" Jack frowned.

"I said, you cook really well. Where did you learn how?"

"My wife," he said glumly.

His wife?

"Your…wife?"

"Yeah. Horrible cook. I had to learn how."

"Yoo-hoo, Jack." Lilly's voice called out and a section of picket fence swung open, scattering wisteria petals. Lilly stepped through and smiled blandly at Jack and Federica, sitting so closely together. "Sorry to bother you, Jack." She innocently held out a canister. "But I've run out of salt."

Federica felt lost. *His wife?*

Chapter Seven

His wife?

Stunned, Federica looked at Jack and Lilly, so alike but so different. Lilly looked curious, Jack looked annoyed and they both looked at her.

His wife.

He was married.

Well, of course he was.

A prime specimen like that. Walking around loose and unattached in this day and age. Unthinkable.

It only confirmed the First Ellen Larsen Law of Love. *The chances of a man being single are inversely proportionate to his attractiveness.* Jack was the most attractive man she'd seen in a long time. Maybe ever. Ergo…

A wife. Federica looked around, as if a wife were something Jack might have temporarily misplaced, like the keys to the house. Where had he put her? Was she hiding up in the attic somewhere, like Mrs. Rochester in *Jane Eyre*? Or worse, was the wife out of town for a day or two and was Jack taking the opportunity to play around a bit?

That thought was so humiliating Federica couldn't even stay in the same place with it.

She bounced out of her deck chair.

"Hi, Lilly." Federica looked around brightly, as if she and Jack had been attending a large dinner party and by sheer chance they were the last people to leave. "Jack and I were just—"

"What did you say you wanted, Lil?" Jack's brow was furrowed. He eyed his sister's belly and got up from the deck chair. "Have a seat."

"No, that's okay, I—"

"Sit."

"No, really—"

"*Sit.*"

"Well…if you insist." Lilly sank down with a grateful sigh and started fanning herself. "Thanks." She reached up and touched her brother's eye. "Swelling's gone down."

Jack smiled faintly at his sister. "I'll live."

Lilly held out the canister. "So…you have any salt, Jack?" she asked.

"Yeah, I've got some salt." Jack stared at her through narrowed eyes. "I seem to remember buying you a two-pound pack the other day."

"I pickled some cucumbers. Used it all up." Lilly said guilelessly. Jack was looking annoyed and Federica was feeling dazed. "I hope I didn't interrupt anything."

"Oh, no." Federica drummed up a smile. "We were just chatting," she looked down at her wristwatch without seeing a thing, "and my, how the time has flown. I guess I should be—"

"We were just talking about my wife," Jack said, coming out of the house with a box of salt and a fold-up chair.

Federica flinched.

"My *ex-wife,*" he said heavily as he opened the chair. Federica could feel the color flowing back into her cheeks.

"Oh, Samantha." Lilly waved her hand. "Water under the bridge. What a bi—" She slanted a glance at Federica, "Business woman. Certainly knew which side her bread was buttered on."

Federica looked at Jack and then Lilly. "Ex-wife?"

"Ex-wife," Jack pronounced the two syllables carefully, as if speaking to a foreigner. "As in divorced. As in—no more."

"Well then." Federica settled back into the deck chair. "You want a pillow for your back, Lilly?"

Two hours later, Lilly stood up, bracing a hand against her back, and winced.

"How's it going, Lil?" Jack asked.

"Not too bad. I had an ultrasound the other day." She smiled secretively.

"Did they see what sex it is?" Jack asked eagerly. He turned to Federica. "Wyatt and I want a boy. We've already booked baseball time. Someone's going to have to take the little tyke in hand. Norman's hopeless at sports."

"Well…they're not entirely sure," Lilly began, then glanced at Jack's face and relented. "But it looks like you and Wyatt will be coaching Little League games in about six or seven years' time."

"Yowee!" Jack gave a rebel yell and hugged her.

"You're such a sexist, Jack," Lilly laughed at him. "Don't you know that there are coed Little League teams now?"

"Yeah, but you can't flick wet towels at girls in the locker room. They'll sue you for harassment. Besides, Wyatt and I already have it all figured out. Your next one will be a girl, and we'll escort her to her coming-out party. You know Norman can't dance, and Wyatt does a really mean foxtrot."

"That's ridiculous. Carson's Bluff doesn't have debutante parties. Your niece will probably be playing soccer in ten years' time. And beating the pants off you."

In ten years' time, Federica thought.

Jack and Wyatt and Lilly and Norman and now the baby—they all knew exactly where they were going to be in ten years' time. Right here, surrounded by family and friends, shouting excitedly in the late summer afternoon as a beloved child made his first home run, or scored her first goal, with the smell of frankfurters wafting on the air.

And she would be…where? In a hotel room alone somewhere, in some foreign city. That was certain. The only uncertainty was which one. Kyoto? Cancùn? Vientiane? Soho? Noho?

Her eyes stung and she blinked.

This is pathetic, she thought. How can I feel sorry for myself? Wherever I'll be, I'll be in a luxury setting, successful, busy and happy.

She'd be happy.

Sure she'd be happy.

Jack frowned at her. "Federica?" He moved away from Lilly. "You okay?"

"Of course." She swiveled in his direction and showed all her teeth in a smile. "I'm just wondering if I should be getting back on—" *Home* lingered on her lips and died. The Folly wasn't home. The big empty beige flat in San Francisco was home. The Folly was temporary, just another hotel room. "To the Folly."

"Do you need anything, Federica?" Lilly asked practically. "Jack's too much of a dense male to think that women might need things. Um, female things. He thinks being at the Folly is all anyone could ever want or need."

Federica was touched. No one ever asked her what she needed. Everyone just assumed that being a Mansion was all anyone could ever want. "No, I'm okay, except…"

"Except?"

Federica looked down at her grubby, stained turquoise shell. "I need some clothes. I don't have anything to wear."

Jack's eyes widened. "You've got a giant suitcase full of clothes."

"I don't have clothes in my suitcase," Federica said. Her suitcase was full of Valentino and Armani and Geoffrey Beene suits. "All I have are uniforms. For going to war. I need *clothes*. Real clothes, like jeans—"

"And T-shirts," Lilly said knowingly. "Maybe a track suit or two. Some sneakers. Sure. I'll drive you down and take you to Kerry's tomorrow afternoon because I know Jack has to run into Shelby for Wyatt. Anything else?"

"Something to read." Federica had a sudden, pleasing image of herself sitting on the Folly's veranda with her feet up on the post, reading a murder mystery. Or maybe a romance. "Nothing too serious, though," she warned. "I want light entertainment. Really light."

"Well," Lilly mused, "Don's got a big mystery section. He's into his religious phase, but he still has a good selection of light reading. We can take a walk around town tomorrow if you're up to it."

"Thanks, Lilly."

"No problem." Lilly yawned, and cupped her rounded belly. "Well, the two of us will be saying goodnight. I need to get back to Norman." Lilly frowned. "Heavens, I hope Norman's not still up. He had strict instructions to turn his laptop off after nine…" Her voice trailed off.

"Gotta watch him, Lil," Jack said swiftly. Unobtrusively, he put a big hand to her back and gently pushed. "Workaholism's the deadliest addiction known to man. Go fix him a stiff drink or something."

But Lilly was already moving. "He's been having a number of relapses, lately," she said worriedly, as she opened the gate. "Oh, dear, the lights in his study are on…" She disappeared in a gentle rain of purple petals.

"Norman will be okay once the baby comes." Jack latched the gate behind Lilly with an inward sigh. "If anything can take his mind off spreadsheets, it's changing diapers."

"And walking the baby at three in the morning," Federica agreed.

Their eyes met, then slid away.

"Well." Jack shifted from one sneakered foot to another, and stuck his hands in his back pockets. "Well."

"Well," she echoed hollowly.

If she didn't know that Jack was a superbly relaxed man, at ease with himself and the world, she'd say he was nervous. But that couldn't be. What did he have to be nervous about? Surely not about…her?

"I guess—"

"I think—"

They both spoke at once, then laughed.

Jack nodded. "Ladies first."

"Um…" Federica looked helplessly at him, his tall broad outline limned by the porch light. He was so beautiful, so incredibly beautiful, and just being near him made her feel so relaxed and excited and above all, happy. And relaxed. And excited.

Nothing like this feeling had ever happened to her before and probably never would again. Good businesswomen seize opportunities, she reminded herself.

I want you to take me inside right now and make passionate love to me. All night, if you can. This might be her last chance at good sex in this lifetime. She opened her mouth, waiting for the words to spill out, but they stuck in her throat.

"It's late, and, um…"

Jack's face was unreadable. He was silent for a long moment, then brought a hand out of his back pocket, stuck it into the front pocket of his jeans and jiggled some change there.

"Yeah." He cleared his throat. "It *is* pretty late. Come on, I'll drive you back."

So much for a night of sex. With a sigh, Federica followed him out to the van.

On the ride up, Federica had a furious argument with Ellen in her head.

So, idiot. Smooth going.

Well, what did you expect me to do, strip him and throw him over my shoulder? He's bigger than I am.

You could have asked to see his house and pretended to faint in his bedroom.

Oh, come on, Ellen. Let's get real here.

I know, I know. Wait. How about this. When you get to the Folly, you invite him up for a nightcap then ask what he'd like for breakfast.

That's really subtle. But it won't work because I don't have anything but mineral water to drink, and he's the one who brings breakfast.

So ask if he wants to see your etchings.

There aren't any etchings at the Folly. Ellen…he's Uncle Frederick's adversary. There's a principle involved here.

Principle. Oh, puh-leeze. Federica, the only principle your Uncle Frederick understands is the kind that earns interest.

Come on, Ellen. Uncle Frederick's not that bad.

There was a long, painful silence in Federica's head.

Okay, okay. But still…

Still what?

Well, suppose…suppose he doesn't want me the way I want him? Suppose I ask him and he says no?

Come on, Federica, you know the way the world works. Women rule and men drool.

That's not true. And anyway, I can't just…ask.

Federica, tell the truth here. Have you ever felt this way about a man before?

Who, moi? I inherited cold Mansion genes. Are you kidding? Never.

Well are you going to do something about it or not?

I don't know, El, Federica thought miserably. *I don't know if I can.*

The van ground to a halt and Ellen disappeared, and Federica felt lost.

"We're here." Jack's deep voice sounded—what? Impatient? Annoyed?

The windows of the van were down and the sounds of the night filtered in. Funny how the night sounds had never bothered her. Federica was not a country person and had no idea what the night sounds were. Still, in all the nights she'd slept out here alone, she'd never once been afraid.

There was something so benign and comforting about the beautiful Folly.

She looked over at Jack. He was barely visible in the dark cabin. Though she couldn't see it, she knew that there were white laugh lines in the tanned skin around his eyes. She knew that the blue of his irises changed hue whenever he felt a strong emotion. Every inch of his face and body was indelibly etched in her mind. She didn't need to see him to know that he was the most attractive, exciting, relaxing man she'd ever met.

"Federica?"

I don't know what to say, she thought in despair. *I don't know what to do.*

But her hand did. All by itself, it reached out and cupped his face.

"Jack," she whispered helplessly.

All of a sudden she found herself dragged halfway across Jack's lap, with the stick shift digging into her thigh and the steering wheel cutting into her back. She didn't care. She didn't even feel it, because Jack was kissing her and she was falling into the kiss as if it were an abyss.

He slanted his mouth over hers, his hand caught in her hair. She threw her arms around his neck and kissed him back. Their tongues tangled and she didn't know who was doing the breathing, him or her, but there wasn't much of it going on because they were both panting when he lifted his mouth.

"Federica." Jack's grip on her hair was strong enough to hurt as he pulled her head back. He looked down at her and she could see his eyes gleaming, pale in the moonless night. "I want you."

Federica spoke three languages well and two languages badly. But at that moment there was only one word in her entire vocabulary. She closed her eyes.

"Yes."

Chapter Eight

Jack flicked on the outside porch light. The big chandelier hanging from the second-story ceiling in the lobby would have shed too much light on the magic and mystery of the moment. The porch light was enough to see by. It was enough to see Federica looking at him. If he was any judge of women's expressions—though Wyatt was the family expert on that—she wanted him as much as he wanted her.

When they crossed the threshold into the Folly, Jack pulled her to him for a brief, fierce kiss. He had one arm around her shoulder and the other hand was fondling her small, rounded bottom, which would have been perfect to swing her up into his arms if he hadn't lifted his head for a moment to look at the long, curved wooden staircase.

Wyatt had done a wonderful job. The wood gleamed a honey blond, each gracefully lathed banister perfectly turned, the steps lacquered and shiny and…steep.

Jack stepped back and smiled down at Federica. "Uh-uh." He shook his head. "No way."

"Okay." Federica sounded breathless and he felt his knees weaken at the sight of that smart, pretty face looking up at him, eyes solemn, lips swollen from his kisses. Maybe he'd try to carry her up, after all. Out of respect for romantic tradition. And because he wanted her back in his arms, badly.

She pushed him in the chest and turned. "Race you up!"

He caught her halfway up the staircase. She squealed and giggled as he caught her by the waist, then managed to wriggle free.

They tangled at the top of the stairs, his mouth on hers, his hands under the silk turquoise shell, her hands clutching his shoulders.

She broke free from his kiss. "Jack." The whisper full of longing and desire was enough to set him off. Stairs were a no-no, but give him even footing and he could play Tarzan with the best of them. He swung her high in his arms.

Plays better in the movies, he thought, as he staggered for a moment, then didn't think anything at all as Federica grabbed his ears and held him still for a long kiss, making those sinful little moans into his mouth.

He staggered again. Not because she was heavy—she wasn't—but because desire had him trembling so badly his knees were starting to give way. Good thing her room was the first one off the stairs. The Folly was being slowly restored by volunteers headed by Wyatt. If they had decided to start by restoring the room at the end of what looked like a mile-long hallway, he wouldn't have made it. He would have sunk to the floor with Federica and they would have made love on the newly varnished parquet flooring, which was shiny and beautiful and a deep honey blond—but hard.

Hard. That was a word he couldn't think about, or his knees really would give way. Federica shifted in his arms and deepened the kiss, and he leaned against the doorpost, trembling.

"You've got to stop this," he gasped.

Her eyes fluttered open. "I do?"

"At least until we get something soft under us."

"Okay." She nuzzled against his neck and bit him, lightly. "But hurry."

God. Jack tried to gather his strength and not think about her tongue, reaching out cat-like to lazily lick his neck.

It had been a long time for him. That was why he felt like he was going to explode, of course.

It was lust—sheer, mind-boggling, adolescent-level lust, something he didn't have that much experience with anymore, but which Wyatt knew all about. And if he felt completely right with Federica, like he were coming home after a long time out in the desert, then it was just hormones. No woman could be right for him. Not after only a few days, anyway.

Then Federica fastened her mouth on his and he was lost.

Jack stumbled forward and by sheer chance met the bed with his shins. He tumbled onto the bed with her and by the time he untangled himself, he was on top of her and she had lost that blue silky thing and her bra.

How had she lost her bra? Had he ripped it off her? His hand covered her breast, and he felt her heart pounding against his hand. His own heart was thumping. He could hear it, a wild jungle drumbeat in his ears.

"Federica," he whispered against her breast.

"Yes," she said. "Oh, yes." She twisted, placing a hard cherry-like nipple right in front of his mouth. He licked it, then suckled, hard. She gave a wild cry, startled and excited at the same time. Her fingers dug into his head, hard, holding him to her breast.

He was going to go crazy if he didn't have her right now. He wanted to go slowly, he wanted to caress her all over, but it was impossible to touch her quickly enough. He only had two hands.

He had to slow down.

He levered himself off her for a second and looked down. She was naked from the waist up, lovely, delicately rounded, skin glowing a pale ivory. Her nipple was red and wet from his mouth. He'd done that to her.

He bent his head and kissed her breasts again, wanting to go slowly this time, but then she sucked in her breath and arched her back, giving a throaty moan. Her hands clutched at his biceps, short fingernails digging in. She was as open as a rose in summer, inviting him in. Fragrance and softness and welcome. For a brief moment, Jack completely forgot roses had thorns and that an unwary man could get hurt.

Federica lifted her head and pulled him up to her mouth, biting his lips. "Now," she whispered against his mouth. "*Now!*"

Jack lost it. In moments, he had stripped her of leggings and panties and shucked off his jeans and was starting to sink into her when something about the feel of bare flesh against bare flesh penetrated the heated fog in his head. He withdrew and scrabbled frantically on the floor with his hand.

"No." Federica's voice was faint. "Don't stop. Please."

"Yes. I mean no." Jack cursed under his breath and reached further out with his hand and grunted when he found what he was looking for, ripping the condom packet open with his teeth. His fingers tangled with hers in a race to see who could put the condom on him first and they both burst into laughter.

Watching her eyes, Jack folded his hand over hers and coaxed her hand into sheathing him with the condom. When the condom was on fully, he lifted his hand away but she didn't. Her fist was still closed tightly over him.

"I can feel your heartbeat here," she whispered.

Jack's entire body was one quivering cell waiting to explode. He tumbled her down onto her back and mounted her. He sank into her completely, groaning, knowing that one second more and he'd have exploded.

She was everything he'd dreamed of, soft, warm, seemingly made especially for him. His face was buried in her neck and he wanted to ask if she was all right, if he was hurting her, but then she turned her head and kissed him and started moving her hips, rocking them gently against his, then more quickly, and every thought flew out of his head. They moved together, wildly, perfectly, as if they had been made for each other, like two halves of a long-separated whole.

He wanted to slow down, draw it out, but then Federica cried out and convulsed softly around him and everything that he was, everything he ever wanted to be, ever dreamt of being, his whole heart and soul poured into her.

He lay atop her shuddering, gasping for breath, lungs fighting to pull in air. It was a long time before the shudders gradually ceased and he was able to loosen his death grip on her hips. He hoped he hadn't crushed any bones. He wanted desperately to talk to her, to tell her that he didn't normally make love with all the finesse of a frenzied warthog. When he got his breath back, he opened his mouth, heard the soft snuffling sounds, closed it again and grinned. He rolled off her, then reached down to pull the crumpled coverlet over Federica's shoulders and gently folded the linen cloth around her.

She'd fallen fast asleep.

She'd had a hard day.

~~~~~

June 3rd

EMAIL FROM: ruswhite@mansent.com

TO: wgreenlee@mansent.com

Will,

Don't bother envying me the trip to Hawaii. I was met at the airport with an asbestos suit instead of a lei and was whisked off in the Muau Loi Mansion Inn SUV to the site of a minor volcanic eruption instead of to a luau. I wasn't even offered a thermos of coffee. Turns out that the problem isn't very serious, though, and I'm hoping to be back in SF in a few days.

I don't really understand why my request for a loan was turned down. I thought Mansion Enterprises employees qualified for automatic loans, to be deducted from salary. Actually, that was one of the reasons I signed on with Mansion Enterprises.

Russ

~~~~~

EMAIL FROM: wgreenlee@mansent.com
TO: ruswhite@mansent.com

Hi Russ,

Your email was the first thing I found when I checked my laptop this morning. I still envy you. You might be out on a lava flow, but it's still a lava flow in *Hawaii*.

I'm really sorry about the loan refusal but orders came from the forty-second floor, and for your information, there is no official Mansion Enterprises policy on personal loans to employees. It's completely discretional.

Shall I pencil in next Tuesday's squash court or not?

Will

~~~~~

Federica woke up lying on something warm, hard and lumpy.

What was warm, hard and lumpy?

She opened her eyes and found Jack's brilliant blue eyes looking at her — well, one blue eye and one black-and-blue eye — and realized what the lump under her stomach was.

Last night shot through her mind and she flushed a bright red.

If it weren't for the ferocious bolt of heat jolting through her as Jack shifted under her, she would have been convinced that last night had happened to someone else entirely. Someone warm and sensuous, a woman skilled in the art of lovemaking with all the right instincts in all the right places. Certainly not *her*, Federica Mansion, heiress to an empire and to the coldest genes this side of Jupiter.

But it must have been her last night, because though there was a bit of fog in terms of memory, and a number of details about last night were hazy, her body knew exactly what it had done. She ached in a number of delicious, intimate places.

Jack smiled. "Good morning." He was so close she could feel his warm breath on her cheek.

"Good morning." Federica was about to make some inane, polite comment—*did you sleep well last night?*—but luckily he ran his hands slowly up the side of her thighs and cupped her bottom, shifting her until she was vitally aware that *he* was having a *very* good morning.

By now, Federica knew what that kind of thing from Jack did to her mind. It destroyed it. Before her thoughts went up entirely in smoke, she cupped her hand around his jaw and brought his face back from where he'd been gently nipping her neck. His jaw was warm and bristly and felt perfect. The perfect jaw. The perfect early-morning bristle.

"I...Jack—stop that," she said breathlessly, when he started exploring her ear with tongue and lips. "I want you to know, Jack—" Federica shivered when he ran one hand up her bare back, slowly over her shoulder and neck, threading his fingers through her hair, holding her head still for an earth-shattering kiss. Early-morning kisses like that should be illegal. No one on Earth would get any work done ever if they all were on the receiving end of morning kisses like that.

"Jack," she sighed.

"Mmmm?"

Federica pulled back and looked him straight in the eyes. Gorgeous, bright blue eyes, with laughter lines starring them. He was a good-looking man, but that wasn't why Federica found herself staring at him with a lump in her throat. She remembered last night with a pang. Nothing that perfect could ever last, and she knew that what she wanted more than anything in the world was to be with Jack Sutter, as often and for as long as was humanly possible. She had never felt this close to another human being in her life. He had slipped into her heart just as surely as he had slipped into her body.

"I want you to know, Jack," she said earnestly, "that last night was wonderful. Absolutely wonderful."

"Yeah, I know." Jack nuzzled the soft skin under her chin. "I was there, too, remember?"

"To die for," she murmured.

"Oh, yeah?" Jack pulled back and looked up at her with interest. "To die for? I had big plans for this morning. I wanted to make up for last night. I got a little…frantic last night, and I wanted to make it up to you." He caressed her rib cage, and Federica's eyelids drooped. "But you've given me a better idea." He nibbled delicately at her earlobe and cupped her breast. Every bone in Federica's body melted. "A long, slow, lingering death…"

~~~~~

EMAIL FROM: ruswhite@mansent.com
TO: wgreenlee@mansent.com

Will,

I've had three showers today and I still can't get the cinders out of my hair. Working on an active volcano is no joke. But the situation is under control.

I won't pretend I'm not disappointed at my loan application being turned down. But maybe *you'd* like to lend me the money, and make a big profit in the bargain. I'll let you in on a sure thing. It's very exciting and top secret and I'll give you the details only in person because security is very tight.

I'll only say two words—*genetic engineering*. Sound good? I can let you in on the ground floor of a deal which will keep you in squash courts 'til the end of time, but I'm a little strapped for capital, which is why I wanted the loan. Think about it.

White

~~~~~

Elizabeth Jennings

EMAIL FROM: wgreenlee@mansent.com
TO: ruswhite@mansent.com

Dear Russell,

I'm glad you're having fun.

Sorry to pass on your wonderful "sure thing", White, but any more of your "sure things" and I can kiss that condo in Marin County goodbye.

You remember those Indonesian bonds you had me buy three days before the tsunami? And the banana futures a week before the coup d'etat? You're jinxed, White, and the sooner you realize that, the better.

The court is booked for Tuesday. If you don't make it, Martinez from Catering will take your place.

Will

~~~~~

"Here's the stuff I want from Shelby." Wyatt sat behind his desk and skimmed a manila envelope across the dusty, scarred surface.

"Right." Jack tore open the envelope and scanned the list of questions to be asked of the U.S. Marshal's office in Shelby while foraging one-handedly in Wyatt's refrigerator.

Gun caliber. Point of entry. Tread mark classifications. Liquid incendiary agents. Car bombs. Wyatt was working again.

Jack grinned and pulled out a bottle of beer.

Wyatt watched him empty half a bottle. "Help yourself to some beer, why don't you, Jack?"

"Don't mind if I do." Jack emptied the rest of the bottle and shifted some papers on Wyatt's desk. The Los Angeles Police Department organization chart fell to the ground. He picked it up, looked at it curiously, placed it on top of the Mellon Law

Manual and shoved the entire pile to one side so he could stack his heels on the desk.

"And make yourself comfortable while you're at it."

"Thanks." Jack settled deeper in the chair, grateful that Wyatt's Scandinavian period was over. While Wyatt had been in it, his house had been full of chairs you knelt in rather than sat on. Now he was in his Americana phase and the chairs were dark, leather and comfortable. "So how did the date with Mary Jane go?"

"Sue Ellen."

"Whatever."

"It went." Wyatt grimaced. "So did I."

"What happened?"

Wyatt fiddled with a paperweight, then put it down when he saw Jack watching him with a small half-smile. He held still a moment, then, uncontrollably, started drumming his fingers.

"I don't know, it was just so—she was—" He stopped drumming and ran a hand through his long, sun-bleached hair. "She talked about mall crawling, and her mom's latest boyfriend. She raved about Ashton Kucher's new movie. You'll be happy to know that there is a new nail polish color called 'Hot Nights'." Wyatt sighed. "The fun's going out of the game, bro, and I don't know what to do about it."

"Well," Jack pointed out reasonably as he popped the top of another beer, "that's what you get when you date girls younger than your Harley-Davidson."

"Is it? I mean, she had a great body and was hinting that her new bedspread matched the nail polish, but I just…I don't know. Right in the middle of the date, I started thinking about deadlines, and did Norman remember to pay my quarterly estimate and then…all of a sudden I found myself leaving Sue Ellen back at her doorstep. What's happening? What's missing?"

Jack remembered meeting Sue Ellen briefly at a county fair where she'd been elected Miss Alfalfa. The girl had seemed nice enough, but a few sandwiches shy of a picnic.

"I think it's called intelligence, Wyatt," Jack said kindly. "You might want to try it in your dates some time."

"But you date an intelligent woman, and then you start getting serious, and then she's got a ring on her finger and you've got a noose around your neck and it's all over."

"I'm not too sure there's such a direct connection between going out with an intelligent woman and death," Jack said thoughtfully.

"There is. And anyway, I already did."

Jack was thumbing through a coroner's manual with interest, grateful that it was out of purely academic interest. Carson's Bluff citizens were more civilized than most people. "Did what?"

"Date a smart woman."

"Oh yeah?" Jack looked up from a particularly gruesome photograph. "When? Who?"

"You remember when I was researching bank fraud last September?"

Jack nodded. It had turned out to be one of Wyatt's best efforts.

"Well, I got a lot of inside information from the Morton Savings & Loan officer."

"So?" Jack frowned as he peered into the empty can. He debated briefly about popping another one, then decided against it. The road down to Shelby was winding and steep and he wanted to make it back—in one piece—before nightfall.

He had things to do tonight.

"Well, the officer was a she. Sort of."

"What the hell does that mean?"

"Well, I mean she looked like a woman and dressed like a woman, but she thought like a barracuda and was so tough she used *aftershave*. She gave me some wonderful tips on how banks work, then spent the rest of the time outlining how she was going to be an executive vice president in ten years' time. Brrrr."

Wyatt shivered. "Am I glad I'm not in her line of fire. She actually talked about 'taking out' the competition and sending her colleagues out to catch 'friendly fire'. I don't need a businesswoman, thank you very much. And all the smart ones are in business nowadays."

"Not all businesswomen are barracudas," Jack said thoughtfully, remembering.

"Well your wife sure was."

"Oh, yeah." Jack stared dejectedly into the empty can, upended it over his mouth to catch a few drops, then crushed it. "I forgot. But she wasn't really a businesswoman. Not really."

"No, she was just greedy." Wyatt looked craftily at Jack. "But you say all businesswomen aren't like her? How do you know?"

"I just know," Jack said, annoyed, hoping Wyatt would leave it at that.

He should have known better.

"Yeah?" Wyatt leaned forward, looking at his brother with interest. "Did you score then? Come on, tell all. What's Federica like?"

Jack glared at Wyatt. "That's not a subject open for discussion," he said stiffly.

Wyatt was unfazed. He slapped the desktop. "Hot damn! I knew it! Come on, bro. You can't hold back. This from the guy who told me Karen Hackensacker's bra size in high school? You even told me all about how Samantha liked to—"

"I'm not talking about it." Jack sat up and folded his arms and met Wyatt's gaze steadily. "And that's that."

Wyatt looked carefully at his brother, and dropped his bantering tone. "Federica's bad news for you, Jack," he said, suddenly serious. "You know that, don't you?"

"I know," Jack said, equally seriously.

He couldn't think about Federica and what he was starting to feel for her, and all the ramifications. He needed to change the subject. Fast.

"So," he said, tilting his chair back and linking his hands behind his head. "You decided to kill off the blonde yet?"

Chapter Nine

Don of a New Age.

Federica looked up, bemused, at the hand-painted wooden sign, depicting a lotus blossom and the slogan, "Take a look and buy a book."

Lilly put a hand at Federica's back and ushered her in through a portal shaped like a Chinese pagoda.

The bookshop was overwhelming, but charming. Delicate rice fans vied for wall space with African masks and Native American spirit catchers. Potted plants covered every surface not already covered with books. Books were piled everywhere. Not just ranged along the shelves lining the walls, but stacked on every available inch of space. There was a faint scent of incense overlaying every booklover's favorite odor—the dusty, papery smell of books.

In a corner sat an enormous silver samovar on top of a Colonial piecrust table badly in need of restoration. The table was next to a broken-down floral print armchair that had seen better days, but still looked sinfully comfortable. Within reach of the armchair, atop a 1920s treadle sewing machine, was a pile of newspapers and magazines.

The ambience was warm and inviting, more comfortable and better-organized than Shakespeare & Co in Paris, but just as offbeat and just as homey.

"Hi, Lil, what can I do for you?" A middle-aged man with a pleasantly ugly face walked forward. His only concession to an alternative lifestyle was a long ponytail and jeans. But his salt-and-pepper hair was thick and clean and the jeans were neatly pressed. He also wore a blue chambray shirt and tie under a sports jacket.

"Hi, Don." Lil leaned casually against a big worktable piled high with bestsellers. "I want you to meet a friend of mine, Federica Mansion. Federica, Don Sellers."

"Hi, Federica. Welcome." Federica had the impression that Don was sizing her up, but in a friendly way. If her name meant anything, he didn't betray it by even a flicker of an eyelash. "Can I help you?"

"Well, I'm here for—" Too late, Federica realized her mistake, though Don's friendly expression remained unchanged. "A…a while," she finished lamely. "And while I'm here I'd like some reading material. Light. Maybe some murder mysteries. A romance or two."

"Sure thing." Don's voice was a soft, pleasant tenor. "Take your time and browse. Mysteries are on the far wall, romances and sagas to your right and science fiction to your left. Straight ahead is humor and self-help. Herbal tea is in the samovar. The magazines are reasonably up-to-date." Though his voice was light, he was observing her closely, his gaze intent, and Federica wondered uneasily what he was seeing.

When Don turned to Lilly, it was like a light switch had been turned off and Federica breathed easier.

Without any self-consciousness, Don reached over and patted Lilly's stomach. "Welcome to you, too, little one. A lot of enlightened little souls are being born right now, and I know you'll be one." He guided Lilly to the armchair, where she settled with a sigh. Don smiled gently. "So, how's she doing?"

"Just fine." Lilly put her feet up on the Moroccan hassock Don placed in front of her. "She's probably going to be a he, though."

"Pity." Don walked to the samovar and opened the spigot. A fragrantly fruity brew poured out into what was clearly a cup designed by Lilly. At least twenty other cups were on a huge, hand-painted wooden tray.

Lilly blew and sipped. "Funny you should say that. Everyone in the family is over the moon that it's going to be a boy. Though to tell you the truth, I was hoping for a daughter."

"And you're right. The feminine principal is destined to rule the Earth. The future is woman. Women are evolving spiritually much more quickly than men. Being a girl would give your child a big advantage."

"Well that's a switch," Lilly blew and sipped again. She should have looked masculine in her maternity jean-overalls and plaid work shirt, but she was the essence of woman as her lips curved in a smile. She curled a protective hand over her belly. "Through most of history, being a girl has been a distinct disadvantage."

"Not now," Don poured a cup for himself and a third one, which he casually handed to Federica. "If it's a boy, he'll just have to scramble to keep up."

Lilly knocked gently on the front of her overalls. "Hear that, in there?" she asked affectionately. "You're going to have to work hard to overcome the handicap of being a male."

Federica tried not to eavesdrop as she walked slowly around the bookshop, making her selections and sipping tea. Mansion Enterprises had an open account at the biggest chain bookstore in downtown San Francisco and she usually ended up doing her book shopping there, since the company picked up the bill. Though she'd spent a fortune in books, the bookshop had a high personnel turnover and none of the salespeople ever recognized her, let alone offered tea or asked how she was doing.

It was fun wandering around Don of a New Age. The store looked chaotic, but after only a short time, she discovered it was surprisingly well-organized. Though the shop was small, much smaller than the chain bookstore, Don had a little of everything, all of it interesting. Federica could have bought half the books in the store.

Don thoughtfully provided wicker baskets for his clientele's purchases, and after half an hour Federica's basket was full. Ellen was the expert on thrillers and mysteries, so Federica stuck to romances and women's fiction by favorite authors, the thicker the better. She was looking forward to many long pleasurable hours reading them.

Then she depressed herself by remembering that she wouldn't be sticking around Carson's Bluff long enough to do it.

But that was thinking about the future. She couldn't think about the future. The future didn't exist. There was only an endless now.

She dumped her selections on the converted butcher's block that served as a counter and Don started ringing up the sales.

"Hey, wait a minute." Federica picked up a slim volume with embossed flowers on the cover. *The Heart's Journey.* She looked it over. "This must have slipped in by accident. I didn't pick it up."

Calmly, Don placed it to one side with her other purchases. "You're not buying it," he said, as he pulled out a recycled paper bag with the lotus-flower logo. "It's my gift to you. Don't get me wrong, but I think you need to read it." He starting putting her books in the bag.

"I—" Federica opened her mouth, then closed it. She studied the book's cover then turned it over to read the blurb on the back. *Many hearts are going on a journey. A journey of discovery, of love, of fulfillment. Is yours?*

Yes, hers was going on a journey. Headed straight for a concrete wall at a hundred miles an hour without a safety belt.

"Um, that's very kind of you, Don—"

"Your aura's green, Federica." Don was looking at her intently. He took her hand in his and it was as if a mild electric current united the two of them, flowing from Don into her.

Federica looked down at herself, though she knew exactly what she'd see. A new pair of soft, comfortable beige cotton slacks, a pink T-shirt and floral sneakers. The sum total of her purchases at Kelly's had been two pairs of jeans, three pairs of slacks, five T-shirts, two sweatshirts, two track suits and two pairs of sneakers. Enough to keep her comfortable for…whatever.

Her mind balked at thinking about the future.

Green, Don had said. There was nothing green in her wardrobe.

"I beg your pardon, but—"

"Green auras are signs of distress and change. Change is necessary for every living creature. You're going through great changes as you start to achieve your destiny." Don took her other hand gently in his and she felt another jolt of electricity as his gaze seemed to pierce directly into her heart. The one that was going on a journey. "Don't fight it. Your heart knows where it's going, even if your head doesn't. Follow your heart, Federica."

He relinquished her hands and the current stopped and she felt suddenly disconnected. As if someone had switched her off. Federica watched, shaken to the core, as Don calmly finished putting her books in the bag.

Don looked up and smiled. "That'll be $89.95. Credit card or cash?"

~~~~~

EMAIL FROM: wgreenlee@mansent.com

TO: pcobb@mansent.com

Dear Mr. Cobb,

I'm emailing this to you because I know that Mr. Mansion is very busy in Prague. You can be the judge as to whether the information should be forwarded to Mr. Mansion or not.

Below you will find seven spreadsheets covering the next semester, using seven different economic scenarios and calculated according to the Karnovsky indices. I don't know if you are up on the latest econometric theories, but Karnovsky's ideas have been applied by a number of Fortune 500 companies, and the predictive factor has been close to ninety-seven percent. All the scenarios postulate different macro- and microeconomic conditions but they all come to the same conclusion. I could wrap it up in techno-speak, but in plain English, Mansion Enterprises will be facing a huge cash deficit sometime early in the new year, even if it foregoes the two big planned purchases for the second semester, the Carson's Bluff property and the Kiev Mansion Inn. With these two purchases factored in — or even with one — we're talking megabucks. Megabucks which we won't have. Since I'm kind of fond of my salary from Mansion Enterprises, I thought I'd just pass word along.

Willard Greenlee, Finances

~~~~~

EMAIL FROM: pcobb@mansent.com
TO: F.H.Mansion@mansent.com

Dear Frederick,

I've just received some rather distressing projections for 2006 from Finances. It looks like our five-year expansion program has been a little over-ambitious. Not to mention the fact that we've lost megabucks due to the fluctuations in exchange rates and the tanking dollar versus the euro. According to Finances, we'll be running into an air pocket early next year if we plan on both purchasing and restoring the Carson's Bluff property and purchasing property in Kiev in the same quarter.

I can send you the figures, but they're so complicated I'm not sure any one human can actually understand them. You need to be a techno-geek like Willard Greenlee, who was the one who first drew my attention to the problem. Anyway, you look them over if you want, but I always tend to the take the experts' advice. Until it lands you in jail, of course. Ha-ha.

Federica still isn't checking her email. Maybe she knows something we don't? Hope things are going well in Prague.

Best, Paul

Federica was miserable.

It was just as bad as she'd feared. Carson's Bluff was perfect, and nothing perfect was destined to last in this imperfect world.

Federica couldn't find anything to fault as she and Lily lazily strolled along the tree-lined streets meandering through the town. Most of the buildings were late nineteenth-century and lovingly restored.

"Beautiful," Federica murmured, as she reached out to touch a delicate pink tea rose. One of the velvety petals fell into her hand. She looked past the rose arbor at a small Victorian home set well back from the road. The workmanship was exquisite, from the freshly painted gingerbread trim to the recently polished brass horsehead knocker gleaming in the noonday sun.

It would have been the perfect yuppie home, right down to the original stained glass transom, if it weren't for an old battered van in the driveway and the swing set and tipped-over tricycle in the front garden.

Though the van was probably old enough to vote, it was too young and battered to be considered a classic car, and much too old and battered to be considered chic. These people weren't rich. Yuppies never let their kids play in the garden because they ruin the flowerbeds, and yuppie kids were too busy with calculus and Japanese lessons to play in gardens anyway.

The whole town was like that—prettified and restored, like an outpost for six-figure professionals. But Carson's Bluff wasn't anywhere near where anyone could earn serious money and Federica didn't know of any mega-corporations in the vicinity.

There were signs of life and kids everywhere. It puzzled Federica. Rich places didn't have any outward signs of life—all life occurred behind tall fences and barricades. There was hardly a fence in all of Carson's Bluff, and every single person they met said hello to Lilly and nodded to her.

The people. They also puzzled her. Not a moussed head of hair in sight. No baggy, hang-off-your-butt designer jeans, no pierced belly buttons, no power suits like those languishing in her suitcase. There wasn't a designer anything in the whole town, or at least not that Federica could see.

And the *shops*. They sold things, real things, necessary things, like food and books and hardware, with nary a frill in sight. It was eerie, being in a place without boutiques, like a science fiction movie. *The Town that Boutiques Forgot*.

Not one wine bar or trendy café, just Stella's with the furniture too recent to be back in style, sawdust on the floor and food to die for.

"You've got some great architecture here." Federica pointed at a particularly fine example of the Beaux Art style.

"That's Harry Carson's doing. When he made his money, he called in some of the finest artists and artisans of his time. Apparently he had a lot of connections back east and he sent out word to all the craftsmen he knew that they would be welcome here in Carson's Bluff. They say a lot of them were on the run or had offended some authority somewhere. Harry Carson made it very clear that they could start over here with a clean slate, no questions asked. They could even change their names, if they wanted to."

"Sounds wonderful," Federica said. Lilly's eyes narrowed at the wistful tone in Federica's voice.

Starting over, no questions asked, changing her name. For a moment, Federica wished she hadn't been born in the century of computerized records. Just running away and changing her name. It sounded heavenly. She shook her head to get rid of the thought.

"Yeah." Lilly glanced at Federica, then looked away. "I guess it's been a Carson's Bluff tradition ever since."

"Running away?"

"Starting over. And living free."

Federica suddenly stopped, as abruptly as if her feet had encountered some particularly potent glue. Chilling thoughts tumbled through her mind. She could be wrong—she *hoped* she was wrong, but all this talk of freedom...individualism...ohgod, ohgod.

"Ah, Lilly?"

"Mmm?" Lilly lifted her face to the warm summer sun and closed her eyes. She opened them to find Federica staring at her. "What?"

Federica was trying not to think of a thousand alarming newspaper and magazine articles. Carson's Bluff's determination to remain isolated...all this talk of independence...and California *was* known for its crazies, after all...

"Federica?" Lilly frowned, worried. "You look like you've seen a ghost."

"Not a ghost, exactly." Federica drew in a long breath and wondered if she should say it. She had a brief, fierce tussle with herself. She had to know. "Who are you people? I mean..." Federica hesitated. She was about to insult a *pregnant lady*, for heaven's sake. "You sound...you sound like the people in Carson's Bluff don't—don't like outsiders. And I know you don't like the outside world intruding too much on your affairs and all..." Federica wound down a little as she looked at Lilly's bright, open, friendly face. Lilly certainly didn't look crazy. But she had to say it. She had to know. "You—you're not all a bunch of survivalists are you?"

Lilly lifted a hand to shade her eyes against the bright sunlight. Federica couldn't read her expression. "Survivalists?"

"You know..." Federica waved her hand vaguely, feeling more and more foolish by the second. "Those right-wing crazies who hole up in the mountains, stockpiling food and AK-47s for when civilization breaks down. Keeping sentry for when the government comes in big black helicopters in the dead of night. There's none of that around here…is there?"

Lilly gaped at Federica. "Survivalists," she said again. Lilly turned her head away and Federica could hear a choking sound. For a panicky moment, she thought Lilly was starting to cry, then she saw that she was struggling not to laugh.

Federica could feel her face flushing. "You read about them all the time," she muttered. "Then the FBI comes and shoots them all."

Lilly finally gave in and threw back her head and laughed heartily. Her throat was strong and tanned.

Federica grew annoyed.

Lilly wiped away a tear. "Survivalists." The thought tickled her. "Not quite. As far as I know, the only guns in town are in Jack's office, under lock and key. And the last time a shot was fired, it was Benny Keller shooting air pellets at a stray that kept overturning his garbage can. Believe me, honey, there is nothing strange or weird about Carson's Bluffers. It's just that we like our peace and quiet and a relaxed way of life."

Federica still wasn't convinced. "So how come everyone here seems to be so…so…" Federica waved her hand in frustration, trying to describe what it was about Carson's Bluff that was so different.

"So what?" Lilly was looking at her with her head tilted, faintly smiling.

"So…normal? Different?" Federica struggled to find the right word.

"Well." Lilly's expression turned serious as she thought about it. "I guess we are all aware that Carson's Bluff is a sort of…sanctuary. It's a friendly place to live in and bring your kids up in and we all make a real effort to keep the stress levels down."

"And if someone…disagreeable moves in?"

"We've had our share of people who love it here, love the friendliness, the relaxed atmosphere. It's safe. Then they move here and end up trying to change the place. They start going to Town Council meetings and talking about upping Carson's Bluff's 'tourist potential' and 'improving the tax base' and attracting growth industries." Lilly shuddered, then shrugged. "So...we booby trap 'em."

"I beg your pardon?"

"Tell you later," Lilly said swiftly. They reached the end of the road and rounded a corner. Federica, who had an excellent sense of direction, realized that they were heading back toward Main Street. "Look at that. That's one of our oldest buildings." Lilly gestured to a three-story gray-and-white building, with an unusual lacy trim.

"Nice." Federica tried to keep the glumness out of her voice. The building was more than nice. It belonged in a coffee table book. *Beautiful Homes of Northern California About to Be Destroyed by Big Business.* "What is it?"

"Old Man Murchisons' place. He deeded it to the town, and the top floors house the town archives. The whole ground floor is the city library. The books are donated, and it's staffed on a volunteer rota basis." Lilly waved at an elderly lady in the bay window of the handsome old building. "I go in the second Tuesday of every month." Federica could barely make out shelves of books lining the walls. The lady waved back and Federica and Lilly ambled on.

They rounded another corner and Federica stopped cold.

"Wow," she breathed.

"Pretty, isn't it?" Lilly smiled. "Morrison Square. We just call it the Square. We're proud of it, though it's Mr. Giannini's work."

"Mr. Giannini?" Federica was barely listening. The central area of Carson's Bluff was a large, irregularly shaped square with tall maples around the perimeter. Federica hurried ahead and Lilly followed leisurely.

Rhododendrons dotted the grounds like colored clouds. Tall hawthorn bushes blocked out the road. Federica ventured further in. A minute into the square and it was like being in the heart of a garden. Not just any garden. Eden. All street sounds were immediately damped and the only things she could hear were leaves rustling and the faint buzz of bees. The square had been designed in such a way that all you could see from any direction were plants.

The Square's grounds weren't formal, but rather a pleasant hodgepodge of colors and varieties in irregular beds meandering in and around the big shade trees. It looked artless, but it wasn't. All the beds were well-mulched and bordered with white paving stones which had been recently painted. All the plants were healthy and planted precisely where they could best grow. Since the Square wasn't formal, it seemed larger than it was and in the center it was easy to forget that there was a town around.

Federica waited for Lilly near a salmonberry bush. "Your landscaper's a genius. We…I mean, Mansion Enterprises pays a small fortune to a gardening service and we can't get results like this."

"We don't pay Mr. Giannini anything." Lilly bent, a little awkwardly, and snapped a wilting gladioli blossom off at the stem. Her mouth quirked when she saw Federica's shock. "It was past its prime. And anyway, the Square belongs to all of us."

"What do you mean, you don't pay anything?" Federica waved her hand. "Keeping this place is a year-round job. Who'd do that for nothing?"

"Mr. Giannini." Lilly twirled the stem. "And we give him a small plot in the corner where he can grow his vegetables. This year it looks like he's going to have a bumper crop in tomatoes."

"Well, that's fair." Federica admired a round box topiary and conjured up a pleasant image of a stooped old man, weather-beaten face curved in a perpetual smile, like the farm workers she'd seen tending the verdant hills around Naples. He'd have a handkerchief tied around his head to keep off the sun, and work in his undershirt. "I guess Mr. Giannini must be a peasant from the Old Country."

"Um, not quite." Lilly smiled. "Marcus Giannini is one of the most elegant men I've ever met. He was a vice president of a big oil company, but he quit after a major polluting incident. He vowed he would never do anything but grow living things again for the rest of his life." Lilly bent to pick up a sheet of paper. She balled it up and tossed it into a trash can. A hole in one.

"Oh. *Oh.*" Federica's heart speeded up as they followed the winding path to a little clearing and she saw what was in it, smooth, gleaming, mysterious and irresistible. She raced to the steel and wood structure and ran a reverent hand over the smooth, curved shape. "This is a Rachel Douglas sculpture, I'd bet on it," she breathed.

"Right first time out."

"How could the town afford a Douglas?" Federica was astonished. Mansion Enterprises had debated buying one for the acre-lot outside headquarters but Finances had balked at the two-million-dollar asking price. The inside of one of the curves was faced with some light-colored material. It opened the sculpture up, making it resemble a giant flower. Sort of. That was the thing about a Douglas sculpture. It was always on the verge of looking like something familiar, something just on the edge of consciousness. It tickled the mind. There was no such thing as ever completely understanding a Rachel Douglas.

Intrigued, Federica laid the flat of her palm along the curve. As always, though Rachel Douglas sculptures were simple in design, they became more complex the more you studied them. Her hand rested on a surface that felt pleasantly warm to the touch. "What do you suppose this material is?"

"Dunno." Lilly shrugged. "You'll have to ask Rachel that. And she didn't sell it to the town. She donated it." Lilly pointed to a house barely visible through the maples. "She lives over there."

Federica's eyes rounded. *"Rachel Douglas lives here?"* The house Lilly indicated stood apart, small, ancient, slightly askew.

"Oh, yeah." Lilly smiled. "Nice old lady. Keeps to herself a lot. Don't be deceived by that Hansel-and-Gretel house of hers. Out back she's got a studio as big as a hangar with machines and tools that would put NASA to shame."

Federica's head was spinning. Horace Milton. Rachel Douglas. *Here*. Who else lived here? She spun around, excited.

"Oh, I get it." Federica could almost whack herself on the forehead for having missed it. That intangible something…something she couldn't quite put a finger on. Why Carson's Bluff seemed so special. The tumblers in her mind spun like a Vegas slot machine. Only this time she was sure she'd hit the jackpot. *"The town is an arts colony*! I don't know why I didn't see it before—it's so obvious that—"

"Chill, Federica." Lilly met her eyes and shook her head slowly. "Right church, wrong pew. Carson's Bluff is a perfectly normal little Northern California town. No right-wing crazies holing up in the hills. No arts colony. Just ordinary people who try to get along and who put lifestyle ahead of income. That's all there is to it."

"And if someone crass and money-grubbing moves in…"

"Simple. We booby-trap 'em." Lilly took Federica's arm. "How about some ice cream? We've got the best ice cream parlor on the continent. My treat."

~~~~~

FAX FROM: Ellen Larsen, c/o Inter Airways, Roissy Airport, Paris

FAX TO: Federica Mansion, c/o Sheriff's Office, Carson's Bluff

Dear Federica,

I can't tell you how worried and anxious I am. Worry and Anxiety are my middle names. You haven't been receiving my faxes so you won't know that my flight had a near miss outside New York, on the way to Paris. After spending eight hellish hours at Kennedy, our flight finally took off, but—get this—*on the same plane*. They did a routine check-up, said it would cost too much to fly out another plane, *so they just decided to take the risk*.

Then they gave the whole crew two days off, thinking it would keep us quiet. Can you believe these jokers? I heard the flight crew talking about it, and they're taking it to the FAA. There's a smell of strike in the air, which would suit me just fine since I've decided to put on my deerstalker, pull out the magnifying glass and play Nancy Drew. See if I can crack The Case of the Missing Heiress. (That's you, by the way.)

I'm trying to keep it light, honey, but actually, I'm worried sick. I hope this fax gets through.

Love, El

FAX NOT RECEIVED/NO SIGNAL

~~~~~

Federica tasted Paradise, but eyed Sin covetously.

"What's Sin like?"

"Divine." Lilly scooped up a carbohydrate-rich spoonful of dark creamy chocolate. "How's Paradise?"

They were in Dora's Ice Cream Parlor, a tiny hole-in-the-wall place, very simply decorated. Not that fancy decor was necessary, given the quality of the ice cream.

Federica dipped into Paradise again, yogurt ice cream and maracuja, and laughed. "Probably not as good as Sin, but delicious anyway. This stuff is really great." Federica eyed the blackboard listing the daily specials. A Deadly Sin for each day of the week. "What do you suppose Avarice is?"

Lilly swallowed and closed her eyes. "Mint and bittersweet chocolate. To die for."

"Next time," Federica promised herself.

Lilly glanced at her, a half-smile on her face. "Next time, Federica," she said slyly, "I'd try Lust if I were you."

Federica dropped her spoon. "I...ah..." Her face bloomed. *Lilly couldn't possibly know about her and Jack, could she?* She felt her pulse pound in her ears as she turned to look at the board and read the description of Lust.

As if she didn't know. Except Dora's version of Lust wasn't six-foot-two, with broad shoulders, black hair, bright blue eyes and a wicked smile. It was nougat and tiramisù.

Federica turned back as soon as she felt her face cool down. "I'm not too fond of nougat."

"Too bad." Lilly peered into her steel cup and scraped up the last of the dark chocolate.

"You want any more, Lilly? Might as well make hay while the sun shines." Dora, the pleasant, thirty-something proprietor materialized beside them.

"I'll have a half-portion of Sloth, thanks Dora. I'm going on a diet as soon as Junior's born. In the meantime," she patted her tummy, "it's well camouflaged." Lilly and Federica watched Dora as she filled the order. "You know, a representative from a big ice cream chain offered her an executive position a few years ago. She thought about it for a while because the offer was very lucrative."

"But she didn't take it," Federica said.

"No," Lilly said, surprised, "in the end she didn't. She thought—"

"—it was better to be her own boss, and live here, rather than earn more money."

"You got it!" Lilly was delighted. "Smart lady. We'll make a Carson's Bluffer out of you yet, Federica!"

Don't I wish, Federica thought.

There was a sudden silence, as both of them remembered at the exact same time why Federica was there.

Federica took a deep breath. In for a penny, in for a pound. "Tell me about Jack's wife."

"*Ex*-wife. Thank God."

"Okay. Ex-wife."

Lilly was silent as Dora slid some Sloth onto the wooden table. She contemplated the double-cream vanilla and maraschino cherries for a long moment. "Jack didn't always live here in Carson's Bluff. For fifteen years he was in the Army."

"The Army?" Federica couldn't quite square her laid-back Jack with the regimentation of military life. "That doesn't sound much like Jack."

"Well, he was." Lilly put her spoon down and leaned earnestly toward Federica. "Jack is deeper than he looks. He's always had a strong sense of duty. It's what makes him such a good sheriff. And it's why he'll probably be re-elected mayor until the day he dies."

Federica just looked at her. She didn't need Lilly to tell her how wonderful Jack was. The fact that he was so wonderful was one of the major problems in her life right now.

"His wife. Okay." Lilly blew out a breath. "Jack—Jack did one of those behind-the-scenes jobs that are really necessary but not glamorous, if you know what I mean. He was a supplies inspector, and he traveled from post to post, and from company warehouse to manufacturing site, making sure everything was up to spec. He traveled a lot with his secretary, Samantha. And he ended up marrying her." Lilly's face screwed up in disgust. "I don't know what he saw in her. Nobody does."

Federica tried making a swan origami out of her napkin. It looked so easy when the Japanese did it. She didn't look up. "I take it Samantha wasn't from around here?"

"You take it right. Not that we'd be prejudiced against outsiders," Lilly added hastily. "It's just that there was something about her…I don't know…we just couldn't get close to her, you know?"

Federica tugged at a paper corner and pulled out an awkward swan, one wing up and one wing down. She hated Samantha already. "So what happened?"

Lilly sighed. "Well, Jack's job took him around the world, on on-site inspections. And he and Samantha would get taken out a lot, by the supply companies. Jack made it clear that his opinion wasn't for sale. But I guess Samantha started getting used to the good life. She liked going to fancy restaurants and nagged Jack into buying her lots of clothes. Anyway, to cut a long story short, a routine audit of the books of one of the supply companies showed that the company had paid almost one-hundred-thousand into Jack's account. He was court-martialed."

"*Jack!*" Federica had started on another napkin origami, a flower this time, but her hands jerked and the paper tore. "I don't believe it! Jack couldn't do anything like that!"

"No, Jack couldn't," Lilly said, her voice grim. "But Samantha sure could. And did. Turned out that she'd been receiving gifts from the president of the company and promised to get Jack to overlook a few irregularities. Which was crazy when you thought about it, because Jack wouldn't do it, and anyway they were barely speaking to each other at that point. I don't know what she was thinking. But the point is that Jack wasn't checking their joint account and didn't notice the money piling up or the expensive presents she was getting. Just like a man. He didn't even notice that she had a diamond bracelet. But the Army lawyers didn't believe him at first. It took all of his savings and then some to convince the court of that. That he was innocent. His name was finally cleared and he quit, but he was financially wiped out. He came back home, divorced and broke." Lilly watched Federica carefully. "About the only thing Jack has to his name now is his house, which belonged to our grandmother, and his salary as sheriff, which is forty thou a year."

Federica was turning over in her mind what Lilly had told her.

"Forty thousand doesn't go very far," Lilly said slowly. "Not nowadays."

Forty thousand dollars was less than Federica's expense account, but Federica wasn't thinking of that. She was thinking that Jack's marriage was really over. She felt a sudden rush of gratitude for this Samantha person's greed. "Crazy woman," Federica said suddenly.

"Who?"

"Samantha."

"You think so?"

"Absolutely. She must be utterly and totally insane. Imagine choosing a few restaurant meals and a bracelet over…over *Jack*. I mean, what sane woman would do that?"

Lilly smiled. "You really mean that?"

"Well, of course I mean it. That woman must have been out of her mind." Federica shook her head in wonder. "Nuts."

"Yeah, nuts." Lilly grinned. She gestured with her spoon at Federica's half-finished ice cream. "Say, are you going to finish that? If not, I'll eat it. I seem to have this enormous appetite lately."

~~~~~

EMAIL FROM: F.H.Mansion@mansent.com

TO: pcobb@mansent.com

Dear Paul,

Thanks for the spreadsheets. I will give them careful consideration. All the more so because we are basing our plans for growth until 2010 on expanding into Eastern Europe. It's going to be trickier than I thought. Even here in Prague, things are not going as well as I had hoped. Nonetheless, this is definitely going to be the fastest-growing part of our business in the future. The question is when? I suppose we can hold off on acquisition of the Carson's Bluff property if it creates a cash-flow problem. Advise Federica to postpone negotiations. We can think about starting to close down the Engineering Department and eliminating Russell White. Stay in touch.

Frederick

~~~~~

Federica finished the chapter with a pleased sigh. Fifty pages into the book and the heroine was still a baby. The book was pleasantly heavy, at least three days' worth of reading. Three days was as far ahead as her mind could stretch, then a little hum would set in, closing off all further thought.

She was sitting on the porch of the Folly, bare feet up on the railing, exactly as she'd imagined it at the bookshop.

The sun was just starting to go down. The Folly was enveloped in a deep, pine-scented peace, the color of the sky an outrageously beautiful turquoise. She had a half-empty bottle of Pigswill on the floor within reach when she wanted a swig. She couldn't remember the last time she felt this happy. If ever. She wriggled her toes and sighed.

Not even the distant rumble of worry in her head could distract her from this immense feeling of peace. Then the rumble grew louder, and she placed the book facedown on her lap and waited contentedly for the van to pull into view.

She didn't stir as Jack braked to a stop and got out. She watched him pull his tall, lanky frame out of the driver's seat, and then something happened. All of a sudden her heart caught in her throat and her stomach clenched as the world seemed to shimmer and stop.

Everything seemed to be suspended in time. Her breathing slowed, the gentle evening breeze died down and Jack seemed to be moving in slow-motion as he walked slowly up the drive with his gunslinger's walk, the gravel crunching beneath his boots, his eyes never leaving hers.

Something swelled painfully in Federica's chest as she watched him watching her, and after a brief stutter her heart kicked into motion and began to beat rapidly. She would have thought that she was having a heart attack if she didn't know that something infinitely more serious, more dangerous to her well-being, was happening.

She was falling in love.

Chapter Ten

"Hi, honey," Jack said softly. "I'm home."

Federica watched him walking up the drive toward her. He felt alive in every single cell of his body. Just seeing here there, short blonde hair ruffled by the evening breeze, bare feet up on the railing, made his chest ache. He felt a tug toward her so strong, it was a wonder the air between them didn't quiver.

Federica suddenly erupted in an explosion of movement, not caring that the book went thudding to the floor, or that the chair tipped over backwards, or that she spilled the beer, or even that the few steps over gravel before she threw herself into his arms must have hurt her bare feet.

He caught her and lifted her up and away from the sharp gravel.

Jack tasted desperation in her kiss and didn't know if it was his or hers. All he knew was that this wonderful creature in his arms, bare feet dangling a few inches off the ground, had been somehow sent to him at a time when his life had started to feel…empty. Full of family and friends, but still empty. And now, here she was. Someone made to measure just for him. The enemy, and she would be gone in a few days.

He tried to remember what he'd been telling himself for the past few days. *Don't get involved. Have a little fling, sure. That's normal, that's natural. Your hormones needed a little stirring. Wyatt tells you that all the time. Just don't get involved.*

Then Federica wriggled in his arms and he forgot the part about not getting involved and lowered his head again. This time the kiss was tender as their tongues tangled slowly and he stroked the silky soft skin of her neck. He retreated in slow, nibbling little bites and pressed her head into his shoulder.

"Did you have a nice day with Lilly?" Jack brushed his cheek over her hair. He inhaled the sweet, lemony smell of her shampoo. She nodded. "Good."

He set her down slowly, so her bare feet rested on his boots.

"Okay, little one. This is the plan." He kissed the tip of her nose. "You go put your shoes on and come help me unload."

She smiled up at him. "And afterwards?"

"Mmm. And afterwards…" His voice dropped and he looped his arms loosely around her waist. He bent down and whispered in her ear. "Afterwards I thought we could…play."

He nipped her earlobe then kissed his way back to her mouth.

"Play," she sighed. "Okay."

"Cards," he said against her mouth.

Her eyes opened. "Cards?"

"Mmm." He loved watching her face. Everything she felt was right there. A second before she had been drifting dreamily. Now she was watching him, head tilted to one side. "An old Carson's Bluff tradition. Saturday night poker."

She blinked, puzzled.

"Strip," he said.

It was perfect. In an instant, the puzzlement turned to surprise and then to delight and before he realized what she was doing, she pulled his head down and gave him a kiss that had his ears ringing.

"Oh, I'm a firm believer in respecting traditions," she said soberly, then stepped off his boots. "Get that deck out."

She walked gingerly back across the gravel and reached for her sneakers. She laced them up and joined Jack at the back of the van. He was unloading bags and boxes. She tilted her head.

"What are you—hey, is that what I think it is?"

"Yup." Jack set down the microwave oven and grabbed her elbow when she moved forward. "No, don't pick that up, it's too heavy. There are some grocery bags farther back. You can haul those in."

Curious, Federica started sorting through the back of the van. "A microwave, a hotplate, dishes, cutlery…"

Jack nudged a box with his foot and smiled at the ping of glass. "And don't forget the case of wine. Dad's best year. Got some bottles of Pigswill, too."

"You planning on opening a store here?"

"Nope." His eyes met hers. "I'm planning on camping out."

"Camping out?" Federica looked around. "Where?"

"Right here. At the Folly." He ran his hands up her arms, then back down again, grasping her hands in his. "All this frenetic traveling you've been doing these past few days." He smiled down at her and brought her hand to his mouth and kissed it gently. "All this to-ing and fro-ing down to Carson's Bluff and back. Why, you must be clocking up a couple of miles a day, easy. Way too stressful. So I thought I'd camp up here with you so you wouldn't have to go out."

"And your job? Jobs?"

"They'll keep. I can take care of business in a couple of hours a day for a few days if I want to. And the van has a car phone for emergencies. I'm all caught up. I can afford to goof off a little for…"

For? Federica didn't dare ask the question. But her eyes did. *For how long?*

"Yes?" she whispered. "For?"

"For a few days." *For as long as we've got,* he thought. "Sound good?"

"Sounds very good," she said softly.

Several hours later, Jack threw down two cards.

"Deal me two," he said, and watched Federica's face carefully. Nothing but mild interest showed.

They were sitting on the bed, cross-legged. Jack found to his chagrin that his cheerfully erotic plan had gone awry. He had planned on beating the pants off her, literally. After all, he'd been playing poker with Dad and his cronies since he'd been old enough to hold a hand of cards. But it hadn't quite worked out that way.

Of course, Federica didn't play fair, either. When he had produced a deck of cards with an exaggerated leer, she had excused herself to go into the bathroom and had come out with four combs in her hair, two scarves and several layers of sweaters. She was still more than decently dressed, though she'd lost the combs, a scarf and her shoes. Not that it would have made any difference to the final result if she'd been dressed in only a few items. She was a killer poker player.

How had he ever thought that pretty face expressive? For the past hour, no expression had crossed her face that he could in any way interpret, whether she won or lost. And she had consistently won. He looked down at himself. He was stripped down to his briefs and one blue cotton sock.

"Aren't you dealing yourself any cards?" he asked suspiciously as he slowly fanned out his hand. Damn. The same pair of deuces was all he held.

"No," she said serenely. She had glanced once, briefly, indifferently at her hand and then had tapped the cards closed.

"You sure you didn't grow up in Vegas?"

"No," she said calmly. "Switzerland."

"Ah." He nodded his head sagely. "That explains it. All those banks, getting richer and richer off other people's money. That's where you learned your trickiness."

Not a flicker of an eyelash. "Who are you calling tricky?"

"You. Anyone who can count shoelaces as items of clothing isn't exactly cutting with a dull tool."

"Well, they are items of clothing. You can't keep your shoes on without shoelaces. Come on, Jack. Don't be such a sore loser. Stop whining and show me what you've got."

What he had was straining against the soft cotton of his briefs. Her eyes jerked up to his face and she blushed a pretty pink.

Jack was delighted that he'd managed to crack that smooth, impersonal façade. "Yeah? You want to see what I've got?" He held her eyes for a long moment, watching her smooth throat muscles work as she swallowed.

He fanned out the cards on the bedspread, his eyes never leaving hers. Suddenly he felt as if he were going to explode. "Pair of deuces."

She folded her cards. "Three jacks. I win."

"Great," Jack muttered, and bent down to pull off his sock, wondering if he could wait long enough to lose the next hand. He had his thumbs hooked in the top of the sock when she put her hand on his.

"Wait." Her voice was husky. She cleared her throat. "Don't the rules say something about the winner getting to choose the…ah…particular item of clothing the loser should remove?"

Not any rules he'd heard about, but he wasn't arguing. "Sure."

He held himself very still as Federica moved forward on her knees until she could touch him. She wasn't quick about it. Her hands rested on his shoulders for a moment, fingers clenching into the muscle. She felt her way over his chest, slowly, thoroughly, as if she were blind and were learning about his body by touch.

She lowered her hand slowly over his stomach muscles, then lower still, to touch the main difference between them, hard and aching. He groaned as she worked her fingers under the waistband and slowly drew them down.

Jack grasped Federica and rolled over with her, intending to get rid of her clothes as quickly as possible. As they moved on the bed, her cards slithered to the floor. Jack was kissing her, engrossed in the softness of her mouth and of her body under his, and it was only as he came up for air and saw the cards on the ground that he realized what she'd done and laughed.

"What?" Federica opened her eyes.

He looked down at her, soft and yielding in his arms. "You didn't have three jacks, did you?"

"No." She hooked her arm around his neck and hauled him back down to her. "I cheated."

~~~~~

June 4th

EMAIL FROM: ruswhite@mansent.com

TO: wgreenlee@mansent.com

Dear Will,

I couldn't believe my eyes when I came back from a lava flow—which against all geological logic is still flowing when it should have stopped two days ago—to find your message. Not a good day.

I resent you saying I'm jinxed, Will. I'm not. There was *no way* anyone could have known about that coup d'etat beforehand. We were *this close* to making a killing in banana futures.

But listen, that's water under the bridge. I seem to have found myself in…a difficult situation. A certain gentleman loaned me some money several months ago and he is very particular about repayments. And I *can* repay him, because there will be a bonus from the Carson's Bluff sale, and because these genetic engineering shares are going to go through the roof when the company goes public. I can't tell you any more, but believe me, Will, this is a sure thing. All I need is a temporary loan of, say, ten thousand so I can buy a stake in the genetic engineering company. Those shares are going to increase tenfold in value in a few weeks, and I'll pay you back the loan at twenty percent. What more could you want?

I'm going to take my fourth shower of the day and turn in. Think about it, Will.

Russell

~~~~~

"Hello?"

"Hello, I'd like to speak to Mr. Willard Greenlee, please."

"Speaking."

"Mr. Greenlee, my name is Ellen Larsen. I don't know if you remember me. We met at the Mansion Enterprises Christmas party last year. I was there with Federica Mansion."

"Yes, of course, Miss Larsen. I remember you quite well."

"Good. Mr. Greenlee—

"Will."

"I beg your pardon?"

"My name is Willard. But my friends call me Will."

"All right...Will. As I was saying—"

"You wore a red dress."

"I—what?"

"You wore a red dress. To the party."

"Oh...I don't really remember. As I was saying, Mr. Greenlee—"

"Will."

"Will. As I was saying...Will...I'm a friend of Federica's. And I can't seem to—"

"You looked very pretty in that dress. You and Federica both looked very pretty. Of course, you two were the only people in the room besides me under sixty. As a matter of fact, we were probably the only ones there with all our own teeth."

"Well, I'm flattered that you remember me, Will...I think...anyway, as I was saying—"

"I had on a green sports jacket."

"I remember that jacket, but I fail to see—"

"You know what I was thinking, Ellen—I can call you Ellen, can't I? After all, we survived a geriatric Christmas party together—I remember thinking it might be fun to go out and continue the party somewhere a bit more…lively, and I thought that we'd look very Christmasy together, you know…you with your red dress and me with my green jacket, but by the time I got up the courage to ask you out after the party you'd gone."

"Well, I'm afraid I don't have such a clear memory of the evening as you do, Mr.…er, Will, but—"

"Yeah, lotta champagne flowed under the bridge that evening."

"It wasn't that. I had just flown in from Paris and I was jet-lagged. By the way, I'm calling from Paris now, Will, and I'd really appreciate some information."

"Paris? Hey, everybody seems to be traveling to glamorous places lately but me. What's the weather like over there?"

"Lousy. It's raining. Now, if you don't mind I'd like some information, *please*."

"Sure. No prob. Shoot."

"Good. I've been trying to get in touch with Federica Mansion for several days now and I'm starting to get really worried. The last time I heard from her was on the 23rd of May and she was in Singapore. She was also very sick. I haven't heard from her since, even though we had a date in San Francisco on the 3rd of June."

"Wait. Let me check my computer files…just a minute…yes, that's correct. Miss Mansion was in the Singapore Mansion Inn on the 23rd of May."

"And then what?"

"What do you mean, and then what?"

"Just what I say. She was very ill when I talked to her. Did she check out of the hotel? And if so, where did she go? Did she fly back to the States? Is she in the States now?"

"She's supposed to be in Carson's Bluff, a small town in Northern California."

"I know that. We were supposed to meet after she came back. But I lost track of her. Did she actually fly out of Singapore?"

"Well, you'll have to wait a second while I check our travel records...though, um, Ellen, I'm actually not too sure I should be giving out this information. Certainly not over the phone. It might be confidential—"

"You listen to me, Mr. Greenlee...Will. I am worried sick about my best friend. She's just slipped off the edge of the world and no one seems to care. Least of all her uncle. She could be anywhere, hurt, in pain, a prisoner. I just don't know. But I damn well intend to find out. I know a lot of journalists, Will, and they would just *love* a story like this."

"Hey, wait a minute—"

"It has all the elements—suspense, a missing heiress, maybe crooked business dealings. I'll throw the works at them. And while I'm at it, I'll make sure that everyone knows that a certain Mr. Willard Greenlee of Mansion Enterprises stonewalled legitimate attempts to locate a missing person. Am I making myself clear?"

"Very. Ooh-kaay. Here we go. Federica Mansion flew back to San Francisco on the 28th of May on Inter Airways Flight WA 3458, departure time 9:52 a.m.—"

"I know that flight. It arrives at San Francisco at 2:10 p.m. What did she do after that? Did she report to work at Mansion Enterprises headquarters?"

"I'm not too sure—"

"Will, let me tell you something you might find interesting. Fred Lawrence is the chief editor of the business section of the *International Herald Tribune* here in Paris. Fred Lawrence happens to be a very good friend of mine. I can call him tonight and tell him that there is very good reason to believe that something nasty might be going on in Mansion Enterprises. That story could hit the newsstands tomorrow morning and create a lot of trouble for everybody, not to mention affect stock prices. Am I making myself clear?"

"Yes, you are. Just give me a minute here…"

"Take your time. My flight doesn't leave for another half hour."

"Your flight? Are you a stewardess?"

"Flight attendant. A *very impatient* flight attendant."

"Okay, okay. There we are…my records show that Federica didn't show up for work. Not on the 28th and she hasn't been here since then."

"Did someone pick her up at the airport?"

"Oh. Well, I guess I'd have to check the car pool records for that."

"*Do it.*"

"Hold on, hold on. Yes. She was picked up by one of our drivers, Erle Newton."

"I know Newton. He usually drives Federica. Where were they headed?"

"To Carson's Bluff."

"She was supposed to go off to work immediately after a *fourteen-hour flight?* When she'd been *ill*?"

"Well, I guess…I mean if you want to put it like that, well yes, that's what it looks like."

"Okay. So she was picked up on the…what? 28th of May?"

"That's right."

"On the 28th. And driven to Carson's Bluff."

"Well…"

"Well, what?"

"That's where they were headed. I mean, I have it right here on my screen. Erle Newton to drive Federica Mansion to Carson's Bluff."

"So? When did they get there?"

"Um…I don't really know. They were due to arrive at around ten at night. But the thing is…"

"What?"

"Er—well, nobody's actually *heard* from Miss Mansion since then. Apparently some faxes have been sent, but the fax machines in the city offices of Carson's Bluff seem to have been turned off. And the car is still registered as out on mission."

"I've been trying to fax her, too. What about her company cell phone?"

"Off."

"And her email?"

"Wait. I'm accessing…no, she hasn't answered any of her emails. It's all backed up."

"So nobody knows if she arrived?"

"Well, actually, I heard that her uncle is pi—angry at her for not being in touch."

"*Angry?* Her uncle's *angry?*"

"Yeah, she's supposed to be reporting back on the negotiations, though I think they might actually be on hold now—"

"Wait a minute. Let me get this straight. Federica arrived on the 28th of May, certainly exhausted, probably sick. She was supposed to have been driven from the airport to this town but nobody knows if she ever even arrived. She hasn't been in touch, nobody knows where she is and her uncle's *angry?* Nobody's worried at Mansion Enterprises? Ohgod, ohgod, Federica could be sick, *dying*, for all anyone cares…"

"Well, she was supposed to be negotiating the sale of a piece of property there. But I'm sure everything's all right, Ellen—"

"…her lifeless body lying by the roadside, eaten by wolves…"

"I'm not too sure there are that many wolves left in California, Ellen."

Click

"So, Ellen, would you like to go out for a drink next time you're in San Francisco? Ellen? Ellen?"

~~~~~

June 5th

EMAIL FROM: wgreenlee@mansent.com

TO: ruswhite@mansent.com

Dear Russell,

Sounds to me like you're fishing without bait. First of all, it's not prudent to offer to pay back loans at twenty percent, since that is basically usury which is…how can I say this delicately…illegal. The only people I know who lend money at those interests are sharks like Gino Gambetti. Come to think of it, I sure hope he's not the guy you owe money to. The guy's nickname is "The Animal" and with him you'd have to watch not only your back, but your front and sides, too.

Frankly, your genetic engineering stock sounds like a bag job to me. My stockbroker takes care of my investment portfolio and so far he seems to be doing okay, at least I haven't gone belly-up as I would have following your advice.

Oh, and by the way, I wouldn't be banking on your bonus from the Carson's Bluff sale — or on your job for that matter — since the word around here is that the sale is off and that your department will soon be history. But you didn't hear it here. I hope you make it back soon. Martinez trashed me on the squash court. At least with you I have a more-than-even chance of winning. Aloha.

Will

~~~~~

June 6th

Jack finished polishing the barrel of his .38. The pungent smell of gun oil filled the small sheriff's office.

Jack made a point of cleaning his guns every week. It was important to him to keep all his guns clean and in perfect working order, though they were never used except for his regular stints on the firing range.

Well, hardly ever used. Jack fondly picked up his .45 and checked the barrel. It was the weapon he'd used to scare off a gang of Hell's Angels who had roared into town one afternoon, hell-bent on setting up shop in pretty Carson's Bluff. Jack had shot the skull-and-crossbones earring off the leader without drawing a drop of blood. Then he had threatened to put out the eye of the Vargas girl tattooed on the leader's chest. The air had smelled of exhaust smoke the entire afternoon after the gang's hasty departure. The memory still made Jack grin.

Luckily, violence was something almost unknown in Carson's Bluff, but you never knew. On his list of priorities, keeping his guns well-oiled and in top condition was right up there with making sure his sheriff's log was up to date, with attending all Town Council meetings and with organizing regular gun safety talks in the schools. It felt good knowing he was doing what he was supposed to do.

The Army had exonerated him from all blame, but the accusation of shirking his duty had stung. Badly.

He finished cleaning his .45 and loaded it. It was the only loaded gun in the sheriff's office, kept in a locked drawer of his desk.

It was time to get back up to the Folly. He'd come down reluctantly to take care of some paperwork and was straining at the bit to get back up the hill.

The door to the office opened.

"Hey." Jack looked up, pleased. He put the gun down and stood up as Federica walked in. "This is a surprise. What are you doing here? How did you get down from the Folly?"

"A pleasant surprise, I hope." Federica closed the door behind her and crossed the room, limping slightly.

"I'll say." Jack walked around the desk and folded her in his arms. "How did you get down? Did Lilly drive you?"

"Nope." Federica pulled away and grinned proudly. "I walked."

"You *walked*?" It was over three miles from the Folly to town. He looked down at her dusty sneakers. "I guess you did walk." Why did she do that? "Nothing's wrong, is there?" he asked.

"No." Federica shrugged. "I just got a little...lonely." Her eyes were soft as she looked up at him. "And I guess I was hoping you'd give me a ride back up."

"Count on it." Jack knew—they both knew—their time together was drawing to a close.

He couldn't help it. He was in his office, anyone could walk in at any moment, and it just wasn't done for the sheriff to be caught kissing in the jailhouse, but he just couldn't help it. He held her head still and bent down. It wasn't possible to keep feeling this sense of excitement, of rightness, every time he kissed her, but he did. After days of kissing her, some of the newness should have worn off. But it hadn't.

His mouth moved on hers, gently, gently.

"We could get a ticket for this," she murmured.

"I'll fix it." He deepened the kiss and let his tongue fill her mouth.

Listen, Jack, a little voice in his head said. It sounded a lot like Wyatt. *See if any of these words ring a bell. Mansion Enterprises. Enemy. Gone. Soon.*

But it didn't make any difference. Federica's mouth soft under his and he forgot all the warnings he kept repeating to himself. Her tongue moved in his mouth and he gripped her head hard, then moved one hand down her back. He was seriously considering clearing his desk with his arm and moving her onto it, when she pulled away.

Her lips were slightly swollen and when she licked them he felt his body clench almost painfully. He should be used to it by now, but it caught him every time.

"So this is where you work."

"Yeah." Work. A word he didn't want to think of. Right up there with duty and future and business.

His hands gripped her arms. "Federica. I—" *Care about you. Am falling in love with you.* The words were there, right there in the air. Probably in his eyes. The air was heavy with them. She plastered a smile on her face and let her gaze roam the room.

"Show me around."

"Okay." Jack released her arms. "This is the front office. It's essentially unchanged from the 1880s." He touched his desk, and ran his hand along a furrow that marred the surface. "Carson's Bluff's first sheriff used this desk. And this is where a prospector took exception to the gold weighing."

"Was anybody hurt?"

"Nah, just the sheriff's pride. The prospector's aim was lousy. And he might even have had a point. They say the gold weighing in those days was…let's say…subjective."

Federica rubbed the furrow in the desk. "Is that how disputes were settled then? With bullets?"

"Well, not quite. Lots of disputes were settled by a round of poker." Jack grinned when he saw the color rise in her cheeks. He looped an arm around her shoulder and hugged her tightly to his side. "Told you poker was an old Carson's Bluff tradition."

"And a good one, too." Federica leaned her head against his shoulder.

"That was how the town got its name, you know."

She looked up, startled. "Carson's Bluff? You mean it's not a—a bluff? I mean—like a cliff or something? I was going to ask you to take me to see it one of these days."

"Not that kind of bluff." Jack pressed her head into his shoulder for a moment. Nothing better to make someone smile than a Harry Carson story. "A poker bluff."

"Sounds like a good one." He'd been telling her Harry Carson stories these past days. There were a lot of them. Some of them were even true.

"It is. It was the start of Harry Carson's fortune. A marathon poker game that lasted three days and three nights, over Christmas, 1879." Jack sat down in his chair and pulled Federica down onto his lap. "Seven men started the poker game but one by one they fell by the wayside. Either they lost all their money or got too drunk to hold the cards. This was Christmas, remember, and the game had gone on throughout the Christmas celebrations, which were pretty rambunctious in those days, believe me. So it's early in the morning on the day after Christmas. Everyone has had time to get drunk and recover from their hangovers. People start drifting into the saloon until they're standing a foot deep around the green poker table. "

If Jack closed his eyes he could almost see the scene. He'd heard the story a thousand times from his father, who had no doubt heard it a thousand times from his father before him.

"There're only two players left by this time, Harry Carson and a prospector who had three sacks of gold on the table and the deed to the mine they came from. Harry had the takings from the table and a promissory note on the saloon he owned. That would be Stella's, by the way." Jack smiled down at Federica, who was listening entranced, her mouth a small O. "So. Imagine the scene. It's about seven in the morning of the third day. Spectators have been drifting in and out all the time, but word spreads that the game is coming to a close and that someone's going to win big, so the room is crowded and smoky and everyone's basically drunk. Harry's won the last three hands. He has maybe twenty thousand on the table—which was a huge sum of money in those days. Enough for a man to live on for the rest of his life. But Harry Carson was a man with a dream and he knew he'd need lots of money for it. So he says he's willing to play two more hands and orders some more bourbon."

"Pretty dangerous," Federica mused.

"Nah. Harry Carson held his liquor well."

Federica laughed at that. She looked up at Jack and batted her eyelashes. "Like a man?" she drawled.

"Yup. Like a man." He kissed the tip of her nose. "So listen. Here we are, two hands from the end. One man will walk away from the table rich, and the other a pauper. Harry lights a cigar, cool as you please."

"Were they playing stud or draw?" Federica asked.

"Draw."

Jack grinned. He loved this story. The one regret of his life was that he had never met Harry Carson, who had died the year his granddad was born.

"So the prospector deals. They're playing for one of the sacks of gold, worth maybe five thousand. Harry ups the ante to another sack and discards two cards. The other guy sees him and deals himself one. He puts down his hand. Two tens and two jacks. Harry puts down his hand. Three aces. He rakes in two sacks of gold and the other guy's down to one sack and his mine. Harry says the next round will be played for the goldmine and the saloon. The prospector hesitates. But Harry's been having a run of good luck. It has to stop sometime. It's Harry's turn to deal. He picks up his cards and lights another cigar. The prospector's sweating. He discards two and looks at Harry. Harry puffs on his cigar and blows the smoke up to the ceiling. He pours himself another glass of bourbon and says he's fine. Then…he ups the ante. Double or nothing. The prospector looks at his hand, looks at Harry and folds. The whole room erupts into cheering. Cool as you please, Harry picks up the two sacks of gold, his table winnings and the deed to the gold mine, and the prospector walks away with the one remaining sack. The bourbon's flowing pretty freely now. Harry doesn't even look up, he's busy stashing away the takings and folding the deed and putting it in his pocket. 'Your luck's really running today,' someone calls out. 'Nope,' Harry answers coolly. 'I bluffed.' The crowd goes wild. And the legend of Harry Carson began."

"What a great story!" Federica enthused.

"Wait. It's not over. The gold mine was a rich one and Harry used the money to build up Libertyville, which was renamed Carson's Bluff. He starts work on the Folly but never gets a chance to finish it. He gets sick and spends a year in bed. Harry Carson did everything in style. He ran his businesses from his sickbed, which had a red satin bedspread, surrounded by pretty saloon girls. But finally, he knows he's dying and he calls in the Town Council. Harry was allergic to authority and never held an official position. He wants to talks to the mayor. The mayor comes up with his hat in his hand. 'You wanted to talk to me, Mr. Carson?' the mayor asks, twisting his hat in his hands. 'Yes, Mr. Mayor,' Harry answers. 'I want you and the rest of the Town Council to know that I bluffed.' The mayor thinks Harry's really lost it now, he can't even remember his finest moment. So he bends down respectfully. 'We know that, Mr. Carson. That's why we named Libertyville Carson's Bluff.' 'No, no.' Harry waves his hand. He's pretty weak by now. 'I mean I really won. I had an inside straight.' And he dies."

Federica digested that for a moment, then laughed in delight. "You mean he bluffed about *bluffing*? He had a winning hand all along?"

"That's about the size of it." Jack watched her. The slight sadness he'd seen in her eyes had been chased away. He'd seen that sadness come and go in the past few days. There was a lot unspoken between them and he knew that soon, soon things would come to a head. But for now, they were a man and a woman enjoying each other's company.

"What a guy." Federica chuckled then looked past Jack's shoulder to the back of the room. Her eyes rounded. "Hey." She nudged him with her elbow. "Those are *bars*."

"Well, it's a jailhouse, honey. Jail cells have bars on them."

She jumped off his lap and walked over, fascinated. The back of the room was closed off by thick floor-to-ceiling steel bars. The door had a big, old-fashioned lock on it and was slightly ajar. The key in the lock looked like it could have opened the gates of a medieval castle. "You use it a lot?" She grabbed the bars and tried to rattle them.

"Nah." Jack stood up and leaned against the desk, amused at her reaction. "Just once in a while when Steve Bond hangs one on. But that's for his own protection. His wife's mighty handy with a skillet and if he's locked up, it gives her time to cool off."

"I wonder what it's like to be locked up?" Federica mused.

"Well, only one way to find out." Jack came away from the desk. He put his hand to the small of her back and pushed her gently the cell. The cell door closed with a loud *snick*. "So. What's it like?"

Federica looked around. The cell was small and clean, with a narrow cot bolted to the floor, a small porcelain sink and a chamber pot with a wooden cover. Federica pointed to the chamber pot. "The prisoners have to use *that*?"

"No. I let Steve use my bathroom, unless he's so pie-eyed he can't aim. Had an offer from an antique dealer passing through town for that chamber pot. Said it would make a wonderful planter." Jack shook his head. "Hundred and fifty dollars. I was tempted, let me tell you."

Federica was looking around. She shivered and moved to the bars.

Jack watched her curl her small hands around the bars. They were so close he could smell her perfume, but separated by the bars. He covered her hands with his and looked down at her. Her hands were soft, but he knew that already. He knew how soft she was all over.

He released her hands and reached through to hold her head still as he started to bend down. "I guess you're my prisoner now," he said, his voice husky.

"Oh, yeah," she whispered.

Jack groaned and pressed up against the bars. He cupped her neck with his hands and used his thumbs to tip her head up.

The door opened and a gust of air filled the small room.

"Unhand that woman, you monster!" cried a woman's voice. Jack twisted his head in surprise and froze for a moment. Then he straightened up and turned around, moving squarely in front of Federica.

An attractive, curvaceous brunette stood in the doorway, wild-eyed and trembling like a leaf. She had picked up one of the guns from the desk and the hand holding it was shaking, too. Damn! It was the .45, loaded and ready for bear. Or worse, loaded and ready for man. And it had a hair trigger.

"Can I help you, ma'am?" Jack kept his voice low, and gauged the distance between them.

"Get away from her!" The woman's voice was shaking, high-pitched and hysterical. "Federica!" she called out. "Are you all right?"

He heard Federica's voice behind him. "Ellen?"

She knew the woman? He turned his head just enough to see Federica as she edged her head past his back. He stepped firmly back in front of her. Federica could sort things out with the brunette later, but right now he had a hysterical, out-of-control woman brandishing a loaded gun and he had no intention of having Federica stop a bullet.

"Let me see her!" The woman's grip on the gun slipped and she caught it in both hands. Jack winced.

"Ah, lady, you want to be careful with that thing—"

"I want to see her! I want to see Federica now!"

"Sure thing, ma'am," Jack said soothingly. "Of course you can see her. But first, why don't you just put that thing down—"

"Ellen, what on Earth are you doing—"

"Let me see her!"

"Just put that gun down—"

Their three voices rose and bounced around the little room.

"Hey, Jack, what's all the noise?" Wyatt stuck his head into the room.

"Wyatt, watch out. That gun's loaded!" Jack barely had time to see Wyatt's startled look and the brunette turning with the gun in her hand before he made a leap. The gun's report made his ears ring and the smell of cordite filled the room.

He wrenched the gun out of the brunette's hand and with a cry she ran to the jail cell and embraced Federica through the bars.

"Oh, honey, I'm so glad you're all right—"

"Ellen, how on Earth—"

"And don't worry, I'll get you out of here—"

"Ellen, I'm so sorry about Springsteen—"

The two women were babbling and crying and making an incredible ruckus. Jack looked at them for a moment and shook his head. Women. His heart was still in overdrive, but Federica was hugging the brunette through the bars. Obviously, there wasn't any immediate danger. Still, he picked up the gun and carefully unloaded it. You never knew. The brunette could turn crazy again.

"Jack?"

His head whipped around. He'd forgotten all about Wyatt, who was standing in the doorway, staring into the room as if he'd seen a ghost. He was clutching his shirtsleeve. A light trickle of blood seeped through his fingers.

"Wyatt!" Jack rushed to his brother's side, trying to push back the spasm of fear. "God, you've been shot!"

Wyatt glanced down at his sleeve absently. "Guess I have," he said carelessly. Then his eyes fixed on the two women again.

Jack gently pried Wyatt's fingers off his upper arm, widened the tear in the sleeve and started breathing again. It was just a nick, really. The bleeding had almost stopped. Probably wouldn't even need stitches. He and Wyatt and Doc

Alonzo could share a beer and a laugh over it at Stella's. It would make for a great story. Wyatt's war wound.

Then he looked at Wyatt's face.

"Wyatt? What's the matter, man? It's not bleeding. It's just a scratch, really."

"I—" Wyatt turned a stunned face to his brother. "Who is that woman? She's gorgeous."

Jack snorted and rolled his eyes. "Oh, shit. Here we go again."

Chapter Eleven

"Unhand that woman." Federica giggled and wiped her eyes. She was still light-headed. She and Ellen had babbled and cried in each other's arms for several minutes after Jack sprang her from jail, but now they were both more in control and beaming at each other. "Honestly, El. Where on Earth did you *get* that line?"

"Great, isn't it?" Ellen grinned proudly. "I don't know. Some old Errol Flynn movie, I think. It just seemed an appropriate thing to say at the time." Her face suddenly turned sober. "God, Federica, it's been awful. I come into the sheriff's office to ask whether anyone in town has seen a Miss Federica Mansion, five-foot-three or so, blonde hair, blue eyes, and then I discover you behind bars, with a man's hands at your throat. I've been so worried about you. I flew to San Francisco and hired a car and just drove straight up, terrified as hell all the way. I—I didn't know if I was coming to rescue you or..."

"Or?"

Ellen swallowed and gave a wobbly smile. "Or...or bury you."

"Oh, El," Federica whispered. Fresh tears welled up and she hugged Ellen again. They rocked in each others' arms.

Jack had had about enough. He cleared his throat. "Ah...gir—" He stopped himself just in time. "Ladies. I hate to interrupt this touching scene, but my brother—"

Both women looked at him as if he'd just disembarked from Mars. Ellen looked to Federica.

"Ellen, I'd like you to meet the sheriff of Carson's Bluff, Jack Sutter. Jack, this is Ellen Larsen, my best friend." Federica turned back to Ellen. "Oh, El, I didn't realize you'd be so worried, I'm so sorry. I just wasn't thinking."

Jack shifted awkwardly from one foot to another. "Ah, Federica, Wyatt here—"

"Well, what did you expect?" Ellen wiped away a tear, then looked at the mascara smear on her handkerchief. She tried to glare at Federica, but it didn't work. "Your emails kept bouncing. I kept phoning and phoning, but the answering service message at your house was always the same, and nobody in this town was answering any faxes—"

"Ladies, my broth—" Jack tried again.

"I know." Federica looked guilt-stricken. "The fax lines were…down."

" —and that creep of an uncle of yours was no help—"

"Ladies, my brother here—"

" —nor was that louse Russell White. Finally, I got in touch with that guy we met at the Christmas party. You know—the nerd?"

"Oh. Willard Greenlee. Of Finances." Federica smiled through her tears. "That was some jacket he wore to the party, remember? Sort of a neon green." Both women were silent for a moment, clearly remembering the jacket.

Jack recognized an opportunity and jumped in. "Federica, Wyatt—"

"Will," Ellen said. "He wanted me to call him Will. Anyway, I phoned him from Paris and he said that no one knew where you were. The company wasn't even completely sure that you'd arrived, can you imagine?"

"Well," Federica said uneasily. "I have been kind of…out of touch."

"Federica, Wyatt's been—"

"I don't care." Ellen planted her hands on her shapely hips. "You'd think that somebody *somewhere* would be worried when

171

someone drops off the face of the Earth for a week. So when I quit—"

"Federica, do you realize that Wyatt—"

"When you *what?*"

Ellen waved her hand. "It's a long story, honey. Tell you some other time. Anyway, I quit and decided that I'd come looking for you myself."

"Would you ladies mind—"

"Oh, *El*," Federica wailed and got a fresh tissue out of her waist pouch. "I'm so sorry. Here I've worried you needlessly and dragged you halfway around the world and now you've lost your job and...and it's *all my fault.*" She blew her nose.

"I didn't *lose* my job, you ninny. Weren't you listening? I quit. And it felt *great.* Do you know what those boneheads in Administration did to us? They flew us out to Paris on—"

He'd had it.

"*Will you two pipe down for one second!*" Jack roared. The women fell silent and two pretty faces turned to him in surprise. "I've been trying to tell the two of you for the past ten minutes that my brother Wyatt's been shot."

Both women looked blank. "Wyatt?" Federica blinked owlishly. "Shot?"

Jack didn't say anything more, just stepped aside. Behind him, a pale Wyatt lifted his uninjured arm and waved his fingers weakly. "Hi."

Jack had practically had to beat them over the head with a stick to get their attention, but once he had it, the response was gratifying. Both women sprang to Wyatt's side and started fussing over him. Of the two, Ellen was the better fusser. While Federica commiserated with Wyatt, Ellen briskly asked Jack where a first aid kit could be found, rooted competently through it, carefully cut away Wyatt's shirt, efficiently cleaned the wound and wrapped a sterile bandage around Wyatt's upper arm.

Wyatt's eyes never left her face.

"There." Ellen stepped back and eyed her handiwork proudly. "I knew those first aid courses they made us take would come in handy some day."

"Ellen's a flight attendant for Inter Airways," Federica offered.

"*Was*," Ellen corrected.

"Oh," Federica said, instantly contrite. "That's right. I forgot."

"Don't fret, honey," Ellen said gently. "It's all for the best." She turned to Wyatt and smiled tentatively at him. "So...I guess it's about time I apologized, Mr...Sutter, is it?"

"Wyatt."

"Wyatt. I was very distraught, you see. I thought that Federica was being strangled—" Ellen stopped and looked at Federica, then Jack, then back to Federica. She narrowed her eyes. "Say, in all the commotion, I forgot to ask how come—"

"Are you *sure* you're all right, Wyatt?" Federica said swiftly. "I mean you're not hurt anywhere else, are you?"

"That's right." Ellen immediately turned back to Wyatt. "Like I said, I'm terribly, terribly sorry. I guess that gun just sort of...went off." She barely stopped herself from wringing her hands. "Does it hurt anywhere else?"

"Yes," Wyatt said. His color had come back and a smile played around his mouth.

Ellen bent anxiously over him, a lock of her shiny black hair falling forward, her full lips pursed. "Where," she asked, placing a gentle hand on Wyatt's shoulder. "Where does it hurt?"

"Here." Wyatt tapped his lips. "Why don't you kiss it and make it better?"

~~~~~

EMAIL FROM: ruswhite@mansent.com
TO: wgreenlee@mansent.com

Dear Will,

WHAT DO YOU MEAN THE CARSON'S BLUFF DEAL IS OFF? I've been working on this fucking project for the last four months. They can't *do* this to me! I'm stuck out here on this godforsaken island, up to my knees in cinders and they shoot the ground right out from under me. They just can't do this. I won't let them. And I can't lose my job now. I just can't. I'm afraid you're right about Mr. Gambetti. And to think that when I first approached him, he seemed like such a gentleman, so understanding.

He's been very…insistent about the repayment of the loan. Threatening, actually.

Will, you've got to help me. Please. Everything's coming apart all at once. Please, Will.

Russ

~~~~~

EMAIL FROM: pcobb@mansent.com
TO: F.H.Mansion@mansent.com

Dear Frederick, I hope things are going well in Prague. But don't worry too much. Time's on our side. They need us more than we need them.

I'm happy to be the bearer of good tidings re our financial situation. Colossal good tidings, actually. The other day on the golf links, I was approached by a representative of Luna films. I know you hate films, but George Luna is the producer of a space opera saga called *Space Battalion*, which has one of the highest grosses in film history. The representative dropped a hint that George Luna wanted to talk to me.

I went out to Santa Barbara and met the Great Man himself. He was older than I imagined, since I still have fond memories of the first *Space Battalion* movie when I was a freshman in high school.

He's this round little man with a salt-and-pepper beard. He'd heard—don't ask me how, but these people are the rulers of the Earth so I suppose they've got good info—that we bought the Carson's Bluff property. One of his scouts had seen the property, and apparently it is just what Luna needs. He's planning another trilogy, this time set in the Old West, and the Carson's Bluff property is just what he's looking for as the set for all three films.

Now get this. He is willing to lease the property from us—I didn't tell him that we aren't actually, technically speaking, the owners of the property—for a sum which would pay us back for the purchase in the first quarter and which would put us heavily in the black by the second quarter.

They would lease it for a three-year period, which would amply cover the Kiev purchase. Not only that. Get this—they don't want a restored property. They want it as-is. At the end of the three-year period, *they will return it to us fully restored.* Which means that we won't have to invest any money in it for the restoration! We milk it, they return it, and we start our plan to turn the property into an executive retreat three years later, several million dollars richer.

Believe me, Frederick. There is a God, after all. And He is a Republican.

Paul

~~~~~

"Well, honey," Ellen said as she threw her Inter Airways flight bag on the bed of the big, homey room Stella had made available. "So how's celibacy?"

It was her usual greeting, but her eyes widened when Federica froze and blushed a bright, glowing red.

"Oh-ho."

"Oh-ho, nothing," Federica answered tightly.

"Nothing? You're the color of the dress I was wearing at the Christmas party." Ellen chuckled at Federica's blank look. "That was that nerd's line. He said he liked my red dress because it went with his green jacket, and it made us look Christmasy together."

"That jacket practically glowed in the dark."

"Yeah, I know. So maybe he's color-blind, too, to go with his other defects. But you're evading the point, honey. So tell me." Ellen sat on the big, comfortable-looking bed. "Who is it? The guy who was throttling you or the other one?"

Federica blinked, but she knew that Ellen knew her too well to be put off. "The one who was throttling me," she said grudgingly.

"And who was the other one? The blond. The one I…"

"Shot?"

"Er…yes. Wyatt was his name, wasn't it?" Ellen asked casually.

"Wyatt Earp Sutter." Federica smiled. "Apparently their mom is a Western history buff."

"And so what does…Wyatt Earp do? Not a gunslinger, I take it."

"No, I think he'd leave all the gunslinging to you, Ellen."

"Federica…" Ellen said threateningly.

Federica felt like laughing for the first time in an hour. She squeezed Ellen's shoulders. "I shouldn't be teasing someone who came rushing so…so…womanfully to my rescue. I'm really grateful, El. I don't know much about Wyatt, actually, except that he's a nice guy. He's the town treasurer and…" Federica's brow furrowed, "…and he brews beer and…"

"And?"

"And…I guess that's it."

"That's *it*? He brews beer?"

"Yeah. Occasionally. And makes wood benches. He's a real…relaxed type."

"Oh." Ellen's shoulders slumped in dejection and she sighed. "A bum. What a pity. He's a looker. So what's the story on the other one, the sheriff? The one who was throttling you."

"Oh. Jack." Federica fell silent.

"Except he wasn't throttling you," Ellen prompted.

"Er…no. Not really."

"He was…"

Federica sighed. "He was kissing me."

"Hallelujah!" Ellen threw two brightly colored silk shirts in the air. "Finally! I never thought I'd see the day. It's about time you got over that jerk Russell."

"Poor Russell." Federica picked up the shirts and folded them. "I feel sorry for the guy."

"*Sorry*?" Ellen exclaimed. "What do you mean sorry? He dated you just so he could get a promotion to head of the Engineering Department and then when he got it, he dumped you. What's the matter with you, Federica? How can you feel sorry for someone like that?"

"Well, his promotion means that now he works directly under Uncle Frederick."

"Oh." Ellen thought about that. "Poor Russell."

They smiled at each other. "I'm so glad to see you, Ellen," Federica said.

"Me too, kid. Particularly since I had visions of finding your body by the roadside. Eaten by wolves."

"I'm not too sure there are wolves in California, El."

"Yeah, that's what the nerd said. So how come you're not happier about this…Jack? That's his name, isn't it? The sheriff?"

"And the mayor." Federica searched for another tissue. "It's very complicated."

"Tell me about it. Life in the twenty-first century."

"It's not that—"

"So what is it? Is he married?"

"He was. He's not anymore."

"So? Jack seems to have all his limbs. Most of his teeth. One head. A job. What else can a girl ask for?"

"Oh, El…" Federica sniffled and held her tissue to her nose. "Oh, El," she wailed, "it's just *awful*."

Ellen pulled Federica down beside her and gave her a handkerchief. "Come on, hon, how bad can it be?"

Federica blew her nose. "Horrible."

Ellen waited patiently.

"I'm going to have to cream him," Federica said finally.

"Okay, this I want to hear. Shoot."

"I'm here to negotiate the sale of a piece of property called Harry's Folly." Federica felt a pang just hearing the name. "It's this gorgeous old mansion a few miles up in the hills around here. It's worth several million dollars but it's like a ripe plum for the taking because it doesn't seem to belong to anyone but the township of Carson's Bluff. There's over $100,000 in tax burden, which makes it onerous property and saleable to the highest bidder."

"So?" Ellen handed Federica another clean handkerchief. "The town stands to gain from the sale, then, doesn't it?"

"You don't understand, El. This place is…magic. It's a real community. Everyone gets on with everyone else. Horace Milton lives here. Rachel Douglas lives here. It's…" Federica shrugged.

"Magic," Ellen supplied. "Okay. Carson's Bluff is a real nifty place. So?"

"So," Federica drew in a big breath. "Imagine what will happen when Mansion Enterprises takes over. And we *will* take over. You know what we're like. We're a juggernaut. We'll take over the Folly, take over the town. Our executives will move in. The town will lose its soul. And I'll lose Jack."

Ellen reflected for a long moment. "Looks like you're in trouble, Federica," she said finally. "Big time."

~~~~~

EMAIL FROM: elucosi@mansent.hawaii.com

TO: pcobb@mansent.com

Dear Mr. Cobb,

My name is Emanuel Lucosi, and I'm the new director of the Muau Loi Mansion Inn. We have just put the head of the Mansion Inn Engineering Department on the red-eye flight to San Francisco. He will be arriving on Flight DA 3506 at 6 a.m. local time. Quite frankly, Mr. Cobb, we're not too sure that having Mr. Russell White here has been that much of a help. He has been distracted and careless in his time here. Thank God, the lava flow stopped of its own accord this morning, otherwise we would have had a disaster on our hands. Mr. White's lava break lasted about two minutes.

This afternoon, Mr. White was mugged in an unusually violent incident, which left him with a broken arm. Believe me, Mr. Cobb, violence is almost unknown here. Mr. White's behavior has been most peculiar. He refused to press charges with the local police and muttered something about "repayments", and then proceeded to book the first flight back. Something tells me he knew the identity of the mugger or muggers.

The lava flow problem is now over—no thanks to Mr. White—but I seriously question Mansion Enterprises' recruiting techniques.

Sincerely,

Emanuel Lucosi

~~~~~

INTERNAL MEMO: Mansion Enterprises
From: Paul Cobb
To: Willard Greenlee

Willard, I've just received word from Mr. Mansion in Prague that we are to proceed with the purchase of the Carson's Bluff property and that it is to be given top priority. Would you please advise Russell White? I'll be out of the office tomorrow. Has anyone heard anything from Federica?

Paul

~~~~~

EMAIL FROM: wgreenlee@mansent.com
TO: ruswhite@mansent.com

Hey Russ,

I understand you're on your way back to SF, minus the use of an arm. Don't say I didn't warn you. You must have known Gambetti worked for IBM (Italian Business Men) and that you don't mess around with those guys. You're lucky it was your arm that was broken and not your head.

All is not lost. You're in luck, my friend. Word has just now come from On High that the Carson's Bluff deal is now back in the pipeline — go figure bigwigs — and not only in the pipeline, but in with a vengeance. It's been given top priority. I'd get myself off to Carson's Bluff — *fast* — if I was you.

Don't ask me why, but I'm willing to bail you out. I'll lend you what you need, at the going bank rate on the day of transfer of the money, plus five percent, with the proviso that you secure the Carson's Bluff deal, since it means a big bonus for me. Come back from Carson's Bluff with the deed in your hand and your troubles are over.

Will

~~~~~

Federica raised her glass of Plonk against the setting sun, admired its ruby color and drained it. She sighed and leaned back against Jack. They were sitting on the veranda, engaging in Federica's favorite activity—watching the sun go down over Carson's Bluff. Jack was sitting on the top step and Federica was sitting one step down, sheltered in the vee of his legs.

Dinner had been elegant and delicious, courtesy of Stella, served on Lilly's plates and heated in the microwave. Smoked breast of duck, fresh steamed green beans, whole wheat bread and cherry cobbler.

"I didn't realize that camping out could be so much fun," Federica said contentedly. "And so elegant. I thought camping was all about hardship and being damp and uncomfortable and trying to light fires with a magnifying glass."

"You've never camped out?" Jack's voice was a pleasant rumble above her head.

"No, never. I went to summer camp once, in England." Federica winced at the memory of her very lonely fourteenth summer. "But mainly they taught us tennis and computer science." She lifted her empty glass.

"You're lucky you didn't have to camp out with my dad." Jack poured some more Plonk into Federica's glass. "Now *that* was hardship. My dad is the gentlest of men, a really relaxed guy except when he's camping, and then he just morphs straight into Attila the Hun. Wyatt and I used to dread it when he'd get that look in his eye. It meant he wanted to go out in the wilderness and commune with nature and bond with his sons. All his sons wanted to do was watch *Charlie's Angels* reruns when we were little, and later on find a girl willing to make out on Saturday nights."

"Sounds tough," Federica commiserated.

"You don't know the half of it. Dad would allow a tent, a knife, a box of matches, a hook and a line. And that was it. We'd have to live off the land for a week, ten days. Wyatt and I used to dream about burgers and corndogs while we skinned rabbits." Jack smiled at the memory, a part of him wondering if he'd ever have a son of his own to torment. Maybe he wouldn't inflict camping in the mud or trying to light a fire out of wet kindling. Maybe he'd just inflict baby boomer torture—a steady diet of Beatles and Rolling Stones.

"Life is hard." Federica leaned her head back against his thigh.

He buried his hand in her hair, savoring the soft curls. "Isn't it?"

The truth was, he'd like nothing better than to go camping with Federica. Comfortable camping, not Dad's variety. Maybe with a camper and a generator. Just take off somewhere, say around Mt. Shasta, maybe as far north as Crater Lake. There were some spectacular places he'd like to show her. Just go and stay away a week…a month…a year. It was crazy. They probably didn't have more than another twenty-four hours together.

"I feel a little guilty being up here and letting Ellen stay down in town, all alone." Federica interrupted his thoughts. "Especially after she came galloping to my rescue."

"Well she can't very well stay here, honey. There's only one bed. And we're occupying it." Jack didn't have to glance down to know that Federica was blushing. "She'll be much more comfortable at Stella's. Don't worry. Wyatt will look after her. He said he'd show her around Carson's Bluff, then feed her."

"It doesn't take much to show someone around Carson's Bluff. A couple of hours is enough."

"Oh, not for Wyatt," Jack said. "And especially not with a beautiful woman. He'll take her through the tri-county area before he's through."

Federica stirred uneasily. "I don't know, Jack," she said. "Do you think—"

"Don't worry, honey," Jack said firmly. He tightened his grip on her shoulder. "Ellen's in good hands. She'll be fed and entertained and taken very good care of, just like I told you. I don't know what kind of impression you might have had of him, but Wyatt is a real gentleman. He wouldn't ever make Ellen uncomfortable in any way…even if she did shoot him."

Federica whipped around. "Come on, Jack, Ellen didn't mean—"

Jack laughed. "Hey, loosen up." He kneaded her shoulder muscles. For the first time in days, her muscles were tense. As tense as when she had first arrived. "Nobody's going to press charges, least of all Wyatt, especially now that he's got a war wound to brag about. We'll never hear the end of it."

Federica polished off the last bite of the cherry cobbler, put the pale pink dessert plate away and leaned back against Jack's thigh, almost purring when he gently stroked her cheek with his forefinger.

"I can't believe you get to live like this all the time," she said suddenly.

"Get to live like what?" He bent to kiss the top of her head.

"Like this." She waved a hand to include the Folly, the woods and the town and searched in frustration for the words to express her thoughts. "I don't know…living in that beautiful little town, working with people you like at a job you like, surrounded by family, making your own hours…"

Jack could almost hear her muscles tensing up. He thought about what to say next. If there was to be any hope for them at all, he had to get it right.

"I live in a small town, Federica," he said finally. His voice was soft, almost dispassionate, and he looked out over the lawn instead of down at her, but he kept stroking her cheek. "Carson's Bluff *is* pretty, and it's true that we all make a real effort to get along, but we're only human and sometimes we get on each others' nerves. The same with family." He took a deep breath. "Don't romanticize me or my life, Federica. I make forty thousand a year and I'll probably never make much more than that. I don't even want to. I'm happy with what I have. I don't need a lot. I live in a small town and lead a quiet life and I will continue to do so until the day I die. This is my life and it's enough for me."

He stroked her cheek, wondering if he should say more. He could. He had the words. But she either understood what he was saying or she didn't. The choice was right there in front of her, down in the valley. Twinkling lights and wood-frame houses. Friends and neighbors meeting up before dinner. Bikes in the driveways, barbecues firing up. No fancy dinner parties, no big events.

It was useless dressing Carson's Bluff up. She either wanted that life or she didn't.

She was either going to stay or she wasn't.

Federica sipped her wine. The sky was a deep turquoise now. Soon, the lights in the valley below would start winking on, one by one. First Stella's, then a few houses, then more, until Carson's Bluff looked like a handful of diamonds against a black velvet backdrop. Funny how in just a short while she had grown used to the rhythms of Carson's Bluff. When was the last time she had spent eight whole days in one place? She couldn't even remember. Now it felt as if she had spent her entire life here, with Jack and Wyatt and Lilly and Stella.

Through a break in the oak stand, she could see the sun's red crescent slip below the Earth. It was officially night now. Maybe her last night of peace. All of a sudden, she felt as if life were slipping through her fingers. Something precious, something irreplaceable was being lost, draining away as surely as the light was draining from the sky.

Leaving blackness.

"Jack." Her voice was urgent as she tipped her face up to his.

"Yeah, honey?" Jack's voice was soft and disembodied in the gathering darkness.

"Jack, make love to me." Federica's voice was shaking. She clenched her hand on his knee, then turned around. She rose on her knees, her arms snaking around his shoulders and pressed her face into his neck. A tear slipped out of her eye.

"Hey." He cupped her face. "What's the matter?"

"I want you to make love to me." Another tear, hot and painful, slipped down. "Now."

"Okay." He kissed her gently, wiping the tears away with his thumb. "There's an old Western custom we respect around here."

"What?" She smiled through the tears.

Jack lowered his mouth. "Never say no to a lady."

~~~~~

June 7th

EMAIL FROM: pcobb@mansent.com

TO: f_mansion@mansent.com

Federica,

I don't know why you haven't been in touch. We had put the Carson's Bluff deal on the back burner for a while, but we have decided to go full speed ahead with it now. As a matter of fact, the old June 15th deadline no longer holds. The sooner we secure the property, the better.

As soon as you cinch the deal, you'll be traveling to New York, London, Hamburg, Copenhagen, Kiev, in that order. We'll want you in Kiev for some time, since we're planning on expanding there. Get going with the sale, it's part of our business plan for the second semester of the year, which looks very busy. We want you out of Carson's Bluff as soon as possible.

Paul

~~~~~

"Hi, Ellen." Federica slid into the booth at Stella's. "You been waiting long?"

"No." Ellen carefully dog-eared the page of the novel she was reading. "And anyway, I had 'The Sleaziest P.I. in L.A.' to keep me company. It's one of Sutter's best. How did you get down? Did you walk?"

"Mmm. Jack left very early. And I've got to do *something* to work off Stella's cooking. I walked down yesterday, too. Today my feet are less sore and I might actually have developed a muscle or two." Federica waved hello to Stella, who was leaning over the counter of the bar, chatting with a customer. "Did you enjoy yourself last night? I felt a little guilty about leaving you alone."

Ellen sipped her coffee. "Well, I certainly understand. The way Jack was looking at you..." Ellen laughed at Federica's blush. "Forget it, honey. And don't worry, Wyatt took very good care of me."

"What did you do?"

"Well, we walked around Carson's Bluff for a while..."

"Did you see the Square?"

"Yeah. It's fabulous. I loved those irregularly shaped flower beds." Like Federica, Ellen had seen most of the world's great gardens, but there was no condescension in her voice. "Then we stopped by Lilly's and had drinks."

"She's great, isn't she?"

"I'll say. Husband's a bit odd, though. He spent the whole time holed up in his room and had to be dragged out by his beard."

"Well," Federica said charitably, "he's a recovering workaholic. Where did you go then?"

"Wyatt took me down to a little town near here called Shelby. There was this great little Mexican tavern. Tacos to die for. He said he wanted to save Stella's for when we could eat with you."

"That was nice of him."

"He's a nice man." Ellen traced a pattern in the napkin with a toothpick. "Very nice."

"It's not every day a girl gets to date a man she's shot."

"Federica," Ellen said warningly. "He was very, very understanding about it."

"That's what people are like around here. Nice and understanding. And relaxed."

"Very relaxed. Though not overly loaded with ambition." Ellen sighed. "What a waste."

"Would you like a refill?" Federica and Ellen looked up to see Stella hovering over them with a coffeepot. "You want some coffee too, Federica, or would you rather have a beer?"

"It's a bit early for beer. I think I'll stick with coffee." Federica took a deep, appreciative sniff at the aromas coming from the kitchen as Stella poured the coffee. "What's for lunch today? Something smells great." With any luck, whatever was causing those mouthwatering smells was going to be picnic lunch at the Folly.

"I'm not too sure. I'll have to check with my new assistant chef." Stella turned her head toward the kitchen and bellowed. "Newton! What's the lunch special today?"

To Federica's astonishment, a smiling Newton appeared at the swinging doors that separated the kitchen from the dining and bar area. He pushed through. Federica gaped. Newton was wearing a real chef's toque and a thick canvas apron, covering his ample chest and reaching almost to the ground.

Grinning, Federica stood up and hugged Newton. She held him at arm's length. "Newton, you look...great. Just great." It was true. He looked handsome and dashing in his chef's outfit, more than when he wore the Mansion Inn livery.

Newton gently returned Federica's hug. "Thanks, Miss Federica."

"Since when do you cook?"

"My momma taught me how. She was a very liberated lady, my momma, said a man had to be able to fend for himself. And since I like to eat well," Newton patted a big stomach which was almost all muscle, "I learned to cook well." Newton stepped back. "I got a little bored just waiting around here and I saw Stella needed a hand, so..." He shrugged massive shoulders. "Thought I'd help out a little."

"More than a little," Stella said. "My regular cook sprained his ankle the other day and I don't know what I would have done if Newton hadn't volunteered. Actually, I'm hoping my cook stays away. Newton's much better than Burt."

"So what's this wonderful smell, Newton?" Federica breathed in deeply.

"Yeah," Stella asked, interested, checking her watch. "It's 11:30. The lunchtime crowd will be coming in soon. What do I write on the blackboard?"

"Cream of asparagus soup, crepes Florentine and chicken gumbo," Newton said with satisfaction. "Now if you ladies will excuse me." He disappeared back through the swinging doors.

"...and chicken gumbo," Stella finished writing on the blackboard. She sighed happily. "God, I love that man."

"Wow, Newton as a chef." Federica shook her head as she settled back into the booth. "Who would have thought it?"

"He looked...happy," Ellen mused. "Certainly happier than when he works for Mansion Enterprises." She looked at Federica with troubled eyes. "So do you."

Federica froze. Jack had loved her out of her anxiety attack the night before, but the future was still this enormous black cloud hovering on the horizon, roiling and building up. She kept it away by sheer force of not thinking about it, but sometime soon… She pushed the thought away.

"Jack's coming to pick me up here in a few minutes. We're going to picnic on the lawn up at the Folly. You want to join us? You haven't seen the Folly yet."

"No, ah, actually," Ellen glanced at her watch, "I'm meeting Wyatt at noon on the Square and I'd better get going. He said something about showing me this little lake up in the mountains. We might be getting back late, too, so don't worry. Wyatt said we should have left early in the morning, but he had something to do." Ellen sighed and gathered her things. "Probably some beer to brew or something."

"Well, he must have made quite an impression," Federica teased, "if you're already walking around with his photograph clutched to your heart."

Ellen looked blank. "I beg your pardon?"

Federica pointed at Ellen's chest. "You've got his photograph—" She stopped.

Ellen took the paperback she clutched in her hand and turned it around.

"You're right," she breathed. "It looks like…" She turned the book to its cover. *Death and the Bogeyman*, by W. E. Sutter. One of her favorite authors. She turned the book back around and looked at Federica in befuddlement. "*Wyatt?*"

Federica grabbed the paperback, turned to the back cover and stared at the studio photograph of Wyatt. She read the author's bio out loud. "W. E. Sutter was born in 1975 in a small Northern California town and has lived there ever since. He is the author of 'The Sleaziest P.I. in L.A.' series, which has enjoyed cult status since the first novel in the series, *Dead Dog*, appeared in 1997. Seven more 'Sleaziest P.I. in L.A.' novels have followed. Incidentally, W. E. Sutter also brews great beer." She stared at Ellen.

"That's Wyatt," Ellen whispered.

"*Our* Wyatt," Federica said, stunned. "How can that be?"

"Hey, ladies." Jack walked in and hugged Federica. "Ellen, Wyatt's waiting for you on the Square. You'll love Lake Clarence. Make sure he tells you the story of how the lake got its name."

"Is it a Harry Carson story?" Federica asked.

"Yup."

"You'll love it," Federica assured Ellen.

Jack kept his arm around Federica's shoulder. "By the way, Ellen," he called out as she reached the door, "try not to shoot Wyatt in the other arm. He'll need both to negotiate the hairpin turns to the lake."

Federica shot her elbow into Jack's side, but he dodged it and chuckled. "Bye, now. Have fun."

"Bye." Ellen looked dazed as she walked out.

"She'll love Lake Clarence." Jack smiled down at Federica. "It's gorgeous this time of year. And they've got the right weather for it."

Federica looked out the window at the buttery sunshine. Beautiful weather seemed to be the norm in Carson's Bluff. Was the weather ever bad here? Maybe it was like Camelot, where it rained only at night.

It was entirely possible.

After all, Carson's Bluff was magic.

"Jack, why didn't you tell me Wyatt—" Federica stiffened.

"Why didn't I tell you Wyatt what?" Jack asked.

But Federica wasn't listening. Her gaze was riveted to the street visible through Stella's big plate-glass window where a tall, good-looking man with his arm in a cast was paying off a taxi.

Slowly, reluctantly, she made her way to the door and beckoned. The man recognized her and made his way impatiently across the street without checking for traffic. A cyclist swerved and teetered for a moment before righting himself. The cyclist looked back in disgust, but the man didn't even break his stride.

"Federica?" Jack came out from Stella's and put a big hand on her shoulder. She wondered if he felt her tension. She was humming with it. "What's the matter?"

Federica felt trapped, like a fly in a web. Any movement would make her situation worse.

"Honey?" Jack shook Federica's shoulder gently and bent to peer at her face. "What is it?"

"Trouble," Federica said.

She'd been dreading it, and here it was. In a way, it was almost a relief that the worst had happened. She'd avoided even thinking about it, but in the end that hadn't done her any good at all.

The future had arrived.

The man walked up the steps of Stella's and looked Federica up and down. He had dark blond hair combed straight back and an arrogant cast to his handsome features.

"Hello Russell," Federica said calmly. "How are you?"

It wasn't an idle question. There was something…odd about him. When she was a little girl, her riding instructor warned her against horses with a wild look to them. If Russell were a horse, he couldn't be ridden.

Usually so controlled, he was quivering with tension. Normally impeccably dressed and groomed, his grey lightweight wool suit was rumpled, as if he had slept in it. The silk burgundy and blue tie had the knot opened down to the second shirt button. He hadn't shaved and he had an angry scrape along one cheek. Federica pointed to the cast on his arm. "What happened to you?"

"Accident," Russell said tersely. His eyes roamed restlessly up and down the street. A tic was beginning in one eye. Abruptly, he brought his gaze back to Federica.

"Where the *fuck* have you been, Federica? You haven't been in touch at all. It's been highly irresponsible of you. Luckily, I brought all your email messages on diskette so you can get caught up."

"Sorry," Federica said softly. "I've been ill."

His jaw clenched and unclenched. "Well, I guess that explains the way you're dressed." His disapproving gaze swept from her sneakered feet to her pink T-shirt. "But you're not sick now, so let's get going. I want to settle this thing as fast as possible and get out of here. I've got business back in San Francisco that needs taking care of."

Federica's heart lurched.

It was over.

* * * * *

Jack sucked in his breath in outrage. How could Federica let this jerk talk to her like that? He looked to Federica for permission to punch his lights out, but she stopped him with a hand on his arm. Her face was remote and composed.

"It's all right, Jack."

She was lying. This wasn't all right.

"Russell, I'd like to introduce you to the mayor and sheriff of Carson's Bluff, Jack Sutter. Jack, this is Russell White, head of engineering for Mansion Enterprises." She drew a deep breath. "Russell will be...helping me in the negotiations. For...the Folly."

Jack froze. Mansion Enterprises. Negotiations.

The moment he'd been dreading was here. What a fool he was. He'd been hoping that when it came to the crunch, what Federica had found here, with him, would be enough. He had it all set in his head, like a movie. The two of them would walk away into the sunset.

More fool him. Instead of telling this creep to buzz off, Federica was standing stock-still, face completely unreadable and as untouchable as if she were a hologram beamed down from the moon.

She turned to him, but her eyes somehow slid off his face and focused on his shoulder. "How soon do you think we can make arrangements to discuss the…" Federica swallowed, "the sale?"

He needed time. He couldn't believe that the lovely woman he had started falling in love with could just disappear right in front of his very eyes and leave this…this *clone* in her place.

He needed time alone with her, time they should have taken before to talk things out, instead of pretending that they were living in Never Land. Time to make plans on how to get rid of this idiot and have a good laugh over it. There was *life* to get on with—the lunchtime picnic, meeting Wyatt and Ellen for dinner…

"I don't know." Jack stuck his hands in his back pockets. He stalled. "We need to book the room in City Hall, I'll have to convene the members of the Town Council…" He searched Federica's face for some clue to what she was thinking.

Give me an idea, honey, he thought frantically. *Let me know what you want to do, what you want me to do, what your plan is.*

There had to be a plan.

"Impossible," Russell snapped. Jack started counting backwards from ten, just like he'd been taught. "Mansion Enterprises will brook no delays, Mr. Mayor."

Brook no delays? What kind of a rock did they find this asshole under?

"If Federica had been doing her duty, negotiations would have already begun." Russell said stiffly.

Federica tightened her hand on Jack's arm.

Hand or no hand, Jack was definitely going to clean this guy's clock.

"She was *sick*, you—" He started forward.

"How about tomorrow morning at 10:00, Russell," Federica said, and took the wind right out of his sails.

"No." The tic around Russell White's eye became more pronounced. "Now." He checked his wafer-thin gold watch and Jack hated him even more. "It's noon. I suggest we meet at four. A lot of time has been wasted already." A polished English shoe tapped an impatient staccato on the wooden porch.

Jack looked at Federica. This was her cue to tell this idiot where to get off. *Come on, honey, this has gone on long enough. It isn't funny anymore. Tell this jerk to crawl back under his rock and we can go do something important, like have our picnic lunch.*

Jack waited.

Federica bent her head. "All right, Russell." Her voice was low.

She turned back and walked into Stella's, passing Jack as if he weren't there.

Russell White remained outside, shoe tapping, eye twitching. Jack followed Federica because he was sworn to uphold the peace and he couldn't do that while his hands were itching to smash that long, aquiline nose into that bland, handsome face.

Federica stopped inside Stella's and took a long look around. Stella must have sensed something because she was standing stock-still, a tea towel in her hand. Federica tried to savor this moment, the last one in which the people here were her friends.

It was all slipping away, like sand through an open-fingered hand and she couldn't do anything to stop it.

She glanced out the window at Russell, whose head was swiveling back and forth, checking out Carson's Bluff.

It's a nice place, Russell, she wanted to say to him. *Let's not spoil it*. But of course, the words would be wasted.

For a moment, she wanted to run away. Hide up in the Folly forever, away from her duty. But duty had found her out, and was waiting outside with a twitch in one eye and a tapping foot.

She could send Russell on his way, but others would follow.

This whole business was larger than she was. Larger than Jack and the Town Council, even. Mansion Enterprises had its eye on the Folly. Whether she chose to participate in the negotiations or not, Mansion Enterprises would buy the Folly, and then they would move in and take Carson's Bluff over.

The Carson's Bluff she knew would disappear.

It was as simple, as inevitable, as the sun rising in the east every morning. She could walk away, but it would happen anyway. If she participated, there was an off chance she could negotiate slightly better conditions for Jack and the others.

It was the least she could do.

"Newton!" Federica called.

"Yes, Miss Federica." A smiling Newton appeared at the kitchen door.

"Newton," she said softly. "I need you to drive me up to the Folly." She turned to Stella. "Sorry."

Stella blinked and looked from Federica to Newton. Her face was an expressionless mask.

Newton stood still for a moment, then he slowly reached behind to untie his apron strings. Carefully, he folded the apron and placed it on the bar counter. "Yes, Miss Federica," he said sadly.

We want you out of Carson's Bluff as soon as possible.

Federica kept looking at the words on her laptop screen until the letters seemed to burn a hole in her mind.

She was in her room at the Folly and she looked around at the beautiful old bed, the big pine dresser that Wyatt had restored, the intricate vase made by Lilly, the handful of summer daisies and baby's breath Jack had gathered for her.

Just another hotel room, she tried to tell herself.

In a day or two, when I'm gone to — she checked the computer screen — *New York, London, Hamburg, Copenhagen, Kiev, I'll hardly remember it here.*

She could only function if she kept a close watch on her emotions, kept them far, far away, where they couldn't hurt her.

It was just another deal. She'd negotiated thousands of them. It was her job, after all. To negotiate deals for Mansion Enterprises. For her uncle, her only living relative. And if it tore a hole in her chest, too bad.

Moving carefully, because she felt as if she was at the brim and moving too fast would make her spill over, she untied the straps in her suitcase and burrowed in the clothes there. Her hands moved past the pastel suits she usually wore and picked up a black designer number. She hardly ever wore it, because though it was beautifully cut, it was a little funereal.

But on this occasion it was quite appropriate, because she *was* going to a funeral.

Her own.

Chapter Twelve

"I hereby declare this meeting open," Jack snarled, and brought the gavel down with enough force to crack open a head.

Pity there wasn't one handy to crack.

He and Lilly were seated at one table, facing Federica and Russell White across a few feet of space at another table. The two tables were perpendicular to the public area.

He looked around. The meeting room in City Hall wasn't large. There were six rows of seats, divided by an aisle behind a waist-high wooden railing.

By some invisible messenger service, the word had spread and people were slowly filing in. Instinctively, the citizens of Carson's Bluff sat together on the right hand side of the aisle. On the left, all the seats were empty except for Newton, sitting stolidly on the front bench, his chauffeur's cap on his lap.

Jack leaned forward and spoke into the microphone.

"Let the record show that an extraordinary Town Council meeting has been called at 4:00 p.m. on this day the 7th of June, 2005. The Town Council is represented by John Augustus Sutter, Mayor and Sheriff, by Lilly Langtry Sutter Wright, Town Clerk—" The door to the room opened. A grim Wyatt and a subdued Ellen walked in. Wyatt marched straight over and took a seat next to Jack. Ellen sat down next to Newton. Jack nodded to Wyatt, grateful for once for the existence of cell phones. "…and by Wyatt Earp Sutter, Town Treasurer." He took a deep breath. "Let the record further show that this extraordinary town meeting concerns the possible sale of Lot 448 of the township of Carson's Bluff, otherwise known as Harry's Folly, to Mansion Enterprises, established at 423 Richmond Row,

Oakland, California. Mansion Enterprises is represented by Mr. Russell White and by Miss Federica Mansion."

Federica listened to the formal opening of proceedings as if hearing the words from a great distance. Her heart was thudding painfully in her chest though she knew her face betrayed no emotion whatsoever. Russell, on the other hand, was almost quivering beside her. His fingers drummed loudly on the table, irritating her.

Russell had handed her a sealed envelope from Paul Cobb with the negotiating parameters. Its contents lay before her, next to the yellow legal pad where she was idly scribbling, pretending to take notes because she couldn't bear to look at Jack and Lilly and Wyatt.

The sealed envelope's instructions bore the distinct imprint of Uncle Frederick's business tactics. Mansion Enterprises was going to play hardball. Good thing Uncle Frederick was away in Prague, because Federica had every intention of negotiating the best possible deal for her friends.

Former friends.

I don't want to be here, she wrote in shorthand, certain that Russell wouldn't be able to read it. Russell would have considered learning shorthand beneath him.

She let her gaze wander over to the public area, filling up with Carson's Bluffers, people she had exchanged friendly words with, people who had smiled at her and wished her good day. Horace Milton sat squarely in the front row, glaring unblinkingly at her. He had his battered black beret on and sat with gnarled hands clenched on the top of his walking cane, chomping angrily on an unlit cigar.

On the Mansion Enterprises side, Ellen and Newton sat alone and isolated.

"Let the record further show that pursuant to state law, the following documents have been entered into the public record..." Jack's voice droned on and Federica tried not to think of the sweet, exciting things that voice had whispered in her ear.

Looking at him hurt.

I want to be somewhere else, she wrote on her legal pad. *The Caribbean maybe, on a beach, lying in the sun and thinking of nothing at all…*

"…document 4035, the deed authorizing myself, John Augustus Sutter, in my capacity as mayor, to act on behalf of the township of Carson's Bluff…"

Maybe not a Caribbean island. My skin doesn't take the sun very well…

"…document 4036, the tax records for the past twenty years of Lot 448…"

I want to be in a big, green meadow somewhere up in the mountains with clean air and a view down to the valley below.

"…and document 4037, the surveyor's assessment of Lot 448."

I know where I want to be, she wrote. *I want to be at the Folly.*

Something in the quality of the silence penetrated her mind and she looked up to find everyone looking at her expectantly.

She leaned forward to the microphone in front of her. "Everything is in order, Mayor Sutter, thank you." The amplification system made her voice sound dead. Almost as dead as she felt. "You may proceed."

Jack leaned back and looked her full in the face. His own face was expressionless, but the skin was pulled tautly over his cheekbones, making them stand out clearly. His eyes were flat. He stared at her for a long moment, his jaw muscles working, then leaned forward again.

"After due deliberation with my fellow members of the Town Council, we have decided that Lot 448 is not for sale." He picked up the gavel. "And I hereby declare this meeting adjourned."

Oh Jack, Federica thought sadly. She knew what was written in her instructions. *You need legal counsel.*

"I'm afraid it is not as simple as that, Mr. Mayor." Federica's soft voice echoed in the speakers around the room. Jack put his gavel down. "I refer you to California property law 4478, subsection 5-C." Jack, Lilly and Wyatt looked at each other in confusion, clearly not understanding what was about to happen. "Lot 448 has an outstanding tax debt of over $100,000." Federica thumbed unnecessarily through her documentation, which she knew by heart. She hated what she was going to have to say. "$127,500 to be exact. This means that Lot 448 is legally 'onerous property' and therefore for sale to the highest bidder starting at double the amount. I have here a cashier's check for $255,000, which would make the property ours unless the township of Carson's Bluff can come up with an amount that would cover the tax burden within twenty days of notification of intent to purchase."

An angry buzz grew from the Carson's Bluff side of the aisle and Jack rapped sharply twice with his gavel and waited for everyone to quiet down.

"I'm afraid, Miss Mansion," he said, his voice bitter, "that we're not a rich community. The amount you mentioned is more than our annual budget for the day care center and the women's clinic combined and I'll be damned...er, I refuse to close those two centers down for some mega-corporation's greed."

Russell stopped drumming his fingers, and started jiggling his leg, bumping his knee against the table. For a moment, Federica contemplated taking a chain saw and chopping his leg off at the knee joint, then was ashamed of herself. It must be the stress. She was not by nature a violent person. She took a deep breath.

"Mansion Enterprises has no desire to see town services shut down, Mr. Mayor. It has always been our policy to live in amity with the communities in which we run our businesses. Mansion Enterprises has always been a very civic-minded organization." Out of the corner of her eye, Federica could see Russell gaping at her in surprise at her description of their company. She slowly unfolded once more her instructions and reread the amount written there. The top offer she was empowered to make was three million dollars, though the Folly was easily worth double that amount. "We could take the Town Council to court, but that would entail legal fees and time and ill feeling, which we have no desire to incur. And that is why we put forward our offer to buy Lot 448 for the amount of…four million dollars." Russell opened his mouth in protest and Federica kicked him sharply in the shins.

So much for non-violence.

A million dollars was the least she could pay Carson's Bluff for what it had given her. Uncle Frederick be damned.

"You can't do that," Russell whispered, scandalized. "That's well over the amount—"

Federica held a finger to her lips and leaned close into him. "New orders," she mouthed.

Jack had covered his microphone with his hand and was consulting with Wyatt and Lilly. Finally, he removed his hand. "I'm sorry, Miss Mansion. But we reject the offer."

Jack, she thought in despair. *Don't make me do this.*

She shouldn't wish for an earthquake to open up the earth and swallow her whole. Carson's Bluff was perilously near the San Andreas Fault and that kind of thinking was dangerous. So…maybe a *little* earthquake. Just a few square feet. Just enough to let her disappear. Now.

Her hand trembled as she drew the microphone nearer.

"To my regret, I must contradict you once more, Mr. Mayor. If you choose to reject Mansion Enterprises' very generous offer, then I'm afraid we have no choice but to take legal recourse. And the first step in that process, Mr. Mayor, is to recuse the Town Council and to sue its representative, in the person of yourself, for nonfeasance in the best instance and in the worst for mal—mal…" The word wouldn't come and Federica put her hand over the microphone and bowed her head for an instant.

Russell impatiently batted her hand away from the microphone and leaned forward. "You'll be sued for malfeasance, Mr. Mayor," he said harshly, his voice echoing from the loudspeakers.

There was a stunned silence. Then pandemonium broke out amongst the spectators.

Jack's gavel went wild.

"Order!" he shouted. "Order! Or I'll have everyone thrown out. Just see if I don't." He turned back to Federica and Russell and his eyes were bleak. "I think this is an appropriate moment to take a break. We will reconvene in an hour's time." He banged his gavel sharply again and stood up.

"Nice park, isn't it?" Federica asked Russell as they walked around the Square.

They had an hour to kill, but going for a cup of coffee at Stella's was out of the question. Most of Carson's Bluff would be there and Federica couldn't bear walking in and seeing everyone look at her with hostility. It seemed as if she had spent a lifetime absorbing hostility toward Mansion Enterprises, instead of just eight years.

"Not bad," Russell said absently.

There was a time when Federica had mistaken Russell's silences for reticence. By the time she had found out his reserve wasn't shyness but a self-centeredness so monumental he was barely aware of the existence of other human beings, it was too late. They had had their affair, she had been dumped and she had wasted perfectly good emotions on the jerk.

Russell had cleaned up a bit in the room he had taken at Stella's. He was clean-shaven and had changed his clothes and looked a little more like his usual handsome self. Federica looked at him as they walked through the Square and mentally compared him to Jack, though it was ludicrous comparing them. The two men might as well have come from different planets.

Federica wondered how she could ever have felt something for Russell. Nothing remained, not even a twinge.

"Do you think we can wrap the whole thing up by this afternoon and leave tonight?" he asked.

"Ah—I'm not too sure," Federica hedged. "Does it make that much difference whether it's today or tomorrow?"

Russell beat an impatient tattoo against his thigh with his fist. He blew out his breath in a gust. "I can't wait to get out of this burg. I hate small towns."

Federica was silent, thinking of what awaited her. The long drive down to San Francisco, the usual debriefing, leaving the next day for New York, then London…or was it Hamburg? She didn't remember. Not that it mattered. Wherever it was, it wasn't Carson's Bluff.

She took in a long, deep breath, trying to steady her nerves and smelled something…odd. She looked around, wondering what the source of the smell could be.

"Is that a Rachel Douglas?" Russell asked as they turned a corner.

"What? Oh, yes. Yes it is."

"It's wasted in this park." Russell stood looking at the sculpture, considering. In addition to the tic, he had taken to fondling his tie. Federica seriously thought about strangling him with it, then realized that she was taking her own frustrations out on Russell. Poor Russell, who reported directly to Uncle Frederick and who was evidently under so much pressure he twitched.

A lot of people under Uncle Frederick twitched.

"It should be up at the property."

Federica blinked. "Excuse me?"

"That's a nice piece of sculpture." Russell nodded at the miracle of lightness and grace before them. "It would look good on that area right in front of the Folly. I've seen photographs of the place and that sculpture would be very impressive on the front lawn, once we've landscaped it. We could design the carport to go behind it."

"You know, Russell, I don't think you can do that," Federica said cautiously. "My understanding is that this sculpture is a donation by Rachel Douglas herself to the town. I don't think you can just…appropriate it and set it up on private property."

Russell gave her a contemptuous look. "Of course we can." He snorted. "This time next year that rube will be out as mayor and one of our people will be in. We'll be able to do whatever we want." He walked on. "Another thing…"

That smell. What was it?

"What Russell?"

He looked around. "The flower beds. They're all over the place. These hicks can't even plant straight. We've got to get our landscaping people out here right away."

The smell of…incense. Of books.

Russell pulled up short. "I can't believe it," he breathed. "Will you look at that?" He waved his hand in disgust at the far corner of the Square. "Those are *tomato plants*."

Federica smiled. "Why, so they are." Neat rows of tomato vines grew on an orderly plot. Judging from the profusion of small green knobs, Mr. Giannini was going to have a bumper crop come fall, just like Lilly had said.

"This is ridiculous," Russell said in disgust. "A tomato patch in a public park."

Incense, books, Don's gentle voice.

"I can't believe these people." Russell crossed his arms and surveyed the Square with disfavor. "What clodhoppers!"

Your heart knows where it's going, even if your head doesn't.

The world seemed to do a slow kaleidoscopic dance around her, shifting things so that what had been hidden was now revealed.

Follow your heart, Federica. Follow your heart.

"These people shouldn't be let out on a leash." Russell's chiseled mouth turned down at the corners in a sneer. "Good thing we're going to take over. That's the kind of thing that's going to have to go."

Oh, no Russell, Federica thought suddenly. *You're the kind of thing that's going to have to go.*

It was a crazy plan, dangerous too, and the timing was very, very tight. If it failed... Federica couldn't even think of the consequences if the plan failed.

For a moment, she had a pang of conscience about Russell, whose career might suffer if her plan was successful.

On the other hand, it might do him a world of good. Maybe he could make failure a learning experience, like in all the New Age books. Maybe adversity would make him grow in spiritual wisdom and turn him into a deeper, kinder human being.

Russell kicked a phlox blossom that had unexpectedly bloomed between the cobblestones.

Then again, maybe not.

No matter. Her mind was made up and there was very little time to waste. She checked her watch. In twenty minutes, they would be reconvening and she needed to get rid of Russell. For now, temporarily. And later, permanently.

"Oh!" she exclaimed.

"What's the matter?" he asked irritably.

"Oh, Russell." Federica brought a hand to her mouth. "I completely forgot! There are some documents I need and I left them...in the car. Yes, in the car. They're in a red folder and I absolutely need them. Would you please ask Newton to unlock the car door for you?"

Finding Newton and hunting through the company Mercedes for a nonexistent red folder would take twenty minutes at least, maybe more.

"Can't you get it yourself? You know where you left it."

"Oh, I just can't, Russell," Federica smiled at him and seriously reconsidered her plan to strangle him with his expensive tie. "I've been ill, you know."

Russell heaved a sigh. "All right," he said ungraciously. Then he peered closely at her. "You don't look like you've been sick. You look just fine in fact."

It was true. Federica had never felt better in her life. Duty and responsibility, an albatross around her neck for so long, had slipped off, just like that. It felt great.

"Must be the mountain air," she said. "It's invigorating. Now go get me that folder, please."

Federica waited until Russell had rounded the corner then took off at a dead run in the opposite direction, heading for City Hall.

Lilly had to be there. She just *had* to. Federica was banking on Lilly's diligence. As town clerk, she was responsible for keeping the records and Federica was hoping that she hadn't gone out for coffee.

Federica ran down the hall to the meeting room, almost sliding on the slick marble floor. She suppressed the urge to punch the air when she saw Lilly bent over her papers, warm chestnut hair falling forward over her face.

Federica peered down the empty hallway, then stuck her head into the room. "Psst, Lilly!" She tried to shout in a whisper.

Lilly looked up in surprise, saw Federica and pursed her lips. She turned back to her documents, her face a stony mask.

"Lil-ly!" Federica dared to call a little louder. She kept an anxious eye on the door to the street. How long would it take Russell to get Newton to open the car for him? Newton knew perfectly well that there was no red folder in the Mercedes. He prided himself on keeping it spotless. Would he recognize the stalling tactic for what it was?

Lilly looked up briefly. "Go away," she said in a normal voice.

"*Lilly*," Federica hissed. Something in her voice made Lilly pause in her work. "Lilly, *please*."

Lilly put down her pen and glowered. "I have nothing to say to you, Federica."

With one last desperate glance down the corridor, Federica stepped into the room. Ten minutes had already gone by. She practically danced with frustration. "Lilly, come with me to the ladies' room, please. We've got to talk undisturbed."

"Why would I want to talk to you?"

"Because," Federica checked that they were still alone, "because I'm going to get us out of this mess, but to do that I need your help, but you can't help me if you don't know what I need."

Lilly frowned, having barely listened. Only one word in Federica's rushed speech made an impact. "Help?" She gave a hollow laugh. "I think you've helped us just about enough, don't you?"

Federica knew she deserved the reprimand and she would be properly repentant.

Later.

"Lilly, I need to talk to you *now*." And with that she turned and walked down the hall, not looking back, hoping Lilly would follow her out of curiosity if nothing else.

"Third door to the right," came a voice from behind her. "It says 'Ladies' on the door," and Federica let out her breath.

The directions were superfluous. The third door to the right had a saloon girl doing the can-can on the door. Federica pushed through and waited for Lilly.

"Okay, Federica." Lilly leaned back against a washbasin and crossed her arms over the swell of her stomach. "What's going on?"

"Listen, Lilly. The threat to the Folly and to Carson's Bluff is real."

"We realize that," Lilly said evenly.

"And so is the threat of a suit. Mansion Enterprises has lawyers that could tie you people in knots and convince any court in the state that the Town Council is made up of dishonest fumblers who should be put away. They can do it and they will, unless—"

"How could you do that to Jack," Lilly interrupted, angry tears welling in her eyes. "I couldn't believe my ears when you accused him of malfeasance. *Jack* of all people. How *could* you?"

"I can't," Federica said simply. "No way. There's no way I can hurt Jack, or you or Wyatt or anyone else in Carson's Bluff. There's no way I'll let Mansion Enterprises take over that beautiful old building up in the mountains. Not as long as I have a breath in my body." Federica stopped and considered. "Or a brain in my head."

The tears had stopped, but Lilly still looked unconvinced. "I don't—I don't understand. In there—" she gestured back at the meeting room.

"Back there was then," Federica said firmly, "and this is now. I'm defecting. As of this moment, I'm going to do everything in my power to save the Folly. But it's not going to be easy, and I'm going to need your help. I'm going to need everybody's help."

Lilly's face was unreadable. "I'm listening."

It was a start.

"Okay. You talked about booby-trapping, no—" She held up a hand. Lilly's expression had immediately grown wary. "Don't worry, I'm not going to turn you in to the Highway Patrol or anything. I need to know—can you get Russell White out of here by nightfall, or by tomorrow morning at the latest?"

"I don't know." Lilly considered the problem. "I'd have to know more about him, his weaknesses, for instance."

"Oh, he's got plenty of weaknesses," Federica assured her. "Pride, ambition, selfishness. Is that the kind of thing you mean?"

"Sounds like you know him pretty well." For a moment, feminine curiosity overcame Lilly's sisterly indignation. "How's that?"

"Well," Federica said uncomfortably, "we sort of had an—" she waved her hand awkwardly in the air, "you know—um, a couple of years ago."

"You didn't." Lilly sucked in her breath and gave Federica a how-could-you look. "With him? With that? *Why*?"

"Well," Federica said defensively, "I was…lonely."

"Nobody's that lonely, Federica," Lilly said firmly. "You should have bought yourself a cat."

"I couldn't, I travel too much," Federica said. "And Russell didn't need a litter box while I was away." Federica checked her watch. Five minutes to go. "But that's not important now. What *is* important is that we get rid of Russell. And then I figure we'll have about twenty-four hours to save Carson's Bluff once he's gone. Maybe less. So—how do we booby-trap Russell?"

"Well, there's always the old standby. Does he like to eat?"

"And drink," Federica assured her. "A lot."

"All right then. Make sure he eats at Stella's tonight. He'll be gone by morning."

Federica opened her mouth to ask, then closed it. She really didn't want to know. "Okay, then right after he's gone, you, me, Jack and Wyatt will need a war room. Someplace with space, and phone and fax and email facilities."

"There's a room in the back at Stella's," Lilly said slowly.

"Great." Federica checked her watch again. It was time. People would be filing back into the meeting room. "That way we won't have to worry about food."

"But—"

"But?" Federica looked up. "But what? Hurry, Lilly, we don't have any time left."

Lilly searched her face. "Why should I trust you after this morning? Why?"

It was an honest question. And it deserved an honest answer. Federica straightened. Nothing less than the truth would do. She looked at Lilly and opened her heart and mind to Lilly's searching gaze. "Because...because I love Jack, that's why."

"You really love him?" Lilly stood stock-still.

"With all my heart." Federica's eyes never wavered from hers. "And I sort of like you guys, too."

"All right." Lilly's eyes started welling again and she reached out and grasped Federica's hand. "I must be crazy, but I believe you. I really do."

Federica fought back tears of her own. She gave in and hugged Lilly, then stepped back. "That's enough of that." She wiped her eyes and checked her makeup in the mirror above the basin. "Now I want you to go back in there and tell that brother of yours to follow my lead. No matter what I do or what I say. You got that?"

Lilly nodded.

"It's time now. Let's scoot." Federica put a hand to Lilly's back. "We've got a war to win."

"I couldn't find the red folder," Russell whispered in annoyance as he slid into the seat to the right of Federica. She suppressed a smile. Russell was breathing heavily. Newton had understood and had detained Russell until the last possible minute. Russell had had to run all the way back.

"Too bad," Federica said. "Maybe I left the folder up at the Folly."

Jack came into the room with Wyatt and Federica felt the breath leave her body, as if someone had siphoned off all the air in the room. He was so beautiful to her, the essence of everything that was good and true, and he had once been hers.

Was it too late?

Lilly put her hand on Jack's arm and he bent his head and listened.

Federica tried to read his expression, but it was impossible. She watched him carefully, trying to understand whether she had lost him forever. He raised his head suddenly and his eyes caught hers from across the room. He stared at her, then bent again to Lilly.

Would he believe her? Had she lost his trust?

Jack and Wyatt made their way slowly through the crowd. Everyone seemed to want to pat them on the back or shake their hand or give them a piece of advice. Federica could see Jack whisper something to Wyatt and then Wyatt, too, stared at her.

Finally, everyone had taken their seats.

Jack brought the gavel down. The sound system came back on with a feedback whine and he winced.

"Let the record show," he said into the microphone, "that we are reconvening the extraordinary Town Council meeting on this day, the 7th of June, 2005, at 6:00 p.m. This meeting concerns the offer made by Mansion Enterprises for Lot 448 of the township of Carson's Bluff. Mansion Enterprises had made a bid of four million dollars for Lot 448, otherwise known as Harry's Folly. After due deliberation—"

"Excuse me, Mr. Mayor," Federica interrupted. Beside her, she could feel Russell stiffen in surprise.

"Miss Mansion?"

"Mr. Mayor, I apologize, but before we proceed, I'm afraid that there is a document missing from the file made available by the Town Council."

Jack stared at her and Federica realized at that moment just how very much she loved him. She'd told it to Lilly, but she hadn't really told herself yet. *Follow your heart*, Don had said, and her heart's journey had led her to a little town in the mountains and to a dark-haired man who was the finest man she'd ever met.

"What's this?" Russell whispered angrily. "What's going on?"

Federica covered the microphone. "We've got a missing document. It's just a formality, but we don't want to give the Town Council a chance to appeal if a court finds against them."

"Oh." The explanation seemed to appease Russell and he sat back. He rolled his cast back and forth on the table and the noise irritated Federica so much she felt like breaking his arm all over again.

"What document would that be, Miss Mansion?" Jack asked. Was it her imagination, or was some of the old warmth creeping back into his voice?

"We don't have the copy of the registration of Lot 448 with the County Land Register," Federica said. It was a minor document, of no real importance. "We insist on having complete documentation, Mr. Mayor," she said, and made her voice prim. "Unfortunately, we cannot proceed without the document. I am afraid that the Town Council of Carson's Bluff has been most remiss."

Federica cupped her hand around the right side of her face so Russell couldn't see her and looked at Jack. Her lips curved in a smile and she winked at him.

Their eyes met and there was silence in the room.

Jack's lips twitched. "In that case, Miss Mansion, I guess we have no choice but to apologize for the oversight and to suggest that we reconvene tomorrow morning with the full set of documents. In the meantime, I suggest that we continue our discussions informally at Stella's Bar & Grill." Jack looked around. "So decided."

He brought the gavel down.

"What are we doing here?" Russell looked with disfavor at the simple décor at Stella's. He hiccupped, automatically covering his mouth with his hand, banging himself on the nose with his cast. He rubbed his nose irritably. "God, I hate small towns."

"Now, Russell," Federica said soothingly, squelching hard the urge to laugh. "I have strict orders to try and stay on good terms with the people of Carson's Bluff, and with the Town Council in particular. This seems like a good way to cement relations."

"Orders to stay on friendly terms?" Russell frowned and sipped some more beer. It was his second bottle. "That doesn't sound much like your uncle."

"No, it was in the letter from Paul Cobb."

"Oh." He drained the bottle. "Well, at least the beer's good."

"You'll like the food, too," Federica assured him. Russell prided himself on being a gourmet. "They say Stella's might be in the next *Good Food Guide*."

"Oh, really?" Russell looked interested for the first time since they'd come into Stella's. "Say, how about another beer?"

Jack was at the bar chatting with Stella and Federica fought down a stab of irritation. It was okay to be relaxed, that was one of the things she loved about Jack, but he didn't seem to understand that their troubles were far from over. They were on a tight schedule. This was no time to be shooting the breeze with Stella.

"I'll get it for you, Russell." Federica slid out of the booth and walked over to Jack and tapped him on the shoulder.

Jack gave her a lazy smile that had her heart turning over in her chest until she remembered that she was annoyed with him. "What's with you?" she whispered. "You people are supposed to be booby-trapping Russell."

Jack glanced behind him at their booth and turned back. "We are." He didn't whisper, but kept his voice low. Stella handed him three bottles and Jack held one out to her. "This is step one."

"*Beer*?" Federica's voice rose and she immediately dropped it back to her stage whisper. "Beer?" she repeated. "You're going to get rid of Russell with *beer*?"

"Check the label, honey."

"I—" Federica blew out her breath in frustration. Jack obviously didn't understand how quickly they had to move and how serious the situation was. A little beer—however good—wasn't going to make Russell have a change of heart about Carson's Bluff, if that was their plan. Russell didn't have a heart.

She looked closer at the label, then tilted her head to one side. On one of the bottles, in a faint sepia wash, was a pig on its back, little trotters in the air and with X's for eyes. Federica looked at Jack in confusion.

"The beer we're giving Russell is Special Pigswill, and it's ninety proof," he said with satisfaction. "And Stella is going to over-salt his food."

"Ninety-proof beer," Federica said wonderingly. "How can that be?"

"I don't know," Jack answered. "You'll have to ask Wyatt. He's a genius when it comes to beer."

"By the way," Federica looked around. "Where *is* Wyatt? And Lilly?"

"Lilly went home to put her feet up. She and Norman will be coming in later. Wyatt is showing Ellen around."

"Showing..." Federica clenched her fist and banged it on the counter. "What's the matter with him? This is no time for romance."

Jack stepped to one side so that his back shielded them from view and curled his big hand around her wrist. "Yes it is." His thumb softly stroked her hand. "It's always time for romance." Federica started to melt, then remembered her anxiety. "Jack—"

"Trust me, honey," Jack said, smiling. "Trust us. We know what we're doing." He gave a sudden pirate's grin. "We've done this before."

* * * * *

"So, Russell," Jack said expansively, looking at Russell's empty plate. "What do you think of the food? I guess an important executive like yourself has eaten in the finest restaurants all over the world."

Russell leaned his head back against the booth seat. "Well, yes," he said and tried to smile modestly. "Of course I've eaten in my share of four-star restaurants. But the food here is very good." He hiccupped. "For a small town, of course."

"Why thank you, Russell." Jack smiled. Russell's eyelids were starting to quiver. Where was Wyatt? It was time. "Have some more beer, why don't you?"

"Well…" Jack could tell Russell was having trouble focusing.

"Come on, pal." Jack poured another glass of Special Pigswill and some of the ordinary kind for himself. "Let's forget business and enjoy ourselves."

Jack watched Russell down his glass and calculated. Russell was about six feet, maybe a hundred and eighty pounds. He was starting to weave slightly in his seat. If Wyatt didn't come soon, Jack would have to do it all by himself.

Russell finished and smacked his lips. They were probably numb by now. "Good," he said and smiled foolishly at Jack and Federica. "Very good beer."

Jack gave him another four, five minutes, tops. Though he had to hand it to the man. Russell was a pompous ass, but there must be more to him than meets the eye. Jack surveyed the tabletop of empty bottles. A lesser man would have been dead by now.

Russell started swaying, as if in a stiff breeze. Where the *hell* was— The door to Stella's opened and Wyatt walked in with Ellen, a grin as foolish as Russell's on his face. They walked over to the booth. The door opened again and Lilly and Norman strolled in.

"About time," Jack muttered to Wyatt. "Say, Russell," he said loudly. "Why don't we step outside for a breath of fresh air? It's a little stuffy in here."

Russell turned his head. His eyes followed a few seconds later. "Spren—er, splendid idea, my man. Little flesh—fresh air would do me a girl of wood." He put his hands on the table to get up and nothing happened. "Say, I seem to be—"

"No problem," Jack said easily and motioned to Wyatt. Between them, they got a shaky Russell to his feet. "You want to wipe some of that lipstick off your chin, bro," Jack said to Wyatt out of the side of his mouth. "Come on now, Russell, you remember how to walk, don't you? Put your left foot out, that's a good boy, now the other one—"

Russell looked in befuddlement at Jack, then at his feet, which weren't obeying. In a slow sort of dance shuffle, the three men reached the door. Jack opened it wide and nudged Wyatt. "I'll take the head, you take the feet," he whispered. He slapped Russell on the back and Russell staggered slightly. "Take a big deep breath, my man," he boomed. "Just smell that clean mountain air."

Russell smiled, took a big breath, and his eyes did a slow roll to the back of his head.

"Timmm-ber," said Jack, as Russell toppled slowly backwards. Jack caught his head, Wyatt his feet and they made for the bedrooms Stella had on the first floor. "Hey Stella," Jack called out, huffing a little. Not one-eighty, more like one-ninety. "Did you change the mattress?"

"Sure did, Jack." A smiling Stella came out from behind the counter. "The oldest, lumpiest one I could find."

"And the hidden tape recorder?"

"Yup. With the most obnoxious music I could find," she said in satisfaction. "Heavy metal and rap fusion. Stole the tape off my son. The guy won't get a wink of sleep."

"I don't think we're talking sleep here," said Wyatt, as they staggered up the stairs with their burden. "I think we're talking coma."

"Okay, then he won't get a wink of coma."

Federica watched them disappear up the stairs and turned to Lilly and Norman.

"Lilly, did you set up the room for tomorrow?"

"Sure, honey. Stella's storeroom. She emptied it this afternoon."

"Good." Federica rubbed her hands and tried to fight off the wave of anxiety. The battle had begun. "Now by tomorrow, I'll need two big wall clocks, two laptops with fax/modems and a good spreadsheet program."

"I've got one I designed myself," Norman said. "It's better than the commercially available ones."

Federica looked at Norman through narrowed, appraising eyes. "How good are you at figures, Norman?"

"Very good." He sighed. "So good it almost killed me."

"And how good are you at lying and cheating?"

"I was a vice president at Longthorn, Pace and Feldstein," he said simply. His eyes slid to his wife. "Of course, I'm reformed now," he added hastily.

"Well, unreform yourself. Fast." Federica drummed her fingers on the counter. "I need you."

Norman fingered his beard and tried to hide the gleam in his eyes. "What exactly were you thinking of?"

"This." Federica outlined her plan while Norman listened, his eyes widening behind his horn-rims. "So what do you think?"

"I don't know, Federica. The timing's going to be tricky..." he started, but there was a noise at the top of the stairs and he lost Federica's attention.

Federica watched Jack come back down the stairs, brushing his hands and grinning, and thought that she had never seen anyone or anything as beautiful as he was. Just knowing that a man like Jack lived in the world made her feel better. The idea that he'd once been hers and maybe might be again took her breath away.

There was a lot left unsaid between them. There'd been no time to talk. Maybe it was over between them. Maybe he was just grateful that she hadn't thrown Carson's Bluff to the lions—or, worse, to Uncle Frederick—but that was it. Maybe what they had couldn't be put back together again. Maybe she had been imagining that he felt as much as she did…or the way she did.

Maybe…

Jack walked toward her and she felt her heart pound in her throat.

He stopped in front of her and stood looking at her. "Come on, honey," he said at last, and held out his hand. "Let's go home."

Federica stepped forward, taking his hand, then she leaned her head against his shoulder, fighting tears. He hugged her fiercely and they started for the door.

Wyatt walked down the stairs and crossed to Ellen.

Norman watched Jack and Federica leave. "Wyatt?" He sounded thoughtful.

"Yeah?"

"If you ever need a role model for a master criminal mind," Norman said, jerking his thumb at Federica's departing back, "there's your woman."

"I thought I'd lost you," Federica whispered and kissed Jack's bare shoulder. Her body was still trembling with the aftershocks of pleasure.

"Me, too." His arm tightened around her. "Don't ever, ever scare me like that again, do you hear?" He gave her a little shake. "You took ten years off my life."

"I know." She wrapped her arms around his broad back, reveling in the strong muscles, reveling in the fact that this was *Jack*. Only a few hours ago, she'd felt as if the world suddenly been emptied of all meaning. She could hardly believe he was here with her, warm and hard and real in her arms.

"I can't believe this is happening," he whispered.

"I was thinking the same thing," she confessed. "I thought we'd never be like this again." The thought had her clutching her fingers into his shoulders.

"When you walked into the meeting room, wearing that little black suit and that cool, remote expression, I thought, I thought—"

"Shh." Federica put a finger over his mouth, then took it away and replaced it with her lips. "Don't say it, don't even think it."

Jack kissed her deeply, then kissed his way down to her breast.

Federica couldn't believe that her body was waking up again, so intensely and so soon. She felt breathless, poised on the edge of a precipice. Jack was licking the spot over her wildly thudding heart and his hands, wicked hands, moved knowingly over her.

Jack lifted his mouth and looked at her. The starlight filtering in through the window bathed him in an unearthly, silvery glow and he looked like a god, sent to Earth just for her. His black hair was tousled from lovemaking and the clean, strong bone structure stood out clearly. She cupped his face with her hands, trembling at the idea of having almost lost him.

I love him so much, she thought, and her heart turned over in her chest as his intent look changed to a smile.

"Federica?" His deep voice sent shivers down her spine. "Will you do something for me?"

"Yes," she whispered. *Anything*, she thought.

"I want you to burn that black suit."

June 8th

"Well, well," Ellen said brightly, as a shaky Russell walked into the meeting room the next morning. "Rise and slime."

Russell shot her a nasty look as he walked past, but his heart clearly wasn't in it. He walked carefully, as if holding a big bowl of water that might spill at any moment. He was wearing a burgundy cashmere cardigan that clashed badly with his green complexion.

Federica looked up from the documents she'd been pretending to read. "Good morning, Russell," she said sweetly. "Did you sleep well?"

He grunted and started to sit down in his usual chair, to Federica's right.

"No, no," Federica said swiftly. She pulled out the chair on her left. "Sit here." Wyatt had told her to try to make sure Russell sat near the public area.

"Why?" Russell asked, suspiciously.

"Er…" Federica thought fast. "You're not looking well, Russell. It's…easier to get out from here," she said delicately, "in case you need to…um…"

It made perfect sense to him. Russell slumped heavily into the chair, just a few feet from the front row of the public area, where Ellen and Newton sat alone. He looked around the room out of hostile, red-rimmed eyes. "How long is this going to take?" He rubbed his forehead. "I can't wait to get out of here. I hate small towns."

Federica patted his hand. "Don't worry," she said. "It'll be over soon."

She looked at Jack, trying not to smile at him, and nodded. He brought his gavel down with a loud crack and Russell jumped, then groaned.

The door to the meeting room opened, and Horace Milton hobbled in. He made his way down the aisle and sat down next to Ellen and Newton. His wide grin showed the black stubs of teeth clamped down on his usual unlit cigar.

"Good morning, ladies and gentlemen," Jack said cheerfully. "We'd like to call the meeting to order, on this bright and sunny day, the 8th of June, 2005. We are all refreshed after the lovely evening offered to the Town Council by Stella last night and let the record show that the Town Council of Carson's Bluff is grateful to her for her hospitality." He brought the gavel down sharply.

"Hear, hear!" Horace Milton banged heavily and enthusiastically on the floor with his cane. Shouts and whistles erupted in the room. Russell slumped further down in his chair, a hand shading his eyes.

It took a long time for the noise to die down. When it did, Jack proceeded to read, slowly and with great emphasis, the proceedings of the day before, verbatim. He eyed Russell and read out, even more slowly, the relevant portions of the California property laws. Russell sat in his chair as if he were nailed to it. Jack started to read out the Carson's Bluff Town Council regulations and nodded at Horace.

With a flourish, Horace brought out an ancient lighter, lit his cigar and started puffing contentedly. Soon his head was wreathed in a noxious black cloud. He blew a long stream of smoke straight ahead and Russell swallowed heavily and scowled at him. Horace smiled happily and blew another stream of smoke. Russell suddenly stood up.

"Federica," he asked urgently, "where's—"

"Turn right outside the door," she replied, as he pushed his chair hastily back, "third door to your left. It says 'Gentlemen' on the door."

"But that's all right, Russell," Ellen called after him as he stumbled down the aisle. "You can use it anyway."

Russell slammed the door closed and there was silence for a long minute.

Federica leaned forward into the microphone. "I think, Mr. Mayor, that we are going to have to suspend proceedings. I'm afraid that something has…er…come up."

Jack ran his hands through his hair. "Whew," he said in relief. "For a moment there, I thought I was going to have to recite the Gettysburg Address."

Federica waited outside the men's room with a satchel in her hand.

The door opened and closed and a pale Russell leaned against it. "God," he said shakily, shutting his eyes. "I *hate* small towns."

Federica almost felt pity for Russell until she thought of the tomato patch. *This one's for you, Mr. Giannini*, she thought.

"Listen, Russell." Federica touched his arm gently. "You're not looking at all well. Why don't you go back to San Francisco and let me deal with this? I've got my instructions and it shouldn't take too long."

Russell opened his eyes. "You think so?"

"Of course, Russell," she said sweetly. "You leave it all to me."

"Well." Russell loosened his shirt collar. "Actually, I really don't feel well."

Federica beckoned to Newton, who was waiting in the corridor.

"Must be the flu," she said. "There's an awful one going 'round. Now don't worry about a thing." She patted his arm. "I'll wrap it up in less than twenty-four hours."

"Thanks, Federica," Russell said gratefully. "I'll owe you one." Newton appeared and Federica nodded to him.

"Newton, please drive Mr. White to his home. He's not feeling well."

"Sure thing, Miss Federica." Newton offered Russell his arm, which he took gratefully.

"You're sure?" Russell stopped and put a hand to his stomach. "Maybe I could—"

"I'm sure Russell," Federica said firmly. "Now go on home and don't worry about a thing."

The two men walked slowly down the corridor, Russell walking very carefully. Federica sincerely hoped that Russell could make this a learning experience. But she doubted it.

"Oh, and Newton?" Federica called.

"Yes, ma'am?"

"Make sure you drive straight back. We'll be needing...sustenance."

Newton grinned. "*Yes, ma'am.*"

As soon as they were out of sight, Federica rushed into the ladies' room and started stripping. She stuffed the little black designer suit, which cost more than Jack earned in two months, into a paper bag and knew, without a shred of regret, that it would probably be the last designer outfit she would ever wear in her lifetime. Hurriedly, she put on jeans, a T-shirt and slipped into her floral sneakers. It felt wonderful.

"Okay, gang." Federica paced back and forth in the spacious room in back of Stella's. There were two big tables with two laptops and two big wall clocks hung on the stuccoed wall, just as she'd asked. One clock showed the correct time. The other ran seven hours behind.

Federica looked at her audience. Jack, Wyatt, Lilly and Norman were sitting in chairs, watching her expectantly. Ellen sat quietly in the back of the room.

Federica wondered if this was how Eisenhower felt on D-Day. Maybe she should be dressed in battle fatigues and carrying a baton.

"The plan is this. Mansion Enterprises wants the Folly. But it wants the Folly for specific economic reasons, not sentimental ones, which gives us a weapon we can use. As a matter of fact, it's the only weapon we have at our disposal, and we'll have to use it to the fullest." She glanced up at the clock behind her. It was noon. "In three hours, it will be eight o'clock in the morning in Tokyo. Norman and I are going to pretend that a Japanese corporation wants to buy the Folly and is engaging Mansion Enterprises in a bidding war which will escalate to the point at which Mansion Enterprises will be forced to give up, because what they will have to pay for the Folly will outweigh the benefits. But it's going to be tricky for two reasons. Firstly, because the bids coming from Tokyo will have to be very carefully calculated to make sure they're plausible. A sudden offer of a zillion dollars would just make them suspicious. Secondly, because we're going to have to move so fast Mansion Enterprises won't have time to send someone up here." Federica put her hands behind her back and felt like George C. Scott in *Patton.* "Any questions, troops?"

"It's not going to work, Federica," Norman said wearily.

"What?" She expected anything but this. "But Norman, I told you last night—"

Norman pushed his glasses up. "I was up half the night looking up the law, Federica. If Mansion Enterprises really wants to play hardball, they have the right to ask for proof of serious intent. In other words, they have the right to ask to see proof that the money being bid is actually there. It's a nasty trick that is seldom pulled, but it's possible. How nasty is Mansion Enterprises?"

"Very." Federica stood still, her mind racing. "What exactly constitutes proof of serious intent?" she asked slowly.

"Well, the law's not very specific. It's just a way of asking for surety that the opposite partner in a bidding war is serious. I suppose you could present a deed of ownership of property worth that amount. Stocks, bonds." He shrugged. "Anything, really, would do. But we're talking millions of dollars here, Federica. No one has anything like that amount of money. If they ask for surety and it's not presented, we could all be sued for fraudulent business practice, which is a felony. Would they do that?"

"Yes." Federica said grimly. "They most certainly would."

Jack, Wyatt and Lilly all started talking at once.

"What are we—"

"Maybe we should give up—"

"Damned if we give up. Before I do that I'd—"

"Wait!" Federica held up her hand for silence. Everyone looked at her expectantly. "Wait." She paced back and forth, thinking furiously. It was a gamble…but maybe it would work.

"Norman, what about a bank account?"

"A what?"

"A bank account. Suppose the deposit in a bank account were to be temporarily transferred to an account opened in a fictitious name. Just for a day, say, just long enough to get a bank statement. Would that be considered surety?"

"Well," Norman fingered his beard. "I guess so. But we're talking about a lot of money. Who has that kind of money in an account?"

"Me." Federica's quiet statement fell into the room like a pebble into a pool of water. There were ripples.

"Millions?" he asked.

"Yes," she answered quietly.

"How much?"

Federica hesitated. "Let's just say it should be…enough."

"That's not all, Federica," Norman said glumly.

"More bad news?"

He nodded. "The law says that…" He paused.

Federica was silent for a moment. "What, Norman?" she asked gently.

Norman sighed. "According to the law, the person or persons posting bond must then prove that they have actually made the purchase."

Jack sat up. "That means—"

"Yes." Norman looked at Federica. "It means that if things go badly, then Mansion Enterprises can force their competitor in a bidding war—in this case Federica—to prove that she purchased the Folly, or be accused of fraudulent practice. In other words, the Town Council would be legally obliged to force Federica to spend every penny she owns to buy a moth-eaten—"

"—termite-infested," said Wyatt.

"—drafty old house in the hills," finished Norman. "And she can't buy it for a penny less than the final bidding price. Are you prepared to do that, Federica? Are you prepared to have to wipe out your bank account? Lose every cent you own?"

"I don't know what to do," Federica whispered. "Norman?"

Norman stared at his clasped hands, then raised troubled eyes. "I'm sorry. I can't advise you, Federica."

"Lilly?"

Federica felt her heart plummet as Lilly slowly shook her head.

"Jack?"

He was watching her out of somber eyes. "It's your call, honey," he said finally.

Federica felt a wild fluttering in her chest. She wiped damp palms on her jeans. If things went badly she'd lose...everything.

"Okay," she said. "This is what we're going to do. Norman and I are going to work out a plausible first bid, ready to send when it's 8:00 a.m. Tokyo time. Jack, Wyatt, would you please go up to the Folly and get some of my things? And someone's going to have to see about food. I have a funny feeling we're going to be bunking here. Lilly, you're going to have to lend me Norman for the duration and he's going to have to fall off the wagon. Sorry."

"Cold turkey when this is over, Norman," Lilly warned. "You're not touching your computer for a solid month."

"What can I do, Federica?" Ellen asked quietly.

"Here." Federica rummaged in her satchel and brought out the paper bag with the crumpled suit. "Burn this for me, would you?"

~~~~~

EMAIL FROM: f_mansion@mansent.com

TO: pcobb@mansent.com

Paul,

I sent Russell White home, since he was feeling ill. There was no problem at the time, because negotiations were just about terminated and there were only a few formalities to take care of. But something serious has come up at the last minute.

I know Uncle Frederick is in Prague but we have to move very fast on this one, so I guess you should lead negotiations on your end.

A Japanese corporation, a large one, has put in a bid for Lot 448. I was able to get the price the Japanese are offering, which is $700,000 more than our own top offer, for a total of $3.7 million dollars. What do we do? The Carson's Bluff Town Council is now locked in discussions with the Japanese and I'm told the signing of the deal is imminent. I'll await instructions.

Federica

~~~~~

"Well," Federica said, sitting back. "Now all we can do is wait it out."

Jack looked at the computer screen, a big hand resting on her shoulder. He put a cup of steaming coffee down beside the laptop.

"I thought your top offer was $4 million."

Federica looked up and gave a weak smile. "I lied."

He squeezed her shoulder and said nothing.

Stella prepared a light lunch, but Norman and Federica didn't eat. They spent their time hunched over the computer screens, going over different scenarios.

At 5:00 p.m., Federica's you've-got-mail tone sounded.

"Here we go," she said.

~~~~~

EMAIL FROM: pcobb@mansent.com
TO: f_mansion@mansent.com

Federica,

Just got your message and it's bad news, indeed. Frederick is very intent on that property. He's in some Czech Schloss somewhere, but I'm empowered to act on his behalf.

Up the price to $4.2 million.

Paul

~~~~~

"Are you okay with that, Federica?" Wyatt asked.

"Mm," she replied.

~~~~~

EMAIL FROM: f_mansion@mansent.com
TO: pcobb@mansent.com

Paul,

This is going to be a long night. I just presented the Carson's Bluff Town Council with our counteroffer. Looks like the Japanese are intent on having this property, too. They bid $4.8 million and will relieve the tax burden, which essentially puts the bid to over $4.9 million. What to do?

Federica

~~~~~

EMAIL FROM: pcobb@mansent.com
TO: f_mansion@mansent.com

Federica,
Offer $5.5 million.
Paul

~~~~~

"Damn," Federica said. "It's not working."

It was 9:00 p.m. Jack and Wyatt had been to the Folly and back, Ellen had burned the suit and Newton had made it back in time to fix hot turkey sandwiches which neither Federica nor Norman had touched.

"Honey, eat something," Jack urged gently.

Federica wrenched her eyes from the screen. "I couldn't eat anything now, Jack," she said. The thought of food made something roil queasily in her stomach.

Jack nodded at the screen. "Do you have enough money to cover that?"

"Mm," she replied.

~~~~~

EMAIL FROM: f_mansion@mansent.com
TO: pcobb@mansent.com

Dear Paul,

The bid from the Japanese has gone up to $6 million. Do we want to continue bidding? After all, the property is in a dreadful state of disrepair. I calculate it would take a million just in structural repair. The road up to the property is almost impassable and needs repaving. The roof is almost completely caved in and the flooring is gone. Is it worth it?

Federica

~~~~~

Jack nudged her. "Tell him about the black widows and giant rattlers."

"Oh, you mean the ones big enough to carry off babies?" Federica looked up at him, tongue in cheek. "Later. We don't want to shoot all our ammunition at once."

She looked around. Ellen was dozing in a chair, her head on Wyatt's shoulder. Lilly had long since gone to bed, pleading fatigue. She'd promised to come back early in the morning. Newton was in the kitchen and kept up a steady supply of coffee, which Federica drank by the gallon, and food, which she couldn't touch.

Only Norman seemed to be happy, lost in his computer screen.

Jack got up and started massaging her tense shoulder muscles. They were hard as rocks. Well no wonder, she was risking everything she owned.

"Better?" he asked.

"Yes." Federica lifted her arm and hooked it around his neck. He bent forward to give her a kiss and Federica's computer beeped.

~~~~~

EMAIL FROM: pcobb@mansent.com
TO: f_mansion@mansent.com

Federica,
$6.5 million.
Paul

~~~~~

"Damn!" Federica said.
"You want to call this off, honey?" Jack's voice was quiet.
"No," she said, and bent over the keyboard.

~~~~~

EMAIL FROM: f_mansion@mansent.com
TO: pcobb@mansent.com

Paul,
I made the offer, but it was turned down. The Town Council has now gone into night session and I get the impression that they want to wrap this up. The Japanese are now offering $7 million. They seem to be very determined, Paul. Do we really want it that badly?
Federica

~~~~~

EMAIL FROM: pcobb@mansent.com
TO: f_mansion@mansent.com

Federica,

Still can't get in touch with Frederick. I'll stay here in the office until I do. It's midnight over here, ten o'clock in the morning in Prague. Sometime today he should be in touch.

I wish we could have wrapped this up sooner, I had tickets to the opera tonight. But never mind. We want that Carson's Bluff property badly. We've had informal talks with George Luna, the film director, who wants to lease the property from us over a three-year period. The terms being discussed are very favorable. We want that property. $7.5 million.

Paul

~~~~~

June 9th, early morning

"Oh." Federica sat up. "So that's it." She pushed her hair out of her eyes, feeling suddenly energized. The sheer financial weight of Mansion Enterprises had depressed her, but this required trickiness. There she was on even ground.

~~~~~

EMAIL FROM: f_mansion@mansent.com
TO: pcobb@mansent.com

Paul,

Sorry you missed your opera date. I'm sorry also to be giving you bad news. The other day I was up at the property, looking a few things over, and two very L.A. types drove up. They asked if they could look around. I had the keys and saw no harm — there's certainly nothing to steal at the property, it's a real wreck — so I let them in.

I guess I should have warned them about the black widows, because one of the men screamed and sprained his ankle trying to jump back. I should also have warned him about the floorboards. They're rotten, you see. The man put his foot straight through the flooring.

Luckily, I was able to call an ambulance on their cell phone, but a tree had fallen across the road and it took the ambulance over half an hour to get there. We were all waiting outside for the ambulance to come and the two men were saying very unflattering things about the property.

I guess I should also have warned them about the rattlers. Local legend has it that the rattlers around here can carry off babies, but that's an exaggeration. Actually, it was only a few feet long and I understand that if you don't disturb them, they won't disturb you. The men really shouldn't have screamed that way.

Then the ambulance arrived. I must say, I always thought movie types were cool, but those two men were very agitated by the time they left. Now I understand what they meant when they said they wanted to do a Western trilogy.

The Japanese are offering $8 million.

Federica

~~~~~

"Eight million dollars," Norman said, coming out of his trance. "That's a lot of money, Federica."

"Yes, it is," she said softly.

"Are you…okay?"

"Mm."

~~~~~

EMAIL FROM: pcobb@mansent.com

TO: f_mansion@mansent.com

Federica,

I was finally able to make contact with Frederick. I have him on the other line. Needless to say, he is very disappointed at the course of negotiations, as am I. We're now well over double the amount we wanted to bid. But still, offer $8.5 million. We'll be waiting online.

Paul

~~~~~

Federica could feel the sweat trickling down her back.

Dawn was breaking. The sky outside was a gentle pink. She felt gritty and longed for a shower and a bed. She felt as if she hadn't slept in a week. Newton came in and poured her another cup of coffee and she smiled at him, wondering at what point she would start sloshing.

Lilly walked in and Ellen woke with a start. She pushed the hair out of her eyes and looked around groggily. "What's happening?" she asked Wyatt.

"We're at eight-and-a-half-million," Wyatt said grimly.

"Federica?"

"Yeah?" Federica turned around. Ellen was looking at her with concern and sympathy.

"Are you going to be...all right?"

"Mm." Federica took a deep breath. The sun slipped over the horizon and a ray of light shot into the room. "Okay, gang. Now is the time for the howitzers. Paul Cobb's got Uncle Frederick on the line. I know the one thing Uncle Frederick hates most." She looked around at all of them. Jack, Lilly, Wyatt, Norman, Ellen. Newton must have sensed something, because he walked in from the kitchen. All the people Federica cared about, here in this room.

There was absolute silence.

"This isn't working," she said. "There's just one more thing I can try."

She turned back to her laptop and started typing.

~~~~~

EMAIL FROM: f_mansion@mansent.com
TO: pcobb@mansent.com

Paul,

I've just come from City Hall. The Japanese have raised the price to $8.6 million. *But*, they're also offering to build and run a Children's Wellness Center for the township of Carson's Bluff. I suppose we could offer to do the same, but it could get very complicated, what with hiring doctors and staff and being involved with the vaccination programs, and the dental clinic, etc. I suppose there would have to be a lot of contact with social workers and the like. They have a whole plan laid out. Should I improvise? Maybe offer $9 million, a Children's Wellness Center and, say, a mental health clinic? Please advise.

Federica

~~~~~

EMAIL FROM: pcobb@mansent.com
TO: f_mansion@mansent.com

Federica,

Just been in touch with Frederick. Under no circumstances are you to offer to open up a clinic, or Wellness Center or whatever. Stop negotiations immediately. We expect you back in San Francisco by late morning. You can leave for New York on the afternoon flight.

Paul

~~~~~

Everyone crowded around the laptop as the message appeared on the screen.

Jack gave a rebel yell and pulled Federica out of her chair, Wyatt kissed Ellen and Norman sat blinking his eyes, smiling.

Federica lifted her mouth and forgot everything for a moment as Jack kissed her.

"Wait," she said breathlessly, and looked into his eyes. What Jack felt for her was right there. Strong and steady and the best thing that had ever happened to her. "Wait. There's one more thing to do."

She pulled away and sat down in front of her computer.

~~~~~

EMAIL FROM: f_mansion@mansent.com

TO: pcobb@mansent.com

Paul,

I have just terminated negotiations with Carson's Bluff, as per your instructions.

Federica

P.S. I quit.

~~~~~

Federica sat for a moment, fingers poised over the keys. She looked over her shoulder at Newton. He nodded and grinned.

P.P.S. Newton quits, too.

Jack hugged her fiercely. Federica jumped when she heard a pop and Wyatt started pouring champagne for everyone.

"Here's to the liberation of Carson's Bluff!" he shouted above the hubbub, and raised his glass. "I knew Federica could do it!"

Federica hated to say it. "It's not over yet," she said quietly.

Everyone stared at her over their glasses. Everyone except Norman.

"Norman? You want to tell them or should I?"

Norman pushed his glasses up his nose and sighed. "I think what Federica means is that the Folly is still extremely vulnerable. Not to mention the fact that sooner or later Mansion Enterprises is going to figure out that it's been had. It's only a matter of time before it starts all over again."

"But," Federica raised a finger and smiled, "I have a plan."

"I thought you might," said Norman.

"But first, I have to know—was Horace Milton born around here?"

They were expecting anything but that. Jack looked at Wyatt. "Hell." He ran his hands through his already tousled hair. "I don't know. Horace is almost a hundred years old and he spent most of his life in Paris—"

"Yes," Lilly said quietly. "I've seen his birth certificate. He'll celebrate his one-hundredth birthday on the fourth of July. The town is going to give him a plaque."

Federica could have hugged Lilly. "Great. So this is the plan. Actually, it's a wonderful idea, and it even has a sort of rough poetic justice, but there's one big problem." Federica looked around her circle of friends, peering deeply into everyone's eyes, first Norman, then Lilly, then Wyatt and finally Jack. She wanted to be able to gauge their reaction. They might actually be repelled by her suggestion and she would find herself out on a limb.

Alone. Again.

"I think it's feasible and if nobody talks, it should work. I don't consider it at all immoral—it's just...it's just..."

Lilly leaned forward, concern etched on her strong features. "It's what, honey?"

Federica blew out a breath. "Illegal."

Norman, Jack, Wyatt and Lilly leaned back in their chairs and looked at one another. Jack laughed.

"Is *that* all?" the sheriff of Carson's Bluff said, relieved. "I thought the problem was serious."

Everyone had gone except Federica and Jack. The sun had come up and the room was bathed in a warm, golden glow. It was going to be another beautiful day in Carson's Bluff.

"So," Jack said softly. He cupped her face, caressing her cheekbones with his thumbs.

"So," she said. "What's next?"

"You tell me." He bent to kiss her lightly. "It's your call. Where do you want to go from here?"

"To tell the truth," Federica said, watching his face carefully, "I don't have all that much choice. I am now officially homeless, jobless and penniless. My apartment is owned by the company. When I quit, I lost it."

"Jobless and homeless, maybe," Jack said. "But certainly not penniless."

"Not quite." Federica stepped out of his arms, opened her fanny pack and took out her checkbook. She checked the stubs. "Mansion Enterprises didn't really pay me much of a salary. I had a free apartment and a very generous expense account. I've got enough in the bank to last maybe a couple of months, not more." She smiled up at him, her heart in her eyes. "Looks like you're going to have to offer me a job. And a home."

"Of course you'll have a home with me —" Jack suddenly stopped. "Wait a minute." He looked at her through narrowed eyes. "Don't tell me you —"

"Yup." Federica smiled smugly. "I bluffed."

July 4th

Article in the Shelby Clarion

There were very special Fourth of July celebrations in Carson's Bluff this year, which also marked the one-hundredth birthday of famous local son Horace Milton. An open-air ceremony in Morrison Square was held and attended by almost all the citizens. The town presented Mr. Milton with a plaque commemorating his one-hundredth birthday and Mr. Milton presented the town with the deed to "Harry's Folly", the mansion built by Harry Carson. In a routine check of archives, the town clerk, Lilly Langtry Sutter Wright, came across the last will and testament of Harry Carson, which had been lost for one-hundred-twenty-four years. Harry Carson had left his Folly, only half-completed by the time of his death, to the father of Mr. Milton, who thus inherited the building. In a generous gesture, Mr. Milton deeded the property to the township of Carson's Bluff in perpetuity. The building will be restored by volunteers and will be run as a community center.

During the celebrations, Sheriff Jack Sutter announced his engagement to Miss Federica Henrietta Mansion, formerly of Mansion Enterprises.

Congratulations Horace, and congratulations Federica and Jack!

The End

Cerridwen, the Celtic goddess of wisdom, was the muse who brought inspiration to storytellers and those in the creative arts.

Cerridwen Press encompasses the best and most innovative stories in all genres of today's fiction.

Visit our website and discover the newest titles by talented authors who still get inspired — much like the ancient storytellers did

once upon a time...

www.cerridwenpress.com